Upon Dark Waters

The Chichester Crime Mysteries

Matthew J. Evans

For Valerie.

Also In This Series

The Dead Beneath Us

Prologue

The thrashing in the icy water ended as abruptly as it began. A few more compressions against her cold breasts, and the bubbles ceased. It was over. The only sound now was the gentle birdsong from the meadows, welcoming the gathering light.

Careful not to cut the skin, the knife made quick work of her jacket and dress. It had to be fast, but numbed fingers struggled with the tights and boots, making them tricky to remove.

When all was done, the stream carried her away like a rose on the water. Her back lightly grazed the creek bed, churning clouds of silt and algae, until she came to a stop, out of sight, beneath the footbridge.

Hurried feet thudded on the wooden boards, then faded along the footpath. As the sun emerged above the horizon, the dark waters settled.

Chapter One

Heather moved away from the bedroom window and knelt beside the bed. Her heart was racing, and her hands trembled. She'd seen Ray busy in the garden, distracted as he sorted out his tools in the shed. It had to be now.

"Come on. No time like the present," she said to herself.

If it weren't for Lily, she would never have found it. That moment of revelation had shattered the facade of her marriage.

Under the bed was an old brown suitcase; its worn tan leather was musty and spotted with mildew from the damp attic. She pulled it out and unclipped the rusty latches. She had taken considerable care to hide Ray's secret beneath a layer of books that had cluttered the dining room shelves for twenty years. They were books his father had left him, all unread.

A creak on the floorboards, and she snapped the case shut.

"What's that you got?" Ray asked, looming in the bedroom doorway. He was light on his feet despite his size.

"Don't you have something to do?" Heather fired back. "It's

3

your father's old books. I'm taking them down to the book bank to declutter the place. Never seen you read them."

His suspicion was obvious. "Why couldn't you just leave them where they were?"

"The new unit's coming on Sunday. We need the space."

"You can't chuck that suitcase."

"It's covered in mould! I'm not having it in this house. I'm fed up with seeing your father's old crap lying around. The only thing he gave you of real value is hidden in your wardrobe. Why don't you sell it or even use it?"

Ray harrumphed and went into the toilet. It was the opportunity Heather needed to haul the suitcase down the stairs. She opened the front door and heaved the case into the boot of her car.

She turned breathless to find him at the door, watching her. "Are you going now?"

"Yes. I've already told you."

He scowled at her again. "What about lunch?"

"Get it yourself! You were a policeman for thirty years. You should be able to make a sandwich."

"You keep hiding the bread," Ray grumbled.

Heather shot back, "No, I don't! It's where it always is." She ran her fingers through her hair. "I'll be going into town, too. I want to go to the charity shops."

"Don't be long," said Ray.

"I'll be as long as I bloody want!" She felt herself raging inside, her pulse throbbing in her ears. Could she do this to him? He would fall apart without her. But then she considered everything he had taken from her. Yes, she could.

She hurried back inside to fetch her coat and scarf, and a shadow appeared behind her in the doorway.

Craig, Ray's friend from next door, flashed an apologetic grin. "Sorry, Heather! Did I make you jump? Just returning this." In his hand was a claw hammer with a grubby yellow handle. He and his busybody wife were always borrowing things.

Heather glanced at the thick plaster on his thumb. "Did you miss?" She offered him a thin smile.

He passed the hammer to Ray, standing close behind her. "You could say that. I'm useless at DIY."

"I would've done it for you, Craig," said Ray.

She found it strange that Ray would help his witless neighbour, but he always expected her to do everything for him. She left them talking, grateful for the distraction.

Without looking back, she slipped into her car, fumbling for her keys in sweaty hands. She started the engine and left her drive, heading towards the city centre. Her mind was racing, her eyes focused on the road. She took shallow breaths, her hands cramping as she gripped the steering wheel.

Instead of going to the book bank, Heather parked in a small car park behind North Street in Chichester. As she calmed herself, she realised this was where it would all begin. She couldn't believe she was doing it.

Using both hands, she lifted the suitcase from the boot of the car and staggered through a short passageway onto North Street. She was relieved the shop was close by. Her arms ached, and she was out of breath by the time she arrived. The bell above the charity shop door jingled as she entered, and she dropped the suitcase in front of her.

Lily was pricing cards behind the counter. She was elegant and model-like. Her strawberry-blonde hair flowed over her shoulders, and her bright blue eyes captured anyone she spoke to. She wore a form-fitting dress with a delicate floral pattern. The winter-weight fabric hugged her slim figure. The dress fell just over her knees, paired with thick black tights and her favourite long boots, making her appear tall and graceful.

The shop was empty apart from Angela, a volunteer who was

busy sorting through the jigsaw puzzles. Lily's face lit up when she saw Heather. She turned to Angela.

"Can you check for any deliveries at the back gate? I meant to do it earlier."

"Sure," Angela said, pushing up her glasses and flashing a smile at Heather.

Lily glanced at the suitcase, her eyes bright with excitement. "Is it in there?"

Heather nodded. "You may want to empty it out the back." She waited for Angela to leave. "It's up to you what you do with it now."

"But what about you?" Lily took Heather's hand in hers, speaking softly.

"I'll be okay. He won't know anything until I tell him, and then I'm going to make him suffer. So it's over to you now. You won't see me for a while, Lily. I'm going to leave him, you see. Sunday's the day."

"Where will you go?"

Heather looked over her shoulder as if Ray were standing nearby. She lowered her voice. "I've always wanted to move to Dorset. Maybe to the coast. I've got my mother's inheritance, and he can't touch that. So, don't worry about me, okay?" She looked up at the clock on the wall. "We'd better get on with it. I'm sure Ray will be spying on me by now."

The two women hugged, and then Lily disappeared into the back of the shop. Heather heard the latches on the suitcase clicking open, and Lily returned less than a minute later.

"You can keep this old thing," Lily said, laughing as she handed the empty case back to Heather. "Yolanda will ask after you."

"Just make something up. She's not talking to me now, anyway. She's jealous of our friendship. Perhaps when it's all sorted, you and I can meet up again." Heather swallowed, fighting back her tears. "I'm so sorry about… everything. I wish I could go back and change it."

Lily nodded. "We all wish that."

"Take extra care."

"I will." Lily hesitated as if she had something more she wanted to say, but Angela had returned and was hovering in the background, tidying the books. "Stay in touch, Heather."

Heather took the suitcase and left without turning around. She couldn't stay any longer. Determined to cover her tracks, she visited three other charity shops. She was certain Ray had put an app on her phone to track her. She made sure the shop staff had seen her, asking them questions, trying on a scarf, looking at old board games and jigsaw puzzles.

As she thought about what she had done, her heart pounded. She felt sick and light-headed. She found a café, sat with a cup of tea, and watched people walking past along the precinct. They were doing ordinary things. She had always envied them. Her life was far from ordinary. A young couple walked past, hand in hand. She almost had that once, but it would never be. Ray had crushed her chance of happiness. She clenched her jaw, squeezing her hand around her cup. At least now, things were going to change. She needed Lily to do what she had to do and to make him pay.

After an hour had passed, she returned to her car, and when no one was looking, she flung the mouldy brown suitcase over a fence. It was Ray's old case, and she didn't want it. And she didn't want him anymore, either. When she drove away, she allowed herself a small, bitter smile.

Chapter Two

Faraday zipped up his trousers, breathless, while she tucked in her shirt. A thin layer of sweat covered his brow as he sat back at his desk, looking up at the ceiling until his heart slowed. The office air was thick with the fug of sex and deodorant. He watched as she composed herself. She was tall, young, and beautiful—just how he liked them.

This wasn't their first time—more like their third or fourth. He'd lost count. But it was the first time in his office. He knew she would have preferred a romantic night in a hotel, but now he was doing her a favour, and she was paying for it.

She gathered her things, threw the used tissues in his bin, and re-clipped her hair, glancing at his door.

"Stop worrying," he said. "It's Friday. No one's here, and the blinds are down."

She nodded and smiled. "I need to use the bathroom, then I must go. Mark will wonder where I am." She tilted her head and looked at the floor. "I'm sure they know."

"Who?"

"My team. I overheard them laughing. They keep giving me funny looks whenever you come into the office."

"You're paranoid."

"After what happened last week, we can't do that again."

"It doesn't matter. You'll be out of here soon. And if Ross Taylor tries to say anything... I'll keep an eye on him. I'll check his phone records if I have to. Stop panicking!"

"I'm sorry. I don't want this to go wrong—that's all."

"That's okay. Trust me." Faraday focused on his computer screen. "See you next week." He sensed her hesitation.

"You're going to make it happen, right? There's no position free anywhere on West, and I want to move on."

"Relax. I've already set things in motion. It'll take three months, and the news of your promotion is imminent."

"Three months!" She shook her head. "I can't—"

"Then find another way, or consider Surrey."

"Surrey! No, thanks."

"Just keep doing what you're doing. It'll be fine."

"Okay. Thank you." She re-fixed her epaulettes and unlocked the door with a twist of the handle. "See you Monday."

Faraday looked back at his screen and checked his emails. Once she'd gone, he lifted the blinds. The corridor outside was dark. He didn't like the reflection staring back at him. What had he become, resorting to cheap thrills to see him through each day? The darkness crept over him again, and his heart sank deeper. He felt his eyes prickling. He needed a drink. Grabbing his wallet and phone, he made a call.

"I'm just leaving," he said. "Need anything from the shop?"

"Hi," said a woman's voice. "No, we just need you. You'll be back in time to read her a bedtime story, won't you?"

"Of course. See you soon. Love you."

~

The hours dragged by as Heather fidgeted in front of the TV, trying to distract herself from her plans and revealing everything to him. He'd spent his entire career reading people's motives and probing their lies. One wrong word, and she would give it all away. She replayed their conversations in her mind, analysing every word and gesture. Each time he spoke, her heart pounded in fear of his cross-examination. He was always accusing her of some sly behaviour, but this time he would be right.

He'd left the room half an hour ago to find a cocktail stick. He'd been picking at his teeth after a stuck piece of gammon. She didn't care—she was glad of the space. She'd heard the floorboards creak above. Was he skulking around the bedroom, rummaging through her underwear drawers again? She'd caught him before, as if he'd found some evil intention in them. She'd packed away all her new knickers and bras somewhere he'd never find them.

She'd checked her mobile throughout the evening. There was still no message from Lily. What if she did nothing at all? That thought worried her. He needed to pay for what he'd done, and Lily was best placed to mete out that justice. She wouldn't let her down.

Heather noticed the loud tick of the clock on the wall, each second a reminder of the time slipping away. Her palms were sweaty, and she wiped them on her trousers. She noticed his empty cup on the table. He never cleaned up after himself. Needing a distraction, she picked it up and carried it to the kitchen to place it in the dishwasher. She groaned. It was full, and she had to switch it on. He couldn't even do that.

"Have you been poking around in my wardrobe?" Ray's sudden presence in the kitchen startled her.

"Someone has to hang up your shirts," said Heather. She knew what he meant, but she didn't look at him. He'd see it in her eyes.

"Not my shirts, woman!" He stepped towards her to look at her face. "The bottom of the wardrobe. My boxes."

"Why would I go near your old rubbish?" She looked away, then snapped, "And can't you put the bloody dishwasher on when it's full? It doesn't run by itself."

"You're changing the subject." He frowned and looked at the dishwasher.

"Whatever goes on at the bottom of your damned wardrobe is none of my business. I don't care how many dirty magazines you keep there. I don't want to know."

He stepped back; she had struck his pride. She didn't know if he still kept them in there, but judging by his reaction, it's likely he had a few stashed away.

The tension in the air was palpable. Heather walked out of the kitchen and back into the lounge. She sat on the sofa and lifted her legs onto the seat next to her. Ray came in and stood over her.

"What is it? I'm trying to watch TV."

"Where did you take my books today?" he said.

"The book bank. I told you."

"You didn't go to the book bank. I checked on the app."

Heather knew he would do that. "Stalking me again, were you? It was closed. I went to the charity shops in the city."

"Which ones?"

"For God's sake, Ray! Does it matter?"

He sat down in his armchair. "They were my books. My father left them to me."

"You never read them, and we need the space, remember?"

He returned with something that took Heather by surprise. "Why don't you love me anymore, Heather? What did I do?"

The rage was rising inside of her. She couldn't let it out. He couldn't suspect, but something had to give. Just enough. "You mean, apart from the beatings, your affairs, your constant jealousy, watching me like a hawk, controlling my friends, who I can

11

see, what I can wear? I kissed Prince Charming, and you turned into the ugly frog. You turned into you, Ray. That's why."

He swore at her and headed into the dining room, slamming the door behind him. Heather let out a long sigh of relief. The confrontation was over. She needed to stay strong—just a little longer, and it would be all over.

Chapter Three

Monday, 8th January

The realisation that Sophia was growing up had blindsided Beniamin Dinescu. He chewed his toast, processing Sophia's announcement while she scrutinised his reaction. He fixed his eyes on hers and felt the peanut butter crunch between his teeth, tasting the bitterness of the carbonised bread. The three of them were sitting around the kitchen table, and Beniamin was ready for work in his shirt and tie.

"Dad?" said Sophia.

He noticed the changed contours of his daughter's face, an echo of her mother's confidence emerging as her chin pushed forward. In that small defiance, he realised she couldn't remain his baby girl forever, but neither was she an adult.

He was aware she was fidgeting more than usual. Placing his elbows on the kitchen table, he looked through the blinds, hoping for some clarity. Daylight broke on the winter morning, and he noticed the smoky haze from the burnt toast had dissipated, though the smell still lingered.

"Don't leave the poor girl hanging!" Lisa said. She gave her husband a look he knew well enough not to ignore. She tightened the cord on her dressing gown and left the table to clear the breakfast things. Beniamin recognised that Lisa busying herself was a sign that she was finding this difficult.

"You're fourteen, Sophia," he said. "Aren't you too young to have a boyfriend?"

"I bet you had a girlfriend at my age," said Sophia, her face blushing a hot pink.

He smiled at her. "The girls—or rather, their parents—wanted nothing to do with a Romanian orphan who barely spoke English."

"Well, I had a boyfriend," said Lisa.

"At fourteen?" he asked.

"Yes, sort of. He was sweet on me, and I knew what my limits were."

Beniamin studied Sophia's face once more. "Who is this boy who wants to date you?"

"*Go out* with me, Dad, not *date*. His name is Charlie, and he goes to the Active One Club." Sophia blushed some more and lowered her fidgeting hands onto her lap.

"Charlie." Beniamin glanced at Lisa, who had sat beside him again.

"Yes. He's sensible and brilliant. His parents are doctors, and he was fifteen last week and plays chess."

Feeling somewhat relieved, he tilted his head. "Chess? Will he give me a game?" Beniamin felt Lisa's foot tapping against his.

"And he's kind and thoughtful, like you, Dad."

He couldn't keep a straight face any longer. He checked his watch. "I really would like to hear more about Charlie, but I must go. I have a long day ahead." As he stood, Lisa straightened his tie. "I trust you, Sophia, but I know what boys are like at that age."

"Ben," said Lisa, flashing a look, "let Sophia and *me* discuss that subject. Perhaps we could invite him to tea."

"Tea?"

"Dad," said Sophia, "it's a boy who's okay with me as I am. Look at me." She looked down at her wheelchair. "I mean—come on!"

"He goes to your club. Does he have a disability?"

"No. His sister does. He goes with her."

Beniamin nodded. "By tea, you mean dinner."

"Yes," said Lisa. "Sophia wants Uncle Kieran to come, too."

"Reinforcements." He winked at Sophia. "Okay, but you two are cooking."

"God, yes!" said Lisa. "I don't want you poisoning the poor boy."

He tried to look offended, but his smile slipped through.

"Perhaps when you're on rest days, Dad," said Sophia. "Can I invite him?"

"Of course you can. I'll try not to scare him."

"Will you be home on time tonight?" asked Lisa. "I'm meeting with my friends from the book group."

"I have a day of important meetings, so I won't promise, okay? You know how it is."

The three hugged, Beniamin in the middle, being squeezed harder and longer so he knew they loved him.

As he put on his police lanyard, the taste of honey from Lisa's lips lingered. The sweetness mixed with regret—he hadn't told her about the offer. He'd spent all weekend considering a letter he'd received from HR in Lewes HQ. It was the written confirmation of an email he was struggling to ignore. He needed more time to consider the consequences for his family. Hadn't he come as far as he wanted in this job? Could he oversee the breakup of his team? His mind was a whirlwind of thoughts as he stepped out into the chilly morning air and unlocked his car. The future seemed uncertain, but one thing was clear: changes were coming, whether he was ready for them or not.

∽

The marsh whispered as Colin Jackman crossed the wooden footbridge, the reeds waving their creamy plumes. The outgoing tide made the mudflats shimmer like silver, the tidal channels tracing a delicate filigree.

He stopped on the bridge to view the course of the creek heading towards the Fishbourne Channel. He removed his gloves and warmed his fingertips with his breath. The light was perfect, and everything was in pin-sharp detail. A blue sky melted into a pale haze on the horizon, with the sun hanging over his right shoulder.

"Beautiful." Colin nodded in agreement with himself. But he knew the ancient marshland could change her mood on a whim, whisking up a waspish squall in an instant. She could not be trusted. She would trick you, trip you into the creek if you didn't pay attention. But not today. Colin knew that, for now, the light was fine for him.

A curlew burst from the reeds. He had to be quick. Setting down his hiking pole, he stuffed his gloves into his anorak. His fingers, still numbed by the cold, fumbled with the zip of the camera bag. The flustered bird circled above and cried out an ominous alarm before flying to the surrounding meadows to preen and take shelter.

"Bugger!" He was too late.

Leaning over the bridge, he watched the water flowing in playful, gurgling swirls. The glint of something gold caught his eye. A watch. How could you lose a watch here? And a gold one at that. Colin resolved to rescue it.

Grabbing his pole, he stepped into the dead reeds, which snapped and cracked underfoot, his boots squelching in the soft, sulphurous smelling mud. He steadied himself by leaning on his pole, which sank deeper. He regretted the idea of retrieving the timepiece. Crouching, he parted the reeds with his pole, his calves burning as he waited for his eyes to adjust to the shadows underneath the bridge.

His attention shifted to a large pallid object in the water, which had snagged on the creek bed, held against the flow. He stretched out his pole and corrected his balance. After poking around the silt, the shape moved with the stream until it cleared the footbridge. Then it stopped.

Shuffling closer, he gazed upon a mermaid-like form, her long, golden hair twisting with the current. Her hands, pale and plump like bars of milky soap, rose and dipped below the surface. Her eyes stared wide and dark at the bright dome of blue above through the rippling, watery glaze.

The realisation struck him. A cold gasp of horror punched his chest.

"God, no!" He fell back breathless, twisting and straining, panicking to get away. The pole slipped. His hands sank into the thick, freezing mud, which tempered every push and pull to extract himself. "Help! Somebody help!" His alarm lifted above the reedbeds.

Colin scrambled up, grasping the brittle reeds. With shaking hands, he clambered back up to the path, away from the face in the water. Peering over the footbridge, he glimpsed her dead eyes staring back. He recoiled. His chest hurt. The chilling image of the lifeless eyes seared into his mind. He had to get help. He had to call the police.

∽

Overlooking the receding tide in the Fishbourne Channel, Joseph McKinley rested on the remains of a fallen tree. Gnarled, weathered, and grey, he looked older than his years. His anger had diminished, and his hands were still. He had been there for some time, but reminiscing only deepened his gloom. He had been betrayed once again, and this time, it had cut him to the bone.

He glanced behind him at a crumbling concrete structure shrouded in brambles. He remembered everything about that pillbox, and the sour stench inside still lingered in his memory. Now, a rotten piece of plywood covered the entrance. The local kids would be inside if they knew it was here, thought Joseph. It had been a long time since he'd slept in there. His back couldn't handle the floor now.

A voice calling for help broke his thoughts, carried on the wind from the north. He stood, his clumsy legs finding their balance. He tucked his grey beard into his coat and pulled down his woollen hat. Following the footpath towards the sound, he halted at the clearing before the footbridge. Something moved on the bridge. Joseph stepped back into the cover of the reeds. He watched a man in a blue anorak look over the side, then stumble back in horror. The man panicked. Rummaging through a black bag, he produced a mobile phone. He looked up and turned towards Joseph. He'd seen him.

"Shit, no!" said Joseph.

Then the nightmare returned—the face in the water, the dead, glazed eyes. His heart pounded as he backed away. He couldn't be here. Not now. He turned and walked away as fast as his stiff knees allowed. Why had he come back? How stupid could he be? To relive this again was unbearable. As he hastened along the path, the biting wind whipped through the reeds, carrying whispers of old secrets and broken promises. A maelstrom of thoughts crushed his head. He pulled his jacket tighter, but it couldn't shield him from the dread. It all ran together in a random stream of confusion. The graves in the forest resurfaced. Fathers and sons buried together, crying out to him again—a scream of still-image memories. Had he done this? The mess in his head! He had to escape, to get away from everything.

Chapter Four

Detective Sergeant Emily Summers was already out of the car and waiting for Gareth Booker in the Bull's Head car park. She wore her green boots and waxed jacket, and her blonde hair was pulled back into a tight ponytail. She was glad to be outside in the fresh air, away from the confines of the office. They had been called to Mill Lane in Fishbourne, a village two miles west of Chichester, famous for its links with Roman Britain.

Summers's phone buzzed with a voice message from Kieran, checking if she was still on for a catch-up drink later. She sighed and looked up at the sky. No distractions. They were friends—just friends—had Kieran got that? She left a brief reply in a voice message. *Something's come up. Sorry.* Why was it so hard to figure out her feelings for him? She had to focus. She slipped the phone back into her pocket with a twinge of regret or maybe relief —she couldn't decide which. And now she felt the familiar churn in her stomach of nervous excitement at the prospect of a new case.

"You just need a labrador and a shotgun over your arm, Sarge." Booker laughed. He was still bent over in the driver's seat with his door open, pulling on his old police boots.

"I was a girl guide, Gareth," Summers quipped. "Always prepared. You should know that by now."

Booker rolled his eyes and scoffed. "You're so keen, Sarge. Don't your batteries ever run out?" He reached into his jacket pocket and pulled out a police beanie hat.

"Won't that mess up your lovely hair?"

His hair and the time he spent on it was a running joke between them.

He stared at the ground in front of him and groaned. "Could've done without coming here. I've got too many jobs on my account already. I can't take on another."

Summers dug her hands into her pockets. "Am I giving you too much to do?"

He shot a look at her. "Feels that way sometimes."

"You have no more than anyone else on the team."

"Really? We're two detectives down, and Sarah swans around from one job to another as if nothing bothers her. Am I the only one who's struggling around here?"

Summers smiled. "That's the way she is—chilled. Unlike you."

"What's that supposed to mean?"

She laughed. "Exactly what I said. Do you need me to go through your account? Come on, Gareth! What's eating you?"

He stroked his beard. "It's just that Chloe and me becoming parents… No, it's okay. You're right. Don't mind me, Sarge."

"Your fiancée? Everything okay, Gareth?" She tilted her head. "Do you need some time out? I'm a good listener."

"No, honestly. We've got this to do." He checked his laces, fixed a smile, and patted the palms of his hands on his knees. "See, I'm fine now—all good."

"Ready, grumpy?"

A gull cried out above them and swooped away south over the reedbeds.

"Yep." Booker stood and locked the car. "Is the boss coming?"

Summers shook her head. "No, he's in the tidy-up meeting for Op Birchwood. It's going to take the best part of the day." And she smiled at that thought. She could take the reins for a short while.

Summers and Booker walked from the pub car park, south along Mill Lane, and past the old mill pond, opposite a picturesque thatched cottage. The mill pond bordered the marshes and Chichester Harbour. A handful of concerned locals had gathered there and had seen them coming. Booker's hat, with *police* written all over it, gave them away.

"Head down and look grim," Summers said to Booker as they approached them. "Don't engage with the natives."

They turned right onto the footpath beside the reedbeds. A single line of blue-and-white police tape barred their way, guarded by a young police community support officer. They identified themselves and signed the crime scene logbook.

"Any problems?" Summers asked the PCSO.

"No, Sarge," he said. "The locals have mostly kept their distance, but some of them have been videoing the SOCOs coming and going, so it will be all over social media soon."

"No worries," said Booker. "It always happens. You're doing a good job."

Summers led the way along the footpath. "See, Gareth, you can be nice." She turned and smiled at him.

"Simple respect," Booker replied. "It's what we all want."

"Who found the body?" she asked.

"Some photographer called it in. Let me see." Booker checked his mobile and scanned a statement. "Mr Colin Jackman. He found something underneath the footbridge and gave it a poke."

"A poke?"

"Apparently."

"You can't just go around poking things. That's how your fiancée got pregnant."

"Not funny, Sarge. We planned it."

They were soon walking between curtains of tall, brown reeds, thin like straw. The light was fading, and the sun would set in an hour. Summers was tired of the short days and longed to feel the warmth of the sun on her face again. Getting up and going home in the dark was getting to her.

They followed the sound of murmuring voices. The path led over a short footbridge, a few yards long, and then to a narrow clearing blocked by another line of police tape.

Summers stopped, took a deep breath, and looked at Booker. "Ready for this?"

"Always ready and prepared, Sarge. I was a boy scout."

She rolled her eyes.

They stood pressed against the tape as she surveyed the scene. A wooden footbridge, about thirty feet long, spanned a creek, which flowed into the Fishbourne Channel several hundred yards east. A handful of muddy SOCOs were busying themselves around the bridge and along the banks of the creek. Summers had walked the marshes and meadows many times before with her ex. She knew this spot was a popular place for dog walkers and bird-watchers. Anyone could have come along at any moment to interrupt the murder. Had no one seen or heard anything? The killer had taken an enormous risk.

She looked beyond the bridge where the footpath went southwards, following the west side of the tidal inlet. She remembered the path split, looping back to Main Road in Fishbourne or towards Bosham. This route could have been another way the killer accessed the footbridge.

"So, why here?" Summers asked Booker.

"Your guess is as good as mine," he replied.

A SOCO in dirty coveralls spotted them and tugged the arm of another standing with a plastic evidence bag. He had somehow kept himself clean. He looked around and lifted a gloved hand to acknowledge Summers.

"DS Summers?" he called out.

She raised her hand. "Yes. And this is DC Booker."

The man met them at the tape.

"I'm Rick Griffin, the crime scene manager." He slipped down his mask, removed his glasses, and blew on them. "We're a bit lacking in decent forensics, I'm afraid. It's hard to keep everything clean. The mud gets everywhere. This is my third set of coveralls this afternoon. People have been walking over the bridge and along the path all day. No clear footprints, I'm afraid. We've got a few to check on the footpath, but I wouldn't hold your breath on those."

"Fair enough. It looks like a nightmare. We've informed the coroner. Have you called out a forensic pathologist?"

"He's just left. He's sent DCI Dinescu an email. Not much more he can say until the victim is at the mortuary. Death was likely from drowning. You don't need a medical degree to tell you that. But there are marks on her neck and shoulders consistent with being forced under the water."

"I don't suppose there's any indication of when?"

Griffin scoffed. "What do you think? She's still quite fresh. His best estimate, without toxicology, is around a fifty per cent probability—between six and twelve hours. It's the cold running water—buggers all the measurements up. If you want a look, the body's still here, waiting to be taken away."

Summers grimaced. "I suppose I should. Wait here, Gareth. Call the response skipper for an update."

She ducked beneath the tape and followed the crime scene manager. They went over the bridge, placing their feet on the SOCO's stepping plates, which were laid in a zigzag line on the bridge.

The body lay under a yellow plastic sheet on the other side. Griffin removed the sheet, and Summers blinked when she saw a dead woman facing upwards, her arms down by her sides. She was in her underwear and appeared to be in her late thirties to early forties, with long strawberry-blonde hair drying in the wind. Her skin was white like marble on the upward-facing side, with purple streaks and blotches closest to the ground. There were dark smudges on her shoulders.

Griffin traced a mark on her left cheek with his finger. "The pathologist highlighted this bruising." Summers felt her toes curl. She tried not to stare into the woman's open eyes. She didn't want to be haunted by them in her sleep. "He suggested someone slapped her before she died."

"Do you know where she entered the water?"

"We do. You can see better from the bridge." She followed Griffin onto the far side of the footbridge. He pointed towards a separation of the reeds labelled by yellow numbered evidence markers. Someone had crushed the reeds underfoot, drawing a line of travel towards the bank of the creek. "I'd say the killer dragged her down there. The victim floated with the current and got stuck under the footbridge. The creek is only a few feet deep here."

She shuddered. The woman's face was still fresh in her mind. "Where did the man who discovered the body go in?"

"Mr Jackman told us he went into the creek on the down-stream side of the bridge." Griffin pointed again. "The patterns of disturbance in the reeds support that. He left his boot marks in the mud, along with his walking stick."

"Was her body underneath the footbridge or not when he found it?"

"Underneath. I've read his account," said Griffin, "and it makes sense. The victim wouldn't have been visible to passersby." He lifted the evidence bag he was carrying and showed Summers.

She frowned. "A watch?"

"He saw it in the water. It was about two feet from the side of the bridge. He went down to the creek to retrieve it, and that's when he saw something underneath in the shadows. He didn't know what it was, so he poked it with his stick."

"As you do," said Summers.

"Precisely. The body then moved a few feet into view. It barely had any buoyancy, so it got stuck again."

She thought for a moment, biting her bottom lip. The icy wind was cutting through her, and she heard the plastic sheet over the corpse fluttering as it lifted. "The watch couldn't have come from her body when she was in the water. It would've just sunk." She squinted as she imagined two figures arguing on the footbridge. "It may have come off in a struggle right here."

Griffin raised his eyebrows. "It appears that way." He moved the evidence bag so Summers could see the watch strap. "The strap is gold, too, with links. It's a woman's watch. There should be masses of DNA from the skin and hair between the links—if the water hasn't washed it away, that is."

"We can match it to the victim if it's hers."

Griffin nodded. "If it *is* hers. Could be her killer's."

"That would be too easy for us," Summers said. "Do we have her clothes?"

"No. We only have the underwear she's wearing. No bag or shoes, either. Hence, no ID."

Summers heard the water trickling below. She imagined drowning in the ice-cold stream—the desperate gasp for air as the water touched her skin. She shuddered. Booker caught her attention, pacing along the path behind the tape on his mobile.

"Is that all you need?" Griffin asked. "I must get on—we'll be losing the light soon."

"Yes, sure. I'll contact the police search advisor, and we'll get a team down here. They'll give us a better idea where to look for the clothes rather than just crashing officers through the reeds."

"Agreed."

They left the bridge and walked back to the police tape. Summers looked at her watch. "It will be dark in less than an hour. Jackman discovered her after two, and she'd been in the water for between six and twelve hours. So, she died between two and eight this morning. It would have got light around eight."

"That's right. According to the pathologist's initial assessment."

"Thank you, Rick. I'll let you get on. I'll be in touch."

Griffin smiled and nodded.

Summers returned to Booker, who had just come off his mobile. They walked back along the footpath towards the car park, and she updated him on what she'd learned.

"No point us both seeing the body," said Summers.

"Thanks," said Booker. "I've just had the response sergeant bend my ear on the phone. He said he was working to a twelve-hour timeframe. They've done a load of house-to-house enquiries along Mill Lane and discovered two houses with video doorbell footage. There's another house with CCTV cameras, but the owners aren't in. Their neighbours say they're away."

"I'll get someone to take on your most urgent caseload, Gareth. We're all on this now. You can go over the statement of the man who found the body. Then it's background checks and the usual. And contact the police search advisor for me and update him. We need the POLSA and a team down here ASAP tomorrow morning. I'll update the boss and call Sarah to get a list of missing persons."

"So, it's a confirmed murder, Sarge?"

"That's what we're working with, Gareth. It's time to roll up our sleeves."

Chapter Five

Yolanda Mellor put the key in the latch and called out as she eased open the front door. "Lily?"

Silence.

Her stomach turned. She knew it was a foolish thing to do. She'd got herself all worked up over nothing.

She walked through the house and found no sign Lily had been home. The kettle was cold. Her yoghurts in the fridge remained untouched. Lily's scent was missing. Was this it? Had she really gone?

The message from the man called Justin was still on the answering machine for Lily. Yolanda had heard him leave it last night. *You can't trust a man like that. Bastard!* She nodded in agreement with herself. She was still clutching her car keys and gazing at them. A pang of regret and doubt came over her, and her eyes filled with tears. Was it too late to save her? Could she bring her back?

They were happy the way they were. How could she have got this so wrong? *Typical of a man to ruin everything!* She squeezed the keys into her palm until it hurt. How was she going to live without her?

She looked over at Lily's chair, and she could still see her there, reading some book she had picked up from her shop. The mantel clock ticked. If only she could turn back time.

The smell of overripe bananas wafted from their bowl on the sideboard next to the photograph of Lily taken before Christmas. She looked so pretty in that green dress, her hair swept from the right side of her face and tucked over her left shoulder. So pretty. Yolanda stroked her neck with her forefinger.

"This is just stupid!"

Lily had gone, and that was her choice.

She dropped onto her sofa and gazed at the coffee table. Her fingers traced the gouge in the surface veneer, one of the casualties from last night's storm of words. Lily's smashed mobile was the other, still where it landed on the floor. If only Lily had been honest with her, it would have blown over. It wouldn't have ended with name-calling and all that followed. But to be so callous was too much after everything they had been through. Everything. Lily had meant everything.

Yolanda removed her coat and school ID card and hung them in the hallway. She poured herself a large glass of cabernet sauvignon and considered running a bath to soak away her worries. Instead, she stared out of the conservatory into the darkness, catching her warped reflection. Lily's works in progress were against the wall, under a large throw. Paintings of the marshes, a boat moored in the water, a grey structure silhouetted against a sunset. Yolanda knew these watercolours well, having watched Lily paint most of them. A few pastels, pencil sketches, and pages of calligraphy were also among Lily's creations.

Then she remembered, and her heart raced. The thought swept her away, spinning her head. Sweat formed on her forehead. She ran up the stairs to the landing and stared at the loft hatch.

"No, I can't! They belong to me!"

The telephone rang downstairs, and it broke her panic. She

returned to the lounge to pick it up before the answering machine kicked in. "Yolanda Mellor speaking," she said, trying to catch her breath.

"Hello, it's Angela from the shop. Can I speak with Lily?" Angela's tone was spiky.

"I'm sorry, she's not here. I'm Lily's friend—we share a house."

"Yes, I know who you are. Lily often speaks about you."

"Really?" She allowed herself a self-gratified smile. "Haven't you seen her today?"

Angela paused. "That's why I'm calling. She never turned up for work."

Yolanda gripped the receiver tighter. "That's unlike her."

"I wondered if she was sick and didn't tell me. I've been on my own all day, and I'm a volunteer." Angela stuttered. "Sh-She can't do this to me. It's simply not fair!"

Yolanda didn't know what to say.

Angela's voice softened. "Is she okay? I don't mean to be cruel."

"She never came home last night, and I haven't heard from her."

"Gosh! This is serious. Have you tried the hospital?"

Yolanda froze, and her stomach flipped over. What if she was? "No. I never considered she could be in there."

"Perhaps you should check. If she does turn up, can you please get her to call me? Tell her I need to speak with her."

"Yes. I will. Bye."

The phone went dead, and she replaced the receiver.

Icy numbness crept from her chest into her neck and face as she stood motionless. What was she meant to do now? Every idea she had only made her feel like she would drown, but she had to do something. She grabbed her coat. Stepping outside, the night air stung her face, and she heard the distant hum of traffic in the city. She knew the way, but what would she say? It had to be done —any normal person would have by now.

When DCI Dinescu reached his office, he put down his coffee and loosened his tie. A throbbing ache stretched around his head. He had just come out of a meeting for Operation Birchwood with the Crown Prosecution Service lawyers. The two linked murders at a private school last year had been a complex case for the team, but it was now ready for trial.

He pulled out his mobile phone and dialled a number. "Looks like I'm going to be late," he said, removing his jacket with one hand and slinging it onto the back of his chair. "A serious job's come in, and I need to speak to Emily. I'm sorry, Lisa. Leave my dinner on the side and kiss Sophia for me. I'll be back as soon as I can. I love you." He ended the call and sighed. He'd been married to Lisa for almost seventeen years and still hated letting her down at the last minute.

He sat at his desk, catching his breath and massaging his left temple. His forefinger traced the ragged contour of the scar on his cheek. Remembering the paracetamol on his desk, he reached for his coffee and realised he'd let it go cold. He took the tablets with it, anyway.

Dinescu was ignoring a call from the media manager at HQ when he saw Summers walk into the department. He pulled down his shirt cuffs—a habit he'd developed many years ago—and left his office to join her.

Summers's desk was closest to Dinescu's office. He noticed her jacket draped over it, together with a baguette she must have bought from a garage. The others' desks were back-to-back behind hers. Two of them were empty. DCs Ross Taylor and

Chester Kirby were away on secondment for three months. It couldn't have come at a worse time.

Dinescu heard laughter and people clapping. He saw the CID team in a meeting through a gap in the screens—someone was leaving to have a baby. Hearing the banter gave him flashbacks of being a DS in the Met, working in the middle of a busy team. Now, his rank meant he was more of a project manager than a doer.

Summers updated the whiteboard, still stained with the faint notes from previous briefings. Dinescu stood behind her, towering over her as he watched. She was muttering to herself and referring to notes she had made on her mobile.

"I followed your updates during the meeting," said Dinescu.

Emily turned, surprised he was standing there. "Ah, boss, how was it?"

"Hard work. The first trial starts in six weeks. Nothing is outstanding for us to do in the meantime."

"That's a great result. We're snowed under here."

Dinescu studied the whiteboard and frowned, making deep furrows appear on his smooth forehead. "Who's checking missing persons?"

"Sarah. And Gareth liaised with the POLSA regarding the search for the victim's clothes in the marshes."

"That's all sorted, Sarge," said Booker at his desk.

"Anything to ID her?" Dinescu asked.

"No, sir," said Summers. "And she was only wearing her underwear. God knows what she went through."

"A sexual motive? That's even more worrying."

Sarah Burgess arrived with a tray of hot drinks and placed it on Summers's desk.

"Just what the doctor ordered," said Booker, looking up from his computer with a smile.

"Come and gather around," said Dinescu, feeling a little less groggy. "Emily, what timeframe do we have?" The others perched on desks near the whiteboard.

"It's unclear, sir," said Summers. "Colin Jackman discovered her around 14:00. The pathologist will only give a fifty per cent probability of a time of death—six to twelve hours before that."

"It's difficult when the body's been in the water," said Dinescu. Images of grey, bloated bodies pulled from the Thames flashed before his eyes.

"We still don't know for sure the victim died in the creek, but it's likely." Summers reached for her baguette and ripped off the wrapper. "There are no witnesses or nearby CCTV. We have potential doorbell camera footage from Mill Lane to look through. It doesn't look promising, though."

Dinescu rocked on the balls of his feet and curled his bottom lip under his teeth. "Why on the marshes? There are easier places to kill someone."

"It's secluded there," she said. "Perhaps it was a crime of passion." She took a bite of her baguette. "Sorry, I'm starving—no time for lunch. Someone lost control, a domestic gone wrong?"

Dinescu looked at the empty desks. "When are Ross and Chester back from secondment?"

Summers swallowed. "Another two weeks for Chester. Crawley CID's running him ragged. I haven't heard from Ross. I hope Worthing Special Ops are treating him well. All hush-hush, I assume."

"We're very short on numbers. I'll talk to Detective Chief Superintendent Faraday. We need to steal more officers from somewhere to help out."

"Thanks, sir, but everywhere is cut back right now. There aren't enough officers anywhere, and the ones we do have are all shiny and new. No experience."

"That's politics for you," said Booker.

"Sarah," said Dinescu, "I assume we have nothing from Missing Persons?"

"No, sir," said Burgess. "No one matching that description. They're going to check with neighbouring forces for us."

"And I've been through all triple-nine calls over the last twenty-four hours in the area," said Booker. "No dropped calls. A couple of violent domestics, but nothing is outstanding."

Dinescu grabbed a fresh cup of coffee while Summers finished her food. "What do we know about the man who discovered the victim?"

"His name's Colin Jackman," said Booker, reading the log. "He's in his mid-sixties, a retired schoolteacher, and a resident of Fishbourne. It was usual for him to be on the marshes. Jackman's a member of a camera club and often photographs the area around Bosham. His only previous dealings with us were for a couple of breaches of the peace and obstruction of the highway. He's an environmentalist."

"That's not a crime," said Burgess.

"No, but shouting abuse at tourists and blocking the road to the Witterings is."

"He was one of those, was he?" said Summers.

"Yes," said Booker. "He has a website with a ton of photos of the marshes and the meadows—lots of animals with fur and feathers."

"You mean *wildlife*, Gareth," said Sarah.

"That's the word. He's written a few opinionated political blogs, but nothing that stands out."

"Thanks, Gareth," said Summers. "You have been busy."

"Emily, house-to-house?" said Dinescu.

"Initial enquiries have so far drawn a blank. No one saw or heard anything on Mill Lane in the early hours of Monday. Are you happy for an appeal for witnesses to be put out, boss? It would be wise to get it out early."

Dinescu nodded. "Yes. ASAP, please. Make sure it's on the local Facebook groups, too. There'll be a limited press release this evening to local media. I don't want any details of the crime scene to be made known. It will fuel unwanted speculation."

"I'll keep an eye on social media," said Booker. "Someone may have inadvertently witnessed something."

"And someone's bound to miss her soon," said Burgess.

"I hope so, Sarah," said Dinescu, rubbing his eyes. He checked the time. "It's getting late, and we all have lives outside this job. We can't do much with this now, and the late shift can cover if anything comes in. I don't know about you, but I need a fresh start in the morning. We'll have a briefing first thing. The coroner authorised the postmortem for tomorrow, and I'll be there. We'll know more about what we are dealing with then."

"Sorry to interrupt, sir." One of the response sergeants appeared in the office. They all turned around to look at her. "A woman has turned up outside Reception on the out-of-hours phone. She's reporting her housemate missing. One of my officers is taking a misper report from Miss Yolanda Mellor from Lapwing Close in Chichester. I'm not sure where the hell that is. Her housemate has been missing since last night." The response sergeant grimaced. "She's a white forty-year-old female named Lily Watson."

Dinescu could feel his team's hearts sinking. This couldn't wait until the morning. "Has she given a detailed description of her housemate?"

"Better than that, sir," said the sergeant. She reached out to Summers and passed her an A5 photograph. "This was taken before Christmas."

Dinescu watched Summers's eyes darken, and her nostrils flare. She nodded for a few moments. "This is our victim. I'll go."

"How certain are you?" Dinescu asked.

"It's her, boss." Summers looked at Booker and Burgess. "If

you need to get off, then that's fine. Sarah, you've got to get back for Rosie."

Burgess nodded. "Thanks, Sarge."

"I'll come with you, Emily," said Dinescu.

"Sir?"

"It's okay."

"I can stay on," said Booker. "My missus is seeing her parents tonight."

"Thank you, Gareth," said Summers. "Get the details of the woman reporting and run some checks on her."

Booker nodded. "I'm on it."

Chapter Six

Summers and Dinescu found Yolanda Mellor in a small, bright room they used for taking statements. She had been waiting with the police officer who had taken her missing person report. Mellor was a short, pale woman—somewhat mousey—whom Summers found hard to age, but at a guess, she was somewhere between forty and fifty. The station was always hot, so Mellor had removed her thick brown coat. Underneath, she wore a thin cardigan with long sleeves.

Sitting opposite the detectives, she played with the frayed end of a sleeve. The shabby state of it suggested to Summers that she often did this, likely due to anxiety. Mellor stared wide-eyed at Dinescu. Summers knew his appearance unnerved some people. He was tall, bald, and broad, with a burn scar on the side of his face.

Holding her pen ready, Summers began in a soft voice. "Hello, Yolanda. This is Detective Chief Inspector Dinescu, and I'm Detective Sergeant Summers."

Mellor gave a thin smile, avoiding eye contact. "What more do you need to know? I've given Lily's description to the policeman."

"I know," said Summers, trying to reassure her. "Thank you. You said you live on Lapwing Close. We're trying to figure out where that is. Is it new?"

"Yes," said Mellor, her voice soft and shaky. "It's a new estate off Old Broyle Road."

Summers tried to put her at ease with a smile. "That explains it." She dipped her head to make eye contact with her. "I know this must be upsetting for you. You're doing really well."

Mellor's dark mop of grey-streaked hair bounced as she nodded. She leaned forward, folding her arms.

"Tell us when you realised Lily was missing," said Summers.

"Lily doesn't do things like this." Mellor shook her head. "She went out yesterday evening. I went to bed early, ready for school —I'm a teacher. When I didn't see her this morning, I checked her room, and her bed hadn't been slept in. She didn't come home last night."

"Did you try calling her?"

"No. She left her mobile phone behind when she went out."

"How about calls to her friends or relatives?"

"I'm Lily's closest relative. Well, we're not blood relatives, but we might as well be. Years ago, people would have called us companions. We travel together occasionally and enjoy each other's company. She has a few work friends and a couple more at the art club she attends, but I don't have their numbers. I was going to try the hospital in case she'd had an accident, but I thought I'd better come here first."

"Does Lily have any social media accounts?" asked Summers.

"She's on Facebook. Braver than me. I wouldn't want my children's parents to find me online."

"And what art club is Lily a member of?" asked Summers.

"Chichester Landscape Art Society. I went to a couple of their exhibitions with Lily."

"So, Lily works. Where is that?"

"The MHCC. It's a charity shop on North Street. She's the manager there—Mental Health Crisis Care."

"Would you say you're her next-of-kin?"

Mellor hesitated, and she gave a slight smile. "I suppose I must be. She moved in with me a few years ago as a lodger, and we've stuck with each other. We've been to Paris together, Morocco, and Madrid—we get along well. We share the same sense of humour, too. I bought a new place a few months ago, and Lily came with me. Neither of us is married—no interest in that sort of thing. Well, I haven't, and I didn't think she had either."

Summers made a note on her pad. "Are you partners, Yolanda? I mean, in the romantic sense."

Her cheeks flushed, and her hand went to her face. "Gosh! What a question! I don't know what Lily would say if she heard you ask that. As I said, we're companions."

Summers smiled and nodded. "Do you know her date of birth?"

"Yes, that's easy. It's the 11th of October. I guess it must be 1983. I remember because my grandfather died on the 11th of October. He was a policeman, too, back in the day. He had a whistle and a cape—and a wooden truncheon. Not like today, eh?" She received polite smiles of agreement from the detectives.

Summers underlined the note she had written.

"We've done a check since you've been here, and we can see that Lily drives. We've checked her driving licence details and they match your address and her date of birth. Miss Mellor—"

"Yolanda, please. The kids at school call me Miss Mellor." She gave a nervous laugh.

Summers took a breath and put a photograph on the table and slid it in front of Yolanda. "This photo you brought with you—can we keep it?"

"Yes, if it helps you find her."

"This image closely matches her driving licence photograph. And Lily looks like this now?"

"Yes." A worried frown ran across Yolanda's face. "Do you know where she is? Is she in the hospital?"

"Yolanda, I have something I must tell you. Someone found a woman matching the description of the one in this photograph on Fishbourne Marshes today. She had drowned in the creek. I'm so sorry."

Mellor's mouth dropped open. She tried to speak, but nothing came out but wheezy air. Her face emptied of colour. Summers thought her reaction seemed genuine enough, but it didn't reach her eyes. Was there some hidden resentment?

Summers touched Yolanda's forearm. "Sadly, I recognise the woman in this photograph as the woman who drowned."

"Lily's dead? There must be some mistake!"

"Would you like a drink of water?"

She shook her head. "It can't be Lily. That's stupid!"

Taking out her mobile phone, Summers produced an image the crime scene manager had sent her. "We found this watch near Lily. Do you recognise it?"

As she studied it, Mellor's left eye flickered as if something had fallen into it. Her bottom lip quivered, and she swallowed hard. "It was a fortieth birthday present from me last year. We only have each other—or I thought we did. It turned out she had so many secrets." She reached for her handbag to get tissues. "How? I don't understand. Did she fall into the water?"

Summers's voice softened. "The postmortem is tomorrow morning, and we'll know more then. It's still too early to be certain. The initial assessment is that she drowned." Summers knew this next part would be difficult. "And we're treating her death as suspicious."

"Someone hurt her deliberately?" Mellor sat back, and her face darkened. "I don't believe that for a moment."

"It's something we're investigating," said Summers. "Did she know that area well?"

"Yes. We both do. Lily paints—she's very talented. Our house is full of her paintings—the marshes in Fishbourne, the harbour, Dell Quay. Why would anyone hurt her? And where's her easel? Was it with her?"

"We didn't find an artist's easel."

"It must be in her car. Oh, God! Lily..."

Dinescu nodded and pursed his lips. "You are being very brave, Yolanda. Any information you give us will help us discover what happened. Where did Lily go yesterday evening?"

Mellor covered her eyes with her palms. "I don't know! I mean, she didn't tell me where she was going."

"Was that usual behaviour?" Dinescu asked.

"No, not at all. You see..." She gazed at the ceiling, and she sobbed.

"Take your time. I know this is hard."

She took a deep breath to stop herself. "We had a tiff."

"A tiff?" Dinescu looked at Summers for help. "What is a *tiff*?"

"It means a falling out, sir," said Summers. "A quarrel—an argument."

"Ah, yes, I understand. What was your *tiff* about?"

"It was stupid," said Mellor. "Some mystery man was showing interest in her. She denied it at first, but I knew she'd been seeing someone on the quiet—telephone calls cut short, walking out to speak privately. Eventually, she said it was Justin she'd been seeing. He owns an art gallery in Bosham. So many little secrets. The thing is, I know the man's married! Or at least has a partner."

"And that caused an argument between you?"

"She tried to keep it from me, and I'd had enough. I told you it was stupid. We shouted at each other, and Lily stormed out. That was the last time I saw her." Mellor's shoulders shook. "No, not Lily. This can't be happening."

"And she didn't take her mobile phone?" said Summers.

"No. It's smashed. She threw it at me, you see. Told me to check her messages myself, or words to that effect. Then she stormed out in a rage."

"Did she take anything with her? Clothes? An overnight bag?"

"I don't know. I heard her go to her room and then come down again. She went straight out of the front door."

"What time did she leave the house?"

"About nine-thirty. Could have been a few minutes earlier."

Summers wrote down the time. "Is that the last time you saw or heard from her?"

"Yes."

"The car she took," said Dinescu, "is it registered to her?"

"Yes. A BMW Mini, black."

Dinescu sighed and leaned forward, his face sympathetic. "All of us have argued with our loved ones and friends. Do you know where she would have gone if she were angry? Somewhere to cool down."

"Not really," she said, wiping mascara-streaked tears from her cheeks. "Perhaps she went to see that Justin in Bosham. I don't know where she went."

"Do you have Justin's contact details?"

"No, but his gallery is near the arts centre on Bosham Lane. He left her a message on the answering machine after she'd stormed out. Probably couldn't get through to her mobile as it was broken. The message was something to do with meeting up with her today."

"Okay, Yolanda," said Summers. "We need to go to your home to collect her mobile phone."

"But it's broken."

"It doesn't matter. We still need it. We also need to search her bedroom and get that answering machine message."

"Search her room? Yes, of course. But the phone…"

"We'll go back to your home with you once we've finished here," said Summers.

"Well, if you must."

"As you're the closest to Lily's next of kin that we know of, could you formally identify Lily for us?"

"See her body?"

"And formally identify her. We have the driving licence photo, but we'd prefer confirmation from someone who knew her."

Clenching her jaw, Mellor nodded. "Yes. I'll do it. There's no one else, anyway. I can at least say goodbye. I never said goodbye, you see."

"It will be tomorrow morning, after the postmortem. I'll let you know. Perhaps you should take some time off work. You shouldn't be on your own. Do you have anyone who can sit with you?"

"No. There's no one. There was only…"

"Okay, Yolanda," said Dinescu. "DS Summers will take over from here. The sooner we recover Lily's phone, the better."

Summers led Mellor back to Reception where she told her to wait. She then found Booker with Dinescu in the Major Crimes office.

"What did you make of her reaction?" she asked Dinescu as she signed out car keys from the CID board.

"I'm not sure," he said. "It seemed genuine. She'd be a talented actress if it weren't."

Summers turned to Booker. "Come on, sunshine. You're with me. We're going to Lily Watson's house to look around and seize her mobile phone."

Chapter Seven

Summers and Booker were behind Yolanda Mellor's blue Fiat, turning off Old Broyle Road. They were on a road with fresh tarmac that snaked for a quarter of a mile, following the line of a new estate. The land was once farmland between Chichester and Fishbourne. The entire estate had been snapped up even before the houses were built. On one side of the road were mounds of earth forming a sculpted park, still muddy and waterlogged from the heavy rains in December.

After several twists and turns, they pulled into Lapwing Close, where Mellor parked in a narrow driveway. They saw the estate was coming to life, with signs of families moving in.

The detectives gathered their things and asked Mellor to wait in her car until they were ready.

"What do you think of these places, Sarge?" Booker asked. "No character, if you ask me."

"Not to my taste," said Summers. "I'm happy with my flat in the city."

Summers and Booker went to the front door and called for Mellor to join them. As she walked towards them, she stopped and looked at the windows.

"I don't remember leaving all the lights on," said Mellor, as she inserted her door key. "The door's not double-locked. I always double-lock when I leave. Is Lily…? No…" She pushed the door wide and stepped over the threshold. "Something's not right."

Summers stopped her from going any further. "Wait outside with DS Booker."

"What's wrong?"

Summers put on her blue gloves and peered through the open lounge door. Cupboard doors were open, a TV was on its side, and sofa cushions were scattered over the floor.

"Looks like you've been burgled," said Summers.

"Burgled!" said Mellor. "On top of everything else!"

"Go and sit in our car." Summers turned to Booker. "Gareth, update Control, then look around the back of the house."

"On it, Sarge," said Booker, ushering Mellor towards their car.

Summers went back inside the house and bellowed. "Police officer! Show yourself!"

The house was silent, and she was relieved there was no response. It was times like this when Summers wished she carried a taser.

She remembered to follow a path through the lounge that the burglar was unlikely to have taken—Rick Griffin would be proud, she thought. She saw a light flashing around the back garden—it was Booker with a torch.

The kitchen door was intact, as was the conservatory. No broken glass anywhere. The search through the house seemed random. They had ignored a glass cabinet filled with trinkets and a presentation case containing an old police truncheon, a whistle, and a set of old epaulettes. Nothing in there was worth taking.

Summers climbed the stairs along the edges of each tread. According to Mellor, Lily's bedroom was at the back of the house. It was a mess, with clothes and paperwork strewn over the floor.

A laptop computer lay in pieces against a wall, its keyboard hanging off. The front bedroom was also upside down. The mattress was on the floor, the wardrobe doors were open, and clothes were ripped from their hangers. On the base of the bed lay an upturned jewellery box with gold necklaces spilling from the lid.

Summers stopped for a moment. She didn't want to disturb anything, but something didn't look or feel right. Why were the gold necklaces still in the jewellery box? Why destroy the computer rather than take it? Her instincts told her this wasn't a typical burglary. There was a sense of hurried chaos, as if the intruder had been searching for something specific. She took note of the haphazard scattering of Mellor's belongings. It made little sense. A frantic search for cash, perhaps. It could be that. But why was there no forced entry? She had attended many burglaries before, but this one seemed different.

She stood at the top of the stairs and updated the police control room on her radio. How was she going to handle this now, and what was messing with her head?

A forensics van was outside Mellor's house, and a SOCO was assessing the front windows with a bright torch.

"Well, the house is a mess," said Summers. "The only thing they didn't touch was Yolanda's display of worthless knick-knacks." She was sitting with Dinescu in a police car parked behind the van. He had arrived a few minutes ago. The only light came from the display on the police radio. "We found jewellery on the bed and a smashed laptop computer. Why weren't they taken?"

"What are *knick-knacks*?" asked Dinescu.

"Trinkets, sir. Souvenirs people buy on holiday."

"Do we know how they got in?" he asked.

"There are no signs of forced entry anywhere. All the doors and windows were closed, and there was no damage. Yolanda noticed the front door wasn't double-locked. She said she always double-locked it. And all the lights were on, too."

"So the burglar had a key. Where is she now?"

"With her neighbour, giving a statement to Gareth. She's shaken up."

"Genuinely?" Dinescu asked.

"As far as I can tell, sir. The neighbour said her porch light came on, but that's it. She saw someone at her front door earlier in the day, but he looked like he was delivering a parcel or something similar."

"Interesting. Did anyone have a spare set of keys?"

"Only Lily and Yolanda had keys to the house," said Summers.

"Were they the first people to move in?"

"Yes."

"So what was taken?" he asked.

Summers shrugged. "Lily's mobile phone is missing. That's what we came for."

Together, they watched a SOCO move a light to illuminate the front door. She began dusting around the door handle and the panels.

"So, the burglar had a door key," he said. "If that's the case, then it's likely this was Lily's killer. They probably took Lily's keys."

"You're suggesting Lily's murderer did this because they wanted the phone?"

Dinescu nodded. "I'd say so. The door key was likely on her keyring with her car key."

"The situation seems off, sir. Yolanda could have faked the burglary as a method to lose the mobile."

"True. But why not fake the forced entry, too? How many faked burglaries have you seen where the supposed victim didn't stage the break-in? A smashed window or broken lock? I've not seen any."

The SOCO brought out some wide, clear tape and lifted a fingerprint from the door panel.

"Have they checked for traces of blood in the house?" Dinescu asked.

"Yes, boss," said Summers. "No blood traces found. There's nothing to suggest Lily was attacked in there. According to Yolanda, a message from Lily's mystery man should be on the answering machine. I'll ask the SOCO to arrange for the device to be examined."

Summers left the car, and Dinescu watched her gesticulate to the SOCO, explaining the situation with the answering machine. He looked at his watch—three hours late off now.

She returned, and Dinescu started the engine. "I'm tired, and you look tired, too. I'll take you back to the station so you can get your things. Need a lift home?"

"I'd appreciate it," she said. "I walked to work today."

He tilted his head and smiled. "I hope you do things for fun when you're not working."

Summers laughed. "Fun? What's that?"

"Policing is relentless. Take a break and enjoy life, Emily. If you need company any time, come over to ours. Lisa would be pleased to see you."

"Will she? She's not upset with me about Kieran?"

Dinescu shook his head. "Not at all! She is protective of her little brother, but she could see it wouldn't work. Anyway, you and Kieran are still friends, and Kieran is fine. So…"

"Your wife is amazing, sir."

"I know." The corner of his mouth lifted. "She tells me every day." He selected first gear. "Let's get you back."

A faint smile appeared on Summers's lips. The car pulled away from Mellor's house, leaving the forensic team still busy at work. She glanced back, her mind already processing the next steps. This case was far from straightforward, and she knew they had a long road ahead.

Chapter Eight

Emily Summers removed her lanyard and closed the front door to her flat. It had been an exhausting day, and her feet ached. Questions from the case troubled her, circling around her mind, desperate to be scratched and examined. The image of Lily's dead face staring into nothingness flashed before her.

"Nope! I'm not having that."

She composed herself and stood still for a few breaths. Her flat was silent, and she was sad there was no one to welcome her home. She'd considered getting a cat once, but it would be stuck indoors all day, and she hated the smell of cat litter. She'd gone for dinner with Ross Taylor and his husband last year. They had two cats, Blue Point Siamese. Una and Dos, they were called. The smell of their litter trays made her feel sick.

She slipped off her shoes, and her feet felt better straight away. She remembered picking up her post from her mailbox and stuffing the letters into her coat pocket. She pulled them out, hung up her coat, and went straight to the kitchen. The fridge was full of ready meals—most of them within their use-by date. But no wine. She was attempting Dry January, although her willpower had already ebbed away.

Choosing a chicken tikka masala, which had to be eaten by today, she put on the kettle, unsure if hot chocolate would go with a curry.

She went through each letter: a reminder that her mobile charges were going up, her fuel supplier was changing, and last, a letter addressed to *Miss Emily R. Summers*. She never shared her middle name. Her mother wouldn't write her a letter, so her next thought was Anthony, her ex. Had he found out where she'd moved to? After leaving him last year, Emily moved in with her mother and found the flat in November. Anthony had tried to contact her at her mother's in the summer, which ended with him being arrested for harassment. He'd be stupid if he tried it again. She opened the letter—it wasn't dated.

Dear Emily,

I hope this letter finds you well. It's been a long time since we said goodbye. I have that memory etched into my mind. I remember how beautiful you looked with your long blonde hair and short red dress. I like to think about that often.

I will be in Portsmouth on January 20th. I'd love to meet you again and catch up. How about where you waved goodbye to me? At midday? Can you do that? You have a special place in my heart, Emily.

Yours always.

The letter was signed in an awkward, rough scrawl that Emily couldn't make out.

"Who the frig is that?" she said to herself. "Creepy!"

She shuddered when she reread it, especially the part about the short red dress. The last time she wore that was before Christmas at the nightclub in Southsea. She'd gone with an old school friend and persuaded Sarah Burgess to go with her. Much of the night was a drunken blur, except for the three Americans staying in Portsmouth at a conference. They tried to convince her to go back to their hotel with them.

"But how do they know where I live? Did I tell them? I need a big dog, not a cat. What is it with men?"

The microwave pinged. She was about to put the letter in the recycling but thought again. Did she need it as evidence?

She looked outside at the street below. Chichester didn't look as busy as usual. No one had the money after Christmas. She peered into the shadows across the road, imagining a man watching her window. She yanked her curtains closed and told herself off for being so stupid. She tried to remember what the three men looked like. Two of them were in their mid-forties. The other was around fifty-something. They wore open-necked shirts and trousers, looking like they'd removed their ties for a night on the pull.

"Yuck!"

She grabbed her curry, mixed it in a bowl, and curled up in front of her TV. Then she remembered the unopened merlot in the cupboard.

With a sigh, Emily got up and retrieved the bottle, deciding that Dry January was officially over. She poured herself a generous glass, swirling the rich red liquid around as she returned to the sofa. The first sip was soothing, warming her from the inside out, and she let out a small, satisfied sigh. The tension of a difficult Monday began to melt away as she took another sip, the wine pairing well with the spicy curry. The warmth of the merlot and the comforting flavours of the tikka masala made her feel a little more secure despite the unsettling letter. She thought about what her boss had said. Policing is relentless. Then she remembered his words regarding Kieran. Maybe she was being too hard on herself. If Lisa understood, then it's likely Kieran did, too.

As she settled back into the cushions, she flicked through the TV channels, trying to find something light-hearted to watch. She landed on an old sitcom, its familiar humour providing a much-needed distraction. But her thoughts kept drifting back to the letter, the unsettling words, and the eerie knowledge of where she lived. She resolved to ask Sarah in the morning about the men they'd met that night and to see if she could help piece together more details. For now, though, Emily allowed herself to relax, her eyelids growing heavy as the comforting buzz of the wine took hold. Her flat, a place of solitude, now felt like a refuge, a small bubble of safety in a world that had just thrown her a curveball.

It was close to midnight. Joseph McKinley had always thought Dean Court smelled like an old people's home. The other residents had gone to their rooms, leaving Joseph sitting alone in a high-backed chair in the communal lounge. The only light was from the emergency exit signs above the side door.

"Lily's dead," Joseph said to himself, but the voices didn't answer him anymore. "What did I do?"

He had never wanted a drink so badly. But it wasn't for the tremors this time. That was long gone. He wanted something to take away the sadness and rage.

A noise came from the corridor. Someone entered the kitchen, turning on the kettle. A shadow appeared in the doorway. It was Jeff, the support worker.

"Joseph?" he said, peering into the dark. "You okay, mate?"

"Not really, fella," Joseph replied. His voice was low and gruff. "But who gives a shit?"

"I'm making a tea. Want one?"

"A whisky would be better."

"Ha! I know, but I'm making tea."

"Yeah. I'll have one with you."

Joseph watched Jeff disappear towards the kitchen. A sharp hissing sound came from the skirting board, followed by the cloying smell of lily of the valley.

Jeff reappeared. "I'll put the small light on, Joseph. Can't see a thing."

"Go ahead."

The dim yellow light on the sideboard came on, and Jeff returned carrying a small tray.

"I come with chocolate digestives. So, be nice to me, eh?"

"I'm always nice to you," said Joseph, giving a wheezy laugh. "You're a fan of lumberjack shirts."

"You noticed? They're easy to iron and hard to see if I spill my dinner." Jeff placed the tray on the small coffee table and opened the packet of biscuits. "Why are you sitting in the dark?"

"I like it."

"Okay. You don't have to tell me," said Jeff. He picked up a couple of biscuits and popped a whole one into his mouth.

"Just reflecting on my life, Jeff." Joseph stroked his beard flat and slurped his tea.

Jeff finished crunching and swallowed. "A birdie tells me you've been wandering around your old haunts. I bet that must be weird."

"Why?"

"Everything's changed so much. New houses everywhere, for a start."

"The pubs are still the same."

"The pubs?"

"I haven't partaken, if that's what you're worried about."

"Nothing to do with me, Joseph."

The two men sat in silence for a few minutes, listening to the radiator pipes ticking on the wall as they cooled.

"Time flashes by," said Joseph. "I was hoping that an old friend would meet me this morning. I thought she'd stood me up."

"A woman. Well, maybe you should try again."

"It's too late now."

"Are you sure? Give them another chance?"

"Very sure."

"Do you think people remember you in Chichester?"

"Nah. Not anymore. A good thing they don't."

Both men took a few more biscuits.

"Perhaps you can make a fresh start," said Jeff. "That's what this place is for."

"I found out something a few weeks ago, Jeff. I thought it would change everything."

Jeff lowered his cup and screwed his eyes. "Okay, go on."

"Someone had some information for me—something to clear my name. I thought they wanted to help me. But I was wrong. I don't blame them. They say blood is thicker than water, but money is thicker still."

"What information did they have?"

"It doesn't matter now—it's all shit. It's not going to happen." Joseph sat forward and lowered his voice. "You see, there's a curse upon those dark waters. They never forget a thing. Just as you think the sun is rising on you, a shadow falls. They remember everything. They remember me, Jeff."

Jeff frowned and paused before answering, "What waters are you talking about, Joseph? Help me understand."

"The Fishbourne Marshes. They remember me. They never forget."

"If you're uncomfortable there, perhaps you should stay away."

"How can I?"

"Have you been there recently, Joseph?"

Joseph wasn't ready for this now. He rose to his feet. "I'm tired. Thanks for the tea and biscuits. You're a good man, Jeff. Shame about the shirt."

He walked out of the lounge, laughing to himself, and disappeared into the shadows of the corridor towards his room.

Chapter Nine

Tuesday

The Major Crimes Office was heaving with detectives and uniformed officers. Dinescu had watched them arrive while he was on the phone, updating DCS Faraday. After ending the call, he gathered his notes and opened his office door. A mixed scent of coffee and cologne hit him. The buzz in the office ceased. It was a cold, dark morning, and the office was gloomy.

DS Jimmy Neil stood with the Chichester CID officers. He nodded to Dinescu.

"We're ready to go when you are, boss," said Summers from her desk.

"Thank you, Emily," said Dinescu. "Someone get the lights, please." The lights flickered on, and Summers stood next to him. He paused to observe the officers present. They were all so young. Where had the old faces gone? "Good afternoon, all. The murder of Lily Watson has now been designated as Operation Brook. I'm DCI Dinescu, the senior investigating officer, and this is DS Summers, my deputy. Hopefully, you'll know by now that Lily Watson was discovered in Fishbourne Creek yesterday afternoon." He outlined what they knew so far about Lily's death and the current status of the inquiry. "I'm grateful for your swift response so far, but we have a lot more ground-work to do starting this morning. We've had hardly any response from members of the public. We need to encourage them to talk to us. I want the house-to-house enquiries expanded to include Main Road and north along Salthill Road and Blackboy Lane."

Dinescu saw a few glances flash towards DS Neil. Eyes rolled at the back of the office, and officers were checking their watches. He picked up the low murmuring and groaning. Glaring at them, he shook his head, his voice cutting through them. "Is this too much trouble for some of you? If you're not up to putting in the work, then you're clearly in the wrong job. We're overstretched across the county, haemorrhaging experienced officers as a result. But we must do what we can with what we have. DS Neil—get a grip on your team!"

DS Neil's face flushed. "Yes, sir."

"Where was I?" The volume of his voice returned to normal. "DS Summers will be collecting responses from the house-to-house enquiries. She'll know if anything has been missed."

The meeting concluded after DS Summers's last update, and the room buzzed with noise and activity. Some officers returned to CID while others hurried to find spare desks, logging onto computers and work mobiles to check their assignments. Leading such a team, especially when resources were stretched thin, demanded decisiveness and positivity.

Dinescu tugged at his shirt cuffs, concealing the scars on his arms, and lingered in the doorway, watching the officers bustling around the office. A young woman in a charcoal-grey trouser suit had listened to the briefing from the back of the room. She had shoulder-length black hair—attractive and somewhat mysterious.

Dinescu watched her study the three remaining members of his team. Why was she so interested in them?

Dinescu tapped Summers on the elbow. "Who is that woman at the back with the black hair?"

Summers leaned towards Dinescu. "Her name's Daisy Irving, sir. She's a hotshot DI from Worthing. She made a beeline for me before the briefing started."

"What's she doing here?"

"She's interested in the case, boss. That's all I know."

When Dinescu looked up, the woman was gone. He grabbed his notes.

"Get the team together. We'll meet in the conference room."

"Yes, sir."

Summers called the core team into the conference room across the corridor. As they filed in, their tired eyes met Dinescu's, each officer clutching a coffee cup and sinking into their seats.

"Are we ready?" he asked.

A weary "yes, boss" echoed across the conference table.

"I need more enthusiasm than that," he said, locking eyes with each detective. "The public is expecting us to work tirelessly until we find Lily's killer. We have a great deal of work to do now, and you've probably seen that the media are all over this, demanding a name. To warn you, we all need to make arrangements to work longer hours this week."

"That's understood, sir," said Booker, glancing at Burgess.

She was frowning, looking out of the window. Dinescu noticed the slight shake of her head, betraying an inner conflict. He knew there were always professional and personal pressures when a case like this kicked off. It hit those with young families the hardest.

"Let's focus on what we know," said Dinescu. "We have a wide timeframe for the murder—somewhere between 02:00 and 08:00 yesterday. According to Yolanda Mellor, Lily was last seen alive at about 21:30 on Sunday. She stated Lily drove off in her car. So, where is it?"

"I've sent the car's details to Roads Policing to make them aware," said Booker. "ANPR hits have her car heading on the Funtington Road during the day, at 13:20 on Sunday, and then heading south through the city past Chichester College at 21:26."

"Which corroborates Mellor's account," said Summers.

"Lily's phone records came through this morning," said Burgess. She picked up a sheet of paper. "She made several calls to a pay-as-you-go phone early on Sunday evening. We don't know who this phone belongs to yet. It's a number she calls regularly." Burgess studied the list in her hands. "Several texts were sent and received near North Street in Chichester. These are for a different pay-as-you-go number. Her mobile phone was switched off at 21:18 while she was home."

"She works in a charity shop on North Street," said Summers. "Do they open on Sundays?"

Burgess shook her head. "Not likely, Sarge, but I can check."

"What about her bank records?" asked Dinescu.

Burgess picked up another sheet of paper. "The last time her card was used was Saturday at a petrol station in Nutbourne. The only thing that stands out is she withdrew a few large cash amounts in November and December. They were withdrawals totalling eight hundred pounds. Nothing else of any concern."

"Christmas presents?" said Booker.

"That's a lot for Christmas presents," said Summers.

"No cash was taken out or cards used on or after Monday," said Burgess. "Nothing to suggest where she was or with whom."

Summers shook her head. "And then we jump to Lily being found in Fishbourne Creek."

"I'm not clear how Lily came to be in the water," said Burgess, running her fingers through her braids. "Was she pushed from the footbridge?"

Dinescu leaned forward in his chair and read his notes. "Evidence points to Lily Watson being dragged through the reeds, down the bank, and into the creek. We don't know yet if there was a sexual motive." He looked at the photograph of Lily on his clipboard. "We must identify the route the killer took onto the marshes. I assume the video doorbell footage has drawn a blank."

"Nothing, sir," said Summers. "Both cameras were set to activate when people walked past them. They wouldn't pick up cars driving by. A house near the entrance of Mill Lane has a CCTV camera. It looks like it's only pointing at their front garden, but it may catch the footpath. We haven't been able to contact the property's owners yet."

"Well, perhaps that will give us something."

"The pub's CCTV cameras don't cover Mill Lane or their car park."

Dinescu flicked his pen onto the notepad and looked up. He could see the team's view of the case was getting foggy. He had to bring some clarity. "Let's go through some hypotheses. First, Mellor's argument with Lily ended in a physical altercation in the house. The pathologist highlighted the bruising on Lily's face. Could that have come from an argument? A slap injury, perhaps?"

"And Mellor could have used the burglary to cover up the mess from a fight with Lily," said Summers. "And to remove the phone when she realised we wanted it."

"A fight, Sarge?" said Booker. "Well, she didn't die at home if it was a fight. Lily drowned in the creek. Mellor would have had to lift her into her car and drag her up the path to the footbridge."

"That wouldn't work," said Dinescu. "Next, Lily had a prearranged meeting with someone she knew on or near the footbridge, and the meeting ended in an altercation. This makes more sense to me."

"It had to be someone she knew," said Booker. "Whoever took Lily Watson's keys knew where she lived and took her mobile."

Burgess nodded. "And what's on a mobile phone that we can't get remotely from cell site analysis and phone provider data?"

"Photos and encrypted messages," said Summers. "Like WhatsApp."

"Yes," said Dinescu. "So, something on Lily's mobile may have identified the killer. Perhaps details of a pre-planned meeting?"

"The only other alternative hypothesis is a stranger murder," said Burgess. "But that's so unlikely. We haven't found anyone fitting that offender profile in the area, so they would have to be someone new."

"And why remove Lily's clothes and take her keys?" said Booker, "Why do the messy search of her house to find her mobile? No, this wasn't some random stranger."

"I agree, Gareth," said Dinescu. "Removing her clothes is hugely significant. It speaks of planning and being forensically aware. Our most likely hypothesis is that she met with someone she knew."

"We're all agreed, sir," said Summers. "We must do more digging around Lily's life and the people she knew."

"Is someone checking Lily's Facebook account?"

"Yes, sir," said Burgess. "Friends and recent messages."

"Good," said Dinescu. He scanned his notes. "The search of the reedbeds and creek is continuing this morning, so the crime scene remains in place. We must identify regular users of the foot-paths across the meadows and marshes—dog walkers and the like."

"We're on that, boss," said Summers. "All recent incidents and intel reports for those locations are also being looked into."

Dinescu nodded. "Excellent. The landlord at the Bull's Head pub is happy for us to set up a mobile incident room in their car park. We should staff that with local officers, but I want us to check in with the incident room during the day."

"Okay, sir," said Summers, scribbling a few notes. "We're putting extensive efforts into tracing Lily's movements after she left Yolanda Mellor on Sunday night, but so far we've drawn a blank."

"Sarge, can I grab some officers to check the CCTV from around the city centre?" Booker asked.

"Yes, sure," said Summers with a sigh. "We're going to be overstretched very soon, boss. We could do with Chester and Ross back here." Dinescu glimpsed the worry on Summers's face.

"Let me see what I can do, Emily," said Dinescu, "but I won't make any promises." He checked his watch. "I have a postmortem to attend. Then I'd like you to get Yolanda Mellor to identify the body."

"Okay, boss," said Summers. "Sarah, go with Gareth to visit the crime scene and get a feel for the place. Look out for any locals walking the footpaths. I also need you to go to the shop where Lily worked and talk to the staff there."

Burgess nodded. Her mobile buzzed, and she checked her phone and frowned.

"Everything okay?" asked Summers.

She shook her head. "My sister has to go out tonight. I don't know what I'm going to do with Rosie."

Booker tutted.

"What?" Burgess snapped at Booker.

He held up his hands. "Nothing. I guess that's the problem with having kids."

"A problem? My daughter is not a problem, Gareth!"

Dinescu saw the horror on Summers's face, but stepping in now wasn't his job. "Emily, I must go and update the senior management team and head to the postmortem."

"No worries, boss."

Booker and Burgess stood to leave, but Summers held up her hand.

"Sit down, both of you," said Summers. She waited until Dinescu had left the room. "Gareth." She prompted him with a glare.

"I apologise, Sarah," said Booker. "I didn't mean it personally." Burgess looked up, and he reached out. "I'll find out what it's like to be a parent soon. I'm dreading being a dad, to be honest. I can't imagine how I'm going to do it. I'm terrified." He pulled at one of her braids. "I have huge respect for you, Sarah. I'll be coming to you for advice real soon. I'm sure."

Burgess smiled and sniffed. "You owe me chocolate."

"Done."

Summers motioned for Booker to leave and waited until the door closed behind him. "Is childcare causing you grief?"

Burgess nodded. "Amongst other things."

"Do you want to talk?"

"It's hard balancing the job, childcare, and finding time for me. It's like I've been written off. I'm a widow, and I'm..." Burgess brought out a tissue and dried her eyes. "I'm a bit down at the moment. I'm on my own. I have to do everything and be everything. If it weren't for my sister, I'd be screwed."

"It must be nice to have a sister like that," said Summers.

"She's wonderful. I love my job, Sarge, but it's not always easy to find someone to look after Rosie if I have to work late."

"If you're struggling to find childcare, then we can work something out. You can take a computer and work from home. It's an option if you want it. But if you can't do it, you can't do it. Your daughter comes first. I don't want to lose you due to stress. And I don't think Gareth meant what he said. It probably sounded different in his head. You know what he's like."

Burgess laughed. "Thank you. I'll think about the option of working from home if things get difficult. "

Summers hesitated and remembered she wanted to ask her something.

"While you're here, Sarah, can I ask you a question about something personal? It's not work-related."

Burgess tilted her head. "Yes, sure."

"Do you remember going to the Black Tiger nightclub before Christmas with me?"

"Yes, but do you?"

Summers laughed. "Barely." She sat forward. "That's what I want to ask you. Three men were there, showing us a lot of interest. Americans. They invited us back to their hotel."

"Invited *you* back to their hotel," said Burgess.

"Just me?"

"Yes, Emily. Just you. I had to pull you away."

"Did you?"

"I did. You were being very... *friendly*. They loved it. You were trying to get them to buy you another drink."

"Oh, God. Really?" Summers put her hands over her face.

Burgess nodded. "They didn't like it when I took you away."

"You rescued me."

"No need to thank me. Why is this?"

"I've received a letter addressed to my flat. I think it's from one of them. They mentioned seeing me in Southsea and remembering my red dress."

"The whole nightclub saw your little red dress. It was nice. If I had small hips, I'd have worn it too. But it's creepy they sent you a letter. Have you kept it?"

"Yes. Did I wave goodbye to them? Tell me I didn't."

"As I dragged you away, you did. You also told them how much you loved them."

"I'm so sorry." Summers buried her face in her hands. "They know my middle initial. I don't even put it on my statements."

Burgess smiled. "Which is?"

"I'm not telling you. You'll be endlessly trying to guess it."

"You tried to buy every drink with your driver's licence. Maybe they saw your name on that."

"This is getting worse! They would have seen my address, too."

"Put the letter somewhere safe, Emily, just in case things start to get awkward."

"You're right. The letter says he wants to meet me again in Southsea a week on Saturday."

"And you're not going anywhere near that place, are you?"

"No. I won't. I promise."

Chapter Ten

Dinescu had found his silver Ford Focus in one of the parking spaces near the workshops. Everyone assumed it was there for repairs. He always parked it there, ready for when he needed it. It was basic, and he kept it topped up with fuel and free of sweet wrappers and empty food containers—unlike the other CID cars. It was also reliable, and he liked reliability.

He left the police station and drove towards St Richard's Hospital. The sad remains of Christmas littered a cold, grey Chichester. The festive cheer had long since faded, and life had moved on.

As he drove, he thought about Sarah Burgess and wondered what had caused her outburst that morning. The extra pressure from resource cuts was hurting everyone across the county, including their team. Although Sarah's behaviour was unusual, he trusted Summers to handle it.

Once at the hospital, Dinescu followed the road to the rear and parked near the mortuary. Entering through the double doors, he found himself in a draughty corridor. By the time he found Doctor Dufour in one of the examination rooms, the postmortem was complete, except for the paperwork. When Dufour saw Dinescu, he covered up Lily's body and stepped away, preparing to scrub hands. A young photographer and a mortuary technician were with him. They stepped aside for Dinescu.

"Good morning, Chief Inspector," Dufour said, his flushed face contrasting with his blue scrubs. "Long time, no see, which is probably a good thing, considering."

Dinescu offered a brief smile. "Good morning, Doctor Dufour."

"You haven't missed much. There are no exhibits to take away. I have some tissue samples for toxicology, and I've sent her underwear to the lab. That's all she had on. As suspected, her death was from drowning. Someone forcibly held her under the water. There are bruises from finger marks on her shoulders and neck—large hands. Likely a man's, but you never know these days. There's an older bruise on her left cheek, too."

"You mentioned that in your email. When you say older?"

"From the colouring, a day or two before. A typical hard slap type of injury by a right-handed person."

"Was she drowned where we found her?"

"The water in her lungs was consistent with the water in the creek. I'll send it away for testing, of course. There's a gash near her left temple. I didn't see it at first. Her hair covered the wound, and the stream cleaned it. I'd say one blow by something heavy and blunt, like a pole or a club. It caused a minor skull fracture and a cerebral haemorrhage. The blow probably knocked her unconscious. There would have been some blood, but she wouldn't have bled profusely. The killer then dragged her to the water." Dufour pointed to his forearms. "She had scratches on her wrists and hands, again washed by the stream. They look to me like thorn injuries. I noticed a lot of brambles in the area. There's some bruising on her left wrist. I guess that's when the watch came off. There are no defence wounds, so the killer probably took her by surprise."

"Okay," said Dinescu. "You're saying there was some kind of altercation, and her watch came off. The killer hit her on the side of her head with something heavy and knocked her unconscious."

"That's my educated guess."

"They dragged her to the creek, stripped off her clothes, and then forcibly held her under the water."

"The clothes could have come off afterwards. It would have been difficult to pull off wet clothes."

"Cut off?" asked Dinescu.

Dufour's face darkened as he nodded. "I've seen it done before."

"Was she sexually assaulted?"

"Not that I can see from a physical examination, but people get off on all sorts of things nowadays. Oh yes, she's had a baby in the past."

Dinescu couldn't hide his surprise. "A baby?"

"Yes, you know, those little people that poop and cry."

"Her housemate never mentioned any other family."

"Sorry, I was being flippant. It's my coping mechanism."

"I know."

"She has a caesarean scar. A long time ago, by the looks of it."

"I see. Any other observations?"

"Only that she lived a healthy life. No sign of excessive drinking or drug taking."

"Thank you, Doctor Dufour. I'll await your email. I assume you can't give us a more accurate time of death."

"Being that she was in cold, running water, it's hard to give an accurate time. The tissue sample results may improve the estimate."

"I understand."

"So, murder it is, then, I'm sorry to say." Dufour scrubbed his hands and arms in a basin. "I understand someone's coming to ID her. She's ready for it. I'll ask the tech to move her into the viewing room."

"I wonder if Lily ever told anyone about having a child," said Dinescu, thinking out loud.

"That's beyond my remit, Chief Inspector."

"Yes, of course. Thank you."

As Dinescu left to wait in the corridor, he puzzled over the scratches on Lily's wrists and hands. Had she been hiding in the bushes from her attacker? Or was she trying to run away?

Dinescu passed the time in the dreary mortuary corridor by rereading that email on his mobile phone. What was he going to do? His time in Chichester had led him towards recovery, especially last year, when he'd faced one of his biggest fears. But now, they were asking him to leave it all behind and work in Surrey. The talk of applying for promotion was just a carrot to lead the donkey. Being a superintendent would further remove him from the sharp end of investigations. But what about his team? How could they be considering absorbing them into Worthing and Horsham? He couldn't let that happen. As individuals, they were all capable officers, but together, they were something special. They had become friends, but most of all, as far as Dinescu was concerned, they were family.

He sighed, feeling the weight of the decision as pressure in his head. He put the phone away and stared in front of him. Someone had tried to bring colour to the walls by hanging a large sunflower print. Bizarre, thought Dinescu, incongruous even. He was waiting for Summers and Yolanda Mellor, and a message from Summers told him they had just arrived in the car park.

In his quietude, he listened to a deep hum, feeling the vibrations through the soles of his feet. Searching his senses and being in the moment was a technique he had learned to deal with rising anxiety from his PTSD. He was okay. Nothing was coming for him today.

Summers would explain the identification procedure to Mellor, so they would be a little longer. This procedure was excruciating. It was confirmation that their loved one had died. The reality could break some people.

The door opened, and they walked in, with Summers leading the way. She slowed and put her arm around Mellor's shoulder for support. Dinescu saw Mellor was pale, with dark rings under her eyes. She asked Summers questions, whispering as if not to wake the dead.

Dinescu greeted them and took them further down the corridor to a window with a closed blue curtain, where they waited. They were silent, lit from above by a line of dim fluorescent lights in the ceiling, giving them all a sallow complexion. This end of the corridor had a chemical and sterile smell. Dinescu saw Mellor trembling as she stood next to Summers.

Summers glanced up at Dinescu. "Ready when you are, sir."

Dinescu nodded. He knew what was coming—he'd done too many of these.

"Where do we go now?" Mellor asked.

"Just here," Summers said in a soft voice. "In a moment, the curtain to this window will open. A person will be lying on a table with her face uncovered. We need you to look carefully and tell us if you can identify them. Take as long as you need. Are you ready?"

Mellor nodded, taking shallow breaths.

Dinescu knocked on a door and whispered to the mortuary technician. A few seconds later, the curtain opened, and Mellor looked through the window. She averted her eyes and staggered back, caught by Summers.

"Yes," said Mellor. "That's Lily." She looked up again, her eyes full of tears. "Bye-bye, Lily, my darling."

Dinescu nodded, and the mortuary technician replaced the cover over Lily's face. The curtains closed.

"I'm so sorry for your loss, Yolanda," said Summers. "That took a lot of courage. Would you like some time alone?"

Mellor shook her head, trembling.

"Let's get some fresh air," said Dinescu.

Summers put her arm around Mellor and led her back through the corridor, with Dinescu following. They left the building and stood together by Summers's car in the cold wind. Mellor dried her eyes on a tissue with shaking hands.

"Before you go with DS Summers," said Dinescu, "I must ask you something. Did Lily ever tell you how she got the bruise on her left cheek?"

"I didn't know she had a bruise. She never said anything to me."

"And what do you know about Lily having a child?"

Mellor frowned. "She didn't have any children. Why do you ask that?"

"According to the forensic pathologist, she had a caesarean scar."

Mellor's jaw dropped, and she shook her head. "No. That's not possible. Your pathologist is mistaken."

"He's a forensic pathologist, Yolanda," said Dinescu. "I trust what he tells me."

Mellor's face reddened. "I'm gobsmacked! Why didn't she tell me?"

"If there's a more immediate family member," said Summers, "we must find them. We need to look through any paperwork Lily had. Can you help me?"

"It's in her room. I tidied it up after the burglary. Take whatever you need."

"Let's get you home. You must see about getting your locks changed, too."

Dinescu sat in his car and watched them leave. There were three things about the postmortem that bothered him: who slapped Lily, where was her child, and how did she get those scratches?

Chapter Eleven

Burgess followed Booker along the footpath that led to the right of the millpond, heading towards the crime scene on the long footbridge. They passed several officers in muddy waders, carrying long poles coming from the opposite direction. The search team had stood down after hours of wading through icy water—they had found nothing.

After talking with Summers, Burgess regained her balance and felt reassured. She didn't know why she had snapped at Booker during the briefing. She had lost focus—lost that stillness. The guy could be insensitive at times, but he didn't deserve that.

"I'm sorry about earlier, Sarah," said Booker. "It was thoughtless of me."

Burgess smiled, her eyes fixed on the footpath. "One word, Gareth—chocolate. Where is it?"

"I haven't had a chance yet. I'll get you some. I promise."

"That's okay. I'm sorry I snapped at you."

The crime scene tape was further along the path now, guarded by two special constables in hi-vis jackets and custodian helmets. Burgess signed herself and Booker in and out of the crime scene, and they followed the path south alongside the Fishbourne

Channel to their left. The sky was slate grey, but the wind was coming from the southwest now.

"This place is so drab and barren," said Booker. "I can't see why anyone would want to spend time here."

"What?" said Burgess. "It's peaceful. Solitude. Perfect, if you ask me. You should come here when the sun's out."

"I'll take your word for it. I prefer shops and pubs."

"You're a heathen, Gareth," said Burgess, laughing.

Booker's phone pinged, and he checked his messages.

"There's an update. Lily Watson's housemate has formally identified her. No press release yet."

They came to the long footbridge over the creek, and Burgess felt a chill come over her. She shuddered, digging her hands deep into her coat pockets. Glancing at the water flowing away towards the channel, she saw the evidence left behind from the SOCO investigation. Further along the path were two uniformed officers looking at the sky. One had *Police Drone Pilot* written on the back of his stab vest. It was then she heard the drone buzzing overhead.

"They're filming the crime scene," said Booker, watching them.

"I don't want to stop here," Burgess said, looking away. "If you don't mind."

"Yes, sure. This place gives me the creeps, too."

They continued along the path and went through a rickety gate. A middle-aged woman with a muddy cocker spaniel came around the bend on the footpath. Booker slowed, making Burgess go in front to meet the dog.

"Oscar!" called the woman. The excited dog froze on the path. "Sorry," said the woman. "He's a jumper. And he especially loves men."

"What's there not to love?" said Booker.

"Do you know if the footpath is open now?" the woman

asked. "The bloody police have been there for ages now and blocked it. Have you come from there?"

Burgess identified herself. "We're from Major Crimes in Chichester. It's not open yet, I'm afraid. We're wrapping up the searches now, so it won't be long."

"Out for a nice jolly, no doubt," the woman said with a wry smile.

"No," said Booker, "we were hoping to meet local walkers, and lo, we have." He tried to be charming, but his sarcasm ruined it.

"We're investigating a woman's death on the marshes yesterday," said Burgess.

"I'd gathered that, young lady."

"Do you live near here?"

"Yes. On Park Lane, back that way." The woman pointed to her left.

"Is this a regular walking route for you?"

"It is. It's just on my doorstep, so why not?"

"You're fortunate," said Burgess. "Have you seen anything on your walks that's caused you concern over the weekend?"

The woman scratched her head. "You mean anyone suspicious?"

"That sort of thing, yes," said Burgess.

"There's been a man."

"A man? But why do you think he was suspicious?" Booker asked, his tone tinged with impatience.

"He was walking up and down this footpath, muttering. Mean-looking chap wearing khaki trousers and a camouflage top, like he was trying to hide. He was by the old wartime defences every time I saw him. It looked very dodgy if you ask me."

"Describe him for me," said Burgess, taking out her mobile phone.

"Don't you want to write it in your pocket notebook?" the woman asked.

"We don't use them anymore. It's all written on our mobiles now."

The woman rolled her eyes. "Dear, dear. How sad. He was tall. About four inches taller than you," she said to Booker.

"Stocky, with a bushy grey and ginger beard and a hat. Looked like a tramp."

"How old?"

"It's difficult to tell. Fifty, sixty? He had a lined face—scared the heebie-jeebies out of me."

"When did you see him?"

"Monday morning. I usually take Oscar for a walk around seven forty-five, just as it gets light. No, wait." She frowned, trying to remember. "I went out later on Monday—had to wait in for the plumber. I'm not sure now what the time was, but it was definitely in the morning."

"How about over the weekend at all?"

"No, he wasn't around then." The woman thought for a moment, screwing up her eyes. "I don't know if he was English or not. Probably a foreigner—Polish or Romanian—an illegal immigrant, no doubt."

"Did you talk to him?" Burgess asked.

"No way, José! Far too scary. Look, nice chatting and all that, but I must get on. Is that it?"

"Can I grab your name in case this is important?"

Burgess took the woman's details before she continued with her dog along the footpath.

"Wartime defences?" said Burgess. "What was she talking about?"

Booker pointed. "Maybe that?" To their right, behind the overgrown brambles, was a concrete structure.

"Is that from the war? I didn't know that was here."

"Invasion defences," said Booker. "It's called a pillbox. I knew there was one on Farlington Marshes, but not here."

"Who's this man she described?"

"He doesn't sound like any of our local homeless, not out this far from the city."

"Might not be homeless," said Burgess.

"If the woman's account is accurate, it could place him here at the time of the murder."

Burgess shrugged, and her phone pinged with a message from Summers. "I need to get back. The sarge wants me to talk to the staff at Lily's place of work. Why don't you head back to the pub car park? The mobile incident room may be there by now. I'm sure you can get a coffee at the pub."

"Sounds like a reasonable course of action to me."

"We should talk to some of the local PCSOs and give them the description of that man," said Burgess. "They may know him."

They turned the corner, where the path ran alongside the millpond and over a sluice gate. A tall figure they recognised was walking towards them with his head down.

"Sir?" said Booker.

Dinescu looked up as if his mind had been somewhere else. "Gareth, Sarah. You two okay?"

Booker nodded.

"All good, sir," said Burgess with a smile. "We've just been talking to a local. Gareth's getting a feel for the place."

"Good. I want to check something. I've just come from the postmortem. Lily has some scratches that are bothering me."

"Okay, sir," said Burgess. "I've got to go to Lily's shop."

"And I'm in the incident room," said Booker. "Anything you need help with, sir?"

Dinescu stared at them as if searching for the words, then said something in Romanian.

"Sir?" said Burgess.

"I said family is the most important thing we have. Don't you agree?"

Burgess glanced at Booker, who looked puzzled. "Yes, boss. I agree."

"Speak to you both later."

Dinescu walked on, leaving Burgess wondering if she had missed something.

"He's got a lot on his mind," said Booker. "I wouldn't worry. He'll sort it out, whatever it is."

"I wonder if he dreams in English or Romanian?" Burgess asked.

Booker pulled one of her braids. "Hey. We're good, yes?"

Burgess laughed and nodded. "Chocolate."

Booker nodded. "This place, Sarah. Don't let what happened here ruin it for you. Come back in the spring. It will all be green and new by then."

Burgess smiled. "You surprise me sometimes, Gareth. Thank you."

Chapter Twelve

After Dinescu left Burgess and Booker, he continued to follow the footpath. Having spent many hours walking around here with Lisa, he knew the Fishbourne Marshes well.

His mind lingered on his family and team, but he had to focus. Signing into the crime scene, he followed the muddy path. He crossed the footbridge and saw the trodden-down reeds and the coloured marks left on the wooden boards by the SOCOs. Stopping to talk with the drone pilot, he looked up at the sky. The drone sounded like a mosquito from this distance, but he could just see it.

"Hello, sir," said the lookout officer when he noticed Dinescu.

"How is it going?" Dinescu asked.

"The wind's a bit strong up there, but my friend here is managing. Dodging the mobbing seagulls at the moment."

"A pain in the arse," grumbled the drone officer, scratching his ginger moustache. "We filmed the scene and looked around for any discarded clothes. We'll give it another fifteen minutes, boss. I don't think there's anything here."

"Thanks," said Dinescu. "I appreciate it."

He left them and veered off the path, walking beside a line of thick brambles until he was on the opposite side of the crumbling concrete pillbox. He crouched down to examine the muddy footprints. His conversation with Dufour had brought him here, and Dinescu knew precisely where to look.

Something caught his eye, fluttering in the breeze. His coat sleeve snagged on the brambles as he reached for the thin strip of torn material trapped in the thorns. It had a lavender-blue flower pattern on the print, frayed where it had ripped. Looking closer, he saw a red tinge had blotted the fabric.

He took a photograph with his mobile phone and called Rick Griffin.

"Chief Inspector! Good to speak to you again," he said with enthusiasm.

"Hello, Rick. I'm at the crime scene site for Operation Brook." He told him about the scratches on Lily's arms and a hunch he'd had about the bramble bushes near the old pillbox.

"How long is the strip of material?" Griffin asked.

"About three inches. It looks like it's torn from a dress or a skirt. There appear to be blood spots on it."

"Interesting. Send me a photo and one of the footprints, too. Let me see if we have anyone free to examine it."

"The pillbox's entrance is blocked off. I doubt anyone has been able to gain access. It doesn't look like they have."

Dinescu could hear Griffin tapping on a computer keyboard. "I have someone who can come up now."

"Thanks, Rick. I'll text you the exact location."

After the call, Dinescu rejoined the footpath, looking back and forth, trying to imagine what could have happened. It may not be Lily's dress, and they didn't know what she wore that morning, but it could be significant.

The marshes seemed hostile that afternoon as he looked over the mudflats and across the narrow channel. Angry even. Lisa had told him once she thought the place played tricks on your mind.

She'd heard as a child that Roman soldiers haunted the marshes—
the *lemures,* she called them—the restless, malevolent spirits of
the dead. He believed it was all nonsense. But there was something uncanny about the place on days like this. Uncanny was
another word he'd heard Lisa use, and now he knew what it
meant.

He returned to the long footbridge where Lily was found and
paid his respects, listening to the creek flowing below him. The
sound of the bubbling water was like a child's laughter and
reminded Dinescu of the stories of the *Iele* from his childhood.
They were the Romanian nymph-like women who lived beside
the streams and danced together, luring men into madness. He
wondered if they had cursed this place. How these stories stay
with us, he thought, and chuckled to himself. He even looked
along the banks of the creek to see if there were the telltale scorch
marks of where the Iele had been.

Dinescu turned to see the pilot packing away the drone, then
glanced at the yellow hi-vis jackets of the special constables in the
distance. He walked over to them.

"Sir?" one of them said, standing up straight.

"Are you going to be here much longer?" Dinescu asked.

"Another couple of hours, then someone's relieving us."

"Could I ask one of you to stand by the old concrete pillbox
beyond the footbridge? It overlooks the water. There's a piece of
material caught in the brambles there. I don't want anyone
touching it until a SOCO arrives. They're on their way now."

The younger special looked lively. "I'll go, sir."

Specials had a less haggard appearance than the paid, full-time
officers—the regulars. Whilst some learned to emulate their mood
and mannerisms, most were happy to serve for free out of love for
the job.

"Thank you," said Dinescu with an appreciative smile. "That's
very helpful."

He returned to his car in the pub car park, behind the mobile incident room. As he drove away, he caught sight of Booker talking to a grey-haired man standing on the steps.

Driving out of Fishbourne, he imagined Lily snagging herself on those brambles. He wondered about the fragment of material he had found. If it was from Lily's clothing, why had she been beside the old pillbox? Was she hiding from someone?

The van had the latest Sussex Police decal on the side, with the words *Mobile Police Incident Room* in large blue letters. Booker had misread the word *incident* as indecent and was chuckling to himself.

"Gareth!" The head of a PCSO he only knew as Bill appeared from around the side of the van. "What's so funny?"

"Nothing, just schoolboy humour. It's just a bloody big campervan," said Booker.

Bill carried a heavy A-frame board and set it up by the pub's car park entrance.

"That's basically what it is," said Bill. "Perhaps I could borrow it to take me and my missus to Devon for the week." He laughed to himself. "They've hooked up a generator, so we have power. Now we can face all the happy members of the public. Talk about dog fouling and parking on the pavement, no doubt."

"Legitimate concerns to them," said Booker, wagging his finger. "Anyway, I hope not. I live in Fishbourne. I don't want to be stopped every five minutes when I leave my flat."

"I'll start up the generator and get the first round. Coffee?"

"Cheers. White, two sugars, please. I need the energy."

Bill set the generator purring behind the van and left for the Bull's Head, while Booker found a spongy seat behind a small table. Although the van was cosy and warm, there was a lingering scent of stale coffee. There was room for two conversations, three if they sat in the front seats. Bill had filled the racks with crime prevention leaflets and arranged them in fanned piles on the tables. Booker knew he was an expert at this.

As he tried logging into an old computer using a dongle, a man in his sixties appeared at the door.

"Can I have a word?" the man asked. He turned as a silver car pulled out of the car park.

Booker smiled. "Yes, come in. This is the incident room for Operation Brook. Do you have any information for us?" He wondered if he sounded too much like an Internet chatbot.

"Yes," said the man with a scornful frown. "Otherwise, I wouldn't be here. I'm Colin Jackman. I found the woman under the footbridge."

"Ah, Mr Jackman. I'm DC Booker, Major Crimes. How can I help?"

Jackman climbed into the van and sat opposite Booker, his anorak swishing as he moved. The seat creaked under his weight. He looked pale and rocked in his seat.

"When I gave my statement yesterday," he said, "I missed something. I only remembered it last night when I went to bed, and I've been worrying about it ever since. I had a terrible night's sleep. Hardly a wink. I kept seeing that woman's eyes in the water. I've seen her before on the marshes—only from a distance, mind. She used to sit with one of those easels. She was an artist. But to think the last thing those eyes saw was her killer. Makes me shudder."

Booker nodded, absorbing the weight of Jackman's words. "These things can really mess with your head. Do you have family or friends you can talk to?"

"I have a daughter, but I don't want to burden her with it."

"What do you want to add to your statement?" Booker glanced down at his screen—his login had failed. Checking his mobile, Booker saw he had no data connection for that either. He pulled out a blank MG11 sheet—a witness statement—from his folder. "I'll have to do this the old-fashioned way, Mr Jackman. Pen and paper don't need an Internet connection. I'm all ears."

"I saw someone."

"Okay. When?"

"Yesterday, when I climbed out of the creek after finding her. I was on the line with the police. He was a tall, ugly bugger." Jackman tutted and shook his head. "He looked like a soldier but had a bushy beard and hat on his head. He was hiding in the reeds. When he realised I'd seen him, he walked off in the other direction."

"When you say he looked like a soldier—"

"I mean, he had a camouflage jacket and green trousers. He looked grim—like he'd crawled out of the marsh."

"Have you seen him before?"

"No."

"How far was he from you?"

"I don't know for sure. Twenty feet, perhaps. I didn't see him fully, as he was trying to hide. But I saw his face, and he was tall."

"How long was he standing there?"

"I don't know. But I think he watched me climb out of the creek."

Booker raised his eyebrows. "That's interesting. Did he say anything to you, Mr Jackman?"

"No."

"Was he carrying anything?"

"Not that I saw. He was watching me—creepy-like. I was already scared out of my wits after finding that poor woman."

"I'm sure you were."

"I don't know what it is about this place. It's like that creek is cursed. Exactly the same place where that copper was murdered."

It took a moment for Booker to register what Jackman had said. "A police officer was murdered?"

"God, you boys have a short memory. PC Wallace. Haven't you heard of him? He was murdered here twenty years ago."

"No, Mr Jackman," said Booker. "Twenty years is before my time."

Jackman frowned at him. "Well, it isn't before mine, I can tell you. I was living in Fishbourne when it happened. A young man with mental problems killed him. They locked him up and threw away the key."

Booker's eyebrows knotted. "He was found in the same creek?"

Jackman sat forward, his eyes intense. "*Exactly* the same place. The bridge was different back then, of course. Just a few planks."

Booker wasn't sure whether the man was trying to spook him. "Give me a few minutes, and I'll write up the changes for you."

Booker finished the statement, and once Jackman signed it, he stood to leave.

"Thank you for taking the time to speak with me, Mr Jackman. You've been a great help. I'll talk to my sergeant and pass on your information."

"Okay," said Jackman. "Good to see the police doing something useful around here for once."

As Jackman walked away, Booker let the backhanded compliment slip away. He was used to them. What was this about a murdered police officer? How could something that happened twenty years ago be relevant to this case?

"There's someone here for you, Mr Croft," shouted Janice from the front of the shop.

Croft, a short, round man in a dark suit and tie, slipped on his glasses and walked sideways through the gap in the glass counter. The spotlights illuminated the cabinets, and their jewel-encrusted watches sparkled. A large Rolex sign, made into a clock, hung on the wall behind him.

Croft's hackles went up when he saw a man in his twenties, with a beard, standing near the door. Dressed in black trousers and a grey fleece top, he shifted his weight from foot to foot—a sure sign to Croft that he was nervous. The young man was not his usual type of customer. Croft glanced at Janice, who had moved behind the counter. He felt annoyed she had let him into the shop.

"Can I help you?" Croft asked from a distance. He gave an exaggerated glance at a CCTV camera on the wall.

"Afternoon," said the young man. He smiled, screwing his eyes a little.

Croft thought he seemed polite enough, but that was how the robbery two years ago began. There were two of them then, and they stole over eighty thousand pounds in watches and diamond rings. He moved behind the counter.

"What are you looking for anything in particular?"

"A month ago, my uncle died. We were very close. He left me a bit of money and this watch." He lifted his hand.

Croft recognised a Rolex Submariner at once. "Very generous, indeed!" He relaxed a little. "Are you considering selling the timepiece?"

"Well, yes," said the young man. "I don't know what to do with it. It looks cool, but I'm petrified of losing or damaging it."

"Quite. May I?"

The young man unclipped the strap and passed it to him. The lustre in the shop lights and the weight of the piece pointed to white gold with a matching strap. He checked the watch's condition, noting its well-preserved bezel and dial and no scratches or damage anywhere. He thought the links could do with cleaning, but nothing of any significance. Turning it over, he found the serial and model numbers between the lugs, confirming its authenticity. Holding the watch to his ear, he listened to the movement—smooth and consistent. He inspected the Cyclops lens and the tiny crown logo using his jeweller's loupe.

"What do you think?" asked the young man.

"It's a fine piece," Croft said. "I need to check its provenance and the register, but I would offer something in the region of thirty thousand for it."

"Thirty!" The man's face lit up. "I didn't expect that."

"Really? Well, as I said, I need to check your paperwork and the register."

"Paperwork?"

"Yes. Your uncle should have passed it down to you with the watch. I'd like to check the serial number against the stolen register, if you don't mind. It will only take a minute."

"I'll hold on to the watch," said the young man in an edgy tone.

Something in the man's eyes made Croft nervous. "It's just easier if—"

The young man licked his lips and held out his hand. "Thank you. But I want to get another opinion. Nothing personal."

Croft frowned and handed the watch back to him. "Well, if you change your mind, let me give you my card."

"I know where you are. Thank you for your time."

He headed towards the front door, and Janice looked at Croft, who nodded. The door latch clicked open, and the young man was gone.

"Save the CCTV," Croft said to Janice. "It may come in useful."

Chapter Thirteen

Burgess parked the car in Northgate Car Park, near the Festival Theatre, and walked south through the underpass, heading towards the shops. She was wrapped in a long, autumn-coloured cashmere scarf and wore the rusty-red gloves Rosie had given her for Christmas, protecting herself against the icy wind. Her vibrancy turned heads as she passed by, bringing light and warmth to an otherwise depressing grey day.

The bitter cold nipped at her cheeks, making her eyes water as she adjusted the scarf around her neck. The city seemed quieter than usual, with fewer people braving the weather.

After a few minutes, she found the charity shop on North Street, a national mental health charity. When she entered, a woman shop assistant was finishing serving someone. Burgess held open the door for the customer, catching a whiff of the vanilla-scented candle she had just bought.

They had filled the shop with bright colours and lined the shelves with books and games, glass ornaments, and fluffy toys. Racks of coats and dresses, trousers, and shirts were against one wall.

As the door closed, Burgess braced herself. She knew the news she was bringing wouldn't be easy to hear.

"Good afternoon," said the assistant. She was a tall woman in her forties wearing glasses and a long, orange dress, identical to one Burgess had in her wardrobe at home. "Are you looking for anything specific or just browsing?"

Burgess reached into her coat and presented her warrant card. "I'm Detective Constable Burgess from Chichester Major Crimes." She smiled to reassure her.

"Oh. Is everything okay?" The woman tilted her head, and a look of concern crossed her face. "I'm afraid my manager isn't in today, but can I help?"

"Is your manager Lily Watson?"

"That's right. I have her mobile number if you want it, but I've tried calling, and she's not answering."

"That's why I'm here. I'm very sorry to have to inform you that Lily was found dead yesterday. I'm here investigating her murder."

The woman staggered back until she found a stool. "Oh, my God! Lily?" She dropped onto the stool, grabbing the curtain of a changing cubicle for support.

"I'm so sorry, but there was no easy way of telling you. Can I get you a drink of water?"

"No, thank you. I'm okay."

"I have some important questions I must ask. So please take your time if you need it."

The woman got up again and went to the shop door, flipped the sign to *closed,* and dropped the door latch.

"How? I mean, what happened to her?"

"That's what we are trying to ascertain. I can't go into details at the moment."

"Have you told Yolanda?"

"We've spoken to her." Burgess took out her mobile phone. "Can I take your details, please?"

"I'm Angela Barton. I'm a volunteer here. I've worked with Lily for four years." Angela gave Burgess her contact details. She became edgy, scratching her arms and scalp. Her neck became red and blotchy. "Forgive me. I have a nervous reaction to stress. I come out in a rash."

"It's okay. It must be a shock. Would you like to call someone to be with you? Or shall I come back a little later?"

"No, it's just hard to believe. Actually, I will get that water." She went behind the counter and returned with a plastic bottle of mineral water. She unscrewed the cap and took several sips. "I'm okay."

"Would you say you knew Lily well?" Burgess asked.

"Well enough, I suppose. I mean, we weren't best buddies or anything. I know she shared a house with someone called Yolanda somewhere in Chichester. I don't think it was a romantic relation-ship—just friends. And I know she was an artist. She even donated some of her work to the shop. They were very good, too."

"Had Lily been her usual self recently?"

"That's a good question. No, she hadn't. Something had distracted her. A friend of hers had brought a pile of old books into the shop just before the weekend. Lily was quite secretive about them. She wouldn't let me sort them at all. She was quite rude when I offered. Touchy."

"Are the books still in the shop?"

"I think so." Angela went to a bookshelf and pulled out a brown hardback. "This was one of them." She handed Burgess a musty-smelling book with a picture of a wolf-like dog on the front. "*White Fang* by Jack London. I remember reading it when I was a girl. A bit bloody in places."

Burgess opened the front cover and read the note written in pencil. *Humphrey Collier, 41 Cowdray Close, Cotisham.*

"Cotisham," said Burgess. "I was there last year. So she wasn't secretive about this particular book?"

"No," said Angela, pushing up her glasses. "I don't know what the secrecy was all about."

"Who brought them in?"

"Someone called Heather. She's an old friend of Lily's."

"Do you have CCTV in the shop?"

"No, sorry. Too expensive, according to Head Office."

Burgess made some more notes on her mobile. "Do you know if Lily was in any trouble at all?"

"Not that she told me," said Angela. "But I think she had a past. It's just the little clues. She was in a relationship that went sour. That's all I know."

"Do you know any names?"

"No, sorry."

"Can you think of anyone who would want to harm her?"

"No," said Angela. "Lily was lovely."

Burgess glanced at the door as someone tried to come in. "Did she have any problems with customers?"

"Nothing out of the ordinary."

Burgess looked around the shop. Posters hung on the walls, advertising wellbeing and counselling services and offering affirming quotations. "How was Lily's mental health?"

"That's the thing—you can never really tell with people. Some people are well-practised at masking their problems."

Burgess smiled and nodded. "What happens to the shop now?"

Angela shrugged. "I guess the charity will appoint a new manager. The show must go on, as they say."

"Of course. Will you apply for that position?"

Angela blushed. "Oh, I don't know. I mean, I've only just found out. I'll have to call Head Office and everything."

Burgess nodded again. "Well, thank you for your help,

Angela. Can you do me a favour? Can I borrow this book? Just until the investigation is over."

"Take it," said Angela.

"Thank you. I'll be back if we have any more questions."

Burgess left with the book under her arm. She walked north, back to her car, and had an idea. She called Summers.

"Sarah," Summers replied. She sounded like she was walking somewhere. "Everything okay?"

"Yes, Sarge. I've just been to Lily's charity shop. Nothing of major significance. I'll update the log later. I'm going to try Lily's art club. What was it called again, and I'll Google it?"

"Chichester Landscape Art Society. They have a website. I'll send you the link."

"Thanks, Sarge."

Burgess could hear the car ticking as it cooled. She was outside a large farmhouse north of Southbourne. She had her phone in front of her and had called up the website of Lily's art club.

The Chichester Landscape Art Society (CLAS) brings together art lovers to celebrate West Sussex's natural beauty. Based in Chichester and the surrounding district, it welcomes experienced and novice artists interested in landscapes. CLAS encourages artistic development through outdoor painting sessions, workshops with renowned artists, and an annual exhibition showcasing member art. Open to all skill levels, the club fosters a collaborative environment in a scenic barn near key landscapes like the South Downs and Chichester Harbour, providing studio space and a place for members to connect.

From the website, the contact name for the club was Gillian Lee, and Burgess had parked in front of her house. Burgess had called ahead, and Gillian was happy to talk to her.

The house was on a long, rough track next door to a converted barn. Burgess could only dream of living in a place like this, surrounded by meadows and bordered by woodland—Rosie could have a pony. She shook her head and smiled to herself. Pipe dreams.

When Burgess stepped out of the car, the front door opened, and a middle-aged woman with fiery red hair, wearing green dungarees, met her in the driveway. They shook hands. It was clear to Burgess that Gillian wasn't sure what to make of her.

"Nice to meet you," said Gillian. "You're a detective?"

"Yes, a detective constable with Major Crimes."

"That sounds rather grim. But I love your hair. It must take you ages to plait it so tightly. And those beads are beautiful. A splendid choice of colour."

Burgess had heard that many times before. "Thank you. It's a beautiful place you have here."

"It is. I have to pinch myself sometimes. You said on the phone you wanted to talk about Lily Watson. Has she made a complaint or something?"

"That's not why I'm here. I'm sorry to say that Lily died under suspicious circumstances yesterday. This is a murder inquiry."

"Jeepers!" She looked up at the sky and puffed out her cheeks. "Shit! How awful. I wondered why she didn't reply to me yesterday. I'm so shocked. How can I help you, Detective Constable Burgess?"

"I'd like to paint a picture of Lily and who she was."

"Paint a picture?"

"I'm sorry, I didn't mean to—"

"It's fine. I knew what you meant. Come with me."

They walked towards a spacious, converted barn covered with brick and flint, featuring large windows and a new slate-tiled roof.

It was an impressive building, and its renovation must have cost a fortune.

Gillian caught Burgess studying the building. "Lovely, isn't it? It's my early retirement project. My partner encouraged me. I sank half my savings into it. Now, I run it as an art school. I allow the Landscape Art Society to use it for a minimal fee."

Gillian unlocked the door, and they entered. The air was heavy with the scent of oil paints and turpentine, mingling with the musty smell of aged timbers. It was clear this was Gillian's territory. She had converted it into a spacious art studio with several seats and easels around the floor. Even on a grey day, light poured in through the large windows facing all directions.

"Was Lily a member for long?"

"Ten years or so. She was one of our better artists. Even helped me out sometimes to teach. I'm sorry she's gone. I don't know who I'll use now."

"How was Lily when you last saw her?" asked Burgess.

"She was her usual focused self," said Gillian. "I saw her last week at the meeting. She was a splendid artist. To be truthful, she was streets ahead of most of the members here, which brought out jealousy and backbiting from some of the women."

"How do you know that?"

"I overheard it—petty, mostly. They won't complain to me, as this is my place. They're all scared of me. I can't imagine why."

"Had Lily made enemies in the club?"

"She wasn't greatly liked, but they weren't what I'd call enemies. They were just a bunch of lonely old women with nothing better to do than bitch about each other."

Burgess smiled and made some notes on her mobile. "Do you have any men who come along?"

"There are three people who purport to be men, yes. They don't say much and have a terrible eye for detail. But they are men, after all."

"Did anyone have a strong grudge against Lily?"

"Not that I know of," said Gillian. "Most of the jealousy was because she was both pretty *and* talented. Apart from selling her marsh paintings, my partner and I had little to do with her, to be honest. Have you seen Lily's work?"

"Not personally."

"Her paintings recently have had the same theme. The Fishbourne Marshes. My partner exhibited them. She ventured into other avenues and was a dab hand at calligraphy and sketching in ink. Then we have her darker work—some of it unpleasant, in my opinion. She kept them here. I don't know who to give them to."

Gillian pulled out a racking unit on wheels with several large black folders stored inside. She opened a folder with two hands, pulled out an A1-sized sheet, and presented it to Burgess. The painting was a blend of purples and blues, depicting a dark, foreboding landscape set against turbulent waters and stormy clouds. In the centre was the silhouette of a man, his hands gripping his head as if in a silent scream towards the horizon. Heavy chains shackled his ankles, anchoring him to the ground. Beside him, a small child crouched over a pool of water, playing with a small stick, a stark contrast to the man's torment. Burgess couldn't help but feel a chill as she studied the painting.

"She painted this?" she asked.

"Yes. She called it *Injustice*." Gillian scoffed. "Not very cheerful, and not my favourite. It was the last thing she painted here."

"Can I take a photo?"

"Of course. It belongs to Lily, so someone will need to claim it."

Burgess photographed the painting with Gillian holding it. "Do you know when she painted it?"

"Last week."

Burgess noticed several unfinished canvases inside the folder, capturing aspects of the marshes. Some were vibrant with life, while others were ominous, with dark, swirling skies. Lily had poured her soul into her work, reflecting her inner turmoil and the beauty she saw in the world around her. Burgess wondered how much Lily had embedded her personal struggles in these paintings. She felt a pang of sadness thinking about the loss of such talent. She hoped that, in some way, she could bring her justice.

Burgess read through her notes. "Thanks for your time, Gillian. It really is a beautiful place you have here." As they left the barn, she handed Gillian her card. "I may ask to see the names of the other members of the club, but I'll let you know. If anything else comes to mind, then call me."

Gillian nodded. "I will do. Anything to help."

As Burgess turned away, she glimpsed anxiety on Gillian's face, as if a mask had slipped.

At the end of a long day, Dinescu caught up with Summers. He had noticed her head buried in a computer for most of the afternoon, coordinating the extra officers and checking the quality of their work.

Summers entered his office carrying two cups of coffee and half a packet of biscuits. She dropped into the chair opposite him. Grateful, Dinescu logged out of his computer and picked up the coffee she had made.

"Thank you," he said. "I needed this."

"Me, too," she said. "There's a strange smell lingering around the office. It smells like someone's died. I'm not sure where it's coming from. Talking about the dead, the mortuary and the ID procedure took it out of me today. I don't know why. Then I had a minor disagreement had to deal with."

"Sarah and Gareth?" asked Dinescu.

"Yes. It's okay, just a *tiff*, sir."

Dinescu smiled. "That's a strange word." He took another sip. "I have some questions, Emily." He counted them out on his fingers. "The slap mark on Lily's face is bothering me. I believe Yolanda did that to her. Is she telling us the complete truth? Another question is Lily's caesarean scar—where is her child? Why didn't she tell anyone? And then we've had no sightings of Lily's car. Whoever has her car has her house keys."

"Her car is a mystery," said Summers. She crunched on a biscuit.

"I went to the crime scene earlier. Those scratches on Lily's hands bothered me."

"Defence injuries?"

Dinescu shook his head. "More like scratches from thorns." He told her about the blood-stained material snagged in the brambles by the pillbox.

"I called Rick Griffin to send a SOCO out to seize it and examine some footprints in the mud."

"If it's connected," said Summers, "perhaps she was hiding there from someone. Or trying to escape."

Dinescu nodded. "I've requested that the tests be expedited. We're running up a nice forensics bill at the moment."

The office was silent, apart from a faint buzz from the lights above them. Dinescu enjoyed working with Summers. After their initial teething problems, she had integrated well with the team and now understood how he worked and thought. He had been there when she split with her partner, and her resilience had impressed him. She worked hard, but he wondered if she played hard, too, or even at all.

"Lily's an enigma, don't you think, sir?" she said. "She had few friends and a relationship with a woman who believed there was more to it than companionship. She had a child she'd told no one about. In fact, no one knows very much about her at all."

"Everyone has secrets," said Dinescu. "But it seems she can trust no one with them."

"No one that we know of."

Dinescu's phone buzzed with a call from Lisa. "Excuse me. I must take this." Summers left Dinescu to take his call, walking back out of his office with her coffee.

"Ben," said Lisa. "We've got a problem."

"I'm listening."

"Sophia is so upset. She's in her room, sobbing her heart out. I don't know what to do. I've tried to talk to her, but she keeps telling me to get out."

"Do you have any idea at all?"

"No. She came home from school in tears."

"Did you manage to speak to her teacher?"

"No. I emailed her. But…"

"Okay." He checked his watch. "I will be home in thirty minutes. Leave her for now. As long as you can hear her crying, she is physically okay. Do you think the kids have been bullying her at school?"

"God, I hope not. Not here. We've been all through that before."

"Try not to worry. Give her some space."

After the call, Dinescu left the office and locked it.

He realised Summers must have noticed something on his face. "Everything okay, boss?"

"I don't know yet. I need to get home. It's okay."

"We're wrapping up here for the night," said Summers. "I can handle the rest."

Dinescu smiled and put on his coat. He knew this was so unlike Sophia—it must be bad. He was glad he wasn't facing a long drive home through rush-hour traffic right now. That wouldn't be the case if he had to transfer to Guildford.

Chapter Fourteen

Beniamin knew at once something was wrong when he entered the house. It was silent. The usual chatter was absent. The front door closing echoed in the hallway.

"Lisa?" he called out.

"In the lounge," she said.

Lisa was curled up on the sofa, reading a book under a lamp. She looked tired and worried.

"The house is so quiet. Is she still in her room?"

Lisa nodded. "It may have something to do with Charlie. He's upset her."

Beniamin sighed. "Don't worry."

He hung up his coat and jacket, removed his tie, and took slow steps up the staircase until he was outside Sophia's bedroom. He closed his eyes and listened, but there was no sound. What had that boy done to her? Anger welled up inside him. Boys can be such idiots sometimes, he thought.

It was then that a memory struck him—his birth mother. They had named Sophia after her. He remembered the last few days he spent with her before she died. One evening, she pointed to a toy donkey embroidered with yellow flowers that had always sat on a shelf near her bed. When he brought it to her, his mother laughed and told him her mother had made it. She had wanted him to have it. Then she said something to him he understood at once, and in that moment, he told her he'd forgiven her for giving him away many years ago.

Beniamin went to his bedroom and returned a few minutes later. He tapped on the door. "Sophia?"

"Please, Dad. I don't want to talk about it." She sounded angry rather than tearful.

"I have a donkey for you." No reply. "It's time I gave it to you." He heard Sophia's bed creaking.

"What are you talking about?" she said.

"Can I come in and give it to you? I won't talk to you unless you want me to."

"Okay."

He turned the door handle and stepped inside her room. It was in semi-darkness, and Sophia was sitting up in bed. He walked over to her, offered the toy donkey, and nodded for her to take it.

"Why are you giving me this?" she said.

He pointed to his lips, which were closed tight.

"Go on, you can talk to me."

"It was my grandmother's in Romania. Then my mother gave it to me."

"Was she calling you a donkey?"

Beniamin caught a slight smile on Sophia's face. "May have been."

"And are you calling me a donkey now?"

"No."

Sophia looked puzzled. "So, why?"

He sat on the edge of her bed. "She said this to me: *All of us are donkeys sometimes, Beniamin. But beating a donkey makes you a donkey, too.*"

"So she was calling you a donkey."

"I had to figure out what it meant, so you can figure it out for yourself."

"I'm not in the mood. Tell me what it means, Dad."

"It means none of us are perfect, and we all do stupid things sometimes. When someone hurts you, they're being a donkey. Try not to let your anger turn you into a donkey, too."

"Are you sure that's what it means? It sounds like you're insulting donkeys."

"I like donkeys," said Beniamin with a smile.

"Even Charlie? He's horrible."

"What did Charlie do to hurt you?"

Sophia took a breath. "When I told him we were inviting him for dinner, he said he only asked me out as a joke, that he was just pretending to be interested in me."

Beniamin groaned. "That was a horrible thing to say to you. Did you tell him how much that hurt you?"

"Yes. And I ran over his foot with my wheelchair. Accidentally, of course."

"Of course."

"I told his sister what he did. She was livid."

"Sophia, was he with his friends at the time?"

"Yes. It was lunchtime, and he was standing with them."

"He's a real donkey, then," he said.

"He is the biggest, fattest, ugliest donkey there is."

Beniamin tried not to laugh, but he couldn't help it. Sophia smiled.

He took her hand. "Would you like me to arrest him and throw him into a cell?"

"Pepper spray him first. Then taser him."

"Sophia, boys at that age can be extremely stupid. They get embarrassed easily around their friends."

"Why does it hurt so much, Dad?"

She leaned against him, and he held her, squeezing her tight, as if he could soak up her pain like a sponge.

"You're worth a million Charlies, my darling girl. He'll learn one day."

She looked up. "His sister's going to kill him. You'll have another murder to deal with."

He sighed, releasing his hold. "Come on. Don't let a stupid boy make you ill. Let me make you some toast."

She laughed. "No, it's alright, Dad. I'll make it. No offence."

"Hey, it's not my fault the toaster's temperamental."

"Only when you use it." She looked at the donkey. "Does it have a name?"

"A name?" He studied the brown, knitted animal and shook his head.

"Charlie," she said. "The donkey's name is Charlie."

Sarah Burgess held the door for Rosie with one hand and reached out to her with the other. "Come on, sweetheart. Try to keep up."

They followed Sarah's sister, Marie, and her children into the Happy Oyster pub, which overlooked the Bognor Regis seafront. It was now under new management and had a new name. The pub was bustling with young families that evening. A cacophony of noise and pub smells, music thumping out from every corner— this was Sarah's idea of hell. As much as she hated it, her daughter Rosie was wide-eyed with excitement. She bounced in, grabbing her aunt Marie's hand, leaving Sarah far behind.

Marie found a table a short distance from the ball pit and play area. Sarah was just happy to be doing something different that evening. Better than sitting at home alone, entertaining a four-year-old, and hanging on until bedtime. She could almost hear her mother's strong Caribbean accent lecturing her. *Life is what you make it, my child*, she would say, wagging her finger. Sarah smiled.

She worked long hours and felt guilty that she relied evermore on her sister's kindness to look after Rosie for her. Working for the police screwed with her family life. The cancelled rest days and long hours were taking their toll on her. Sarah often wondered if there would ever be a time when she didn't feel torn between duty and motherhood. The guilt gnawed at her, an ever-present reminder of the sacrifices she made.

"You hungry?" Marie shouted above the music.

"You bet," said Sarah. "When's your Nathan coming?"

"He'll be here in a few minutes. He's got someone from work coming with him."

Sarah wasn't in the mood to make small talk with strangers, but as Marie was paying, she couldn't object. She prepared herself for another round of forced pleasantries.

She felt a finger tap her arm. "Can I take Rosie to the ball pit?" asked Sarah's fourteen-year-old nephew, Jordan. He pushed his glasses up and gave a broad smile. "We won't go deep."

"Yes, sure. We'll call you when the food gets here."

"Jordan loves Rosie so much," said Marie. "He wants to be her big brother."

"I know. He's growing to be a wonderful young man."

Marie studied Sarah's face. "You look stunning! Is there anyone you haven't told me about?"

Sarah rolled her eyes. "Marie, you know I can't. It's too soon. Anyway, I'd tell you."

"Three years, Sarah. Three years."

"Three years tomorrow." Sarah felt that pressure in her head again. "I'm not saying never, but I can't imagine being with anyone else. You know that."

A waitress took their drink order.

"I think you're working too hard."

"It's that murder in Fishbourne yesterday. Thanks for everything you do for me, Marie, having Rosie so much."

"We're family, and Rosie is so easy. I'm worried about you. Nathan said he'd heard about what happened. He'd been into the Fishbourne Centre, doing fire safety checks. There's talk that it's some freaky old man wandering the marshes at night."

Burgess laughed. "A marsh monster! If only."

"Just be careful out there, sis!"

"I will."

"He spoke to one of the managers at the club, who said the dead woman was one of their regulars. She had a friend who worked there, and she hadn't turned up for work."

"Who's that?"

Marie shrugged. "That's all Nathan said." Someone coming in through the entrance caught Marie's attention. She stood and bounced like her niece. "Nathan! Over here!"

Her husband, Nathan, a tall, handsome man with dark skin and an athletic build, walked towards them. With him was a shorter man with lighter skin and cropped hair. He held his head high with his shoulders back and focused on Sarah. Glued to him was a young boy, about five or six years old. He held onto—she assumed—his father's leg and looked up at her.

"Hey, Sarah," said Nathan with a broad smile. "Looking good! Where's Rosie?"

"Hey, Nathan. She's with your beautiful boy in the ball pit. Jordan's being her big brother."

He glanced at the man next to him. "This is Louis from work. He has his son, Frankie, for the week. So…"

Sarah welcomed him and felt her sister's eyes probing her reaction. "Hey, Louis and Frankie." This was the second time Marie and Nathan had done this in three months—bringing random men to nights out. She didn't know what they'd told Louis about her, but he was smiling back.

He took the empty seat next to Sarah. Marie had a self-satisfied grin, and Sarah gave her a secret glare.

"Nice to meet you, Sarah," said Louis. "I didn't know this place existed."

"Neither did I," said Sarah. She could smell Louis's aftershave —subtle and expensive.

"It's new," said Marie. She stood. "Nathan, let's check what Jordan wants to eat."

Marie took her husband's hand and dragged him to the ball pit.

Louis sighed when they'd gone. "Look, I'm sorry, Sarah. They're as subtle as a brick through a jeweller's shop window."

Sarah laughed out loud. "Oh, thank God! They do this to you, too?"

"All the time. I'm a divorced father, so I must be *looking for love*."

"I'm a widow. The last thing I need or want is bloody romance."

Louis smiled and pointed. "Wait a minute. This isn't some kind of double-think, is it? Where you pretend not to be looking and—"

"I promise you, Louis," said Sarah, "I'm not interested." She looked away. "We'll just be nice and grateful and play their game. I love my sister so much. She's only trying to be helpful."

"I know. It looks like neither of us needs that complication right now. I'm happy just to have Frankie."

Louis's sincerity struck a chord with Sarah. She felt a rare moment of connection, understanding that both of them were navigating similar paths. She nodded but wondered if she had protested too much.

Colin Jackman cleared away his dinner things and made himself a hot chocolate using a saucepan, preparing for bed. He didn't like those instant drinks from a plastic tub. This was the proper stuff—not too bitter or too sweet.

The heating had come on that evening, so he knew it must be cold outside. He had kept the thermostat as low as he could before the cold made his joints ache, but with fuel prices so high, he had little choice.

When he was at home, he spent most of his time in the kitchen. He had a decent-sized table with a sturdy chair and a small TV. His computer desk fitted into an alcove where a fireplace had once been. The kitchen was his refuge, a place where he felt both productive and comfortable. He enjoyed the familiarity of the space. The light from the small TV flickered against the walls, and the gentle hum of the fridge provided a constant, soothing background noise.

After talking with DC Booker earlier that day, he had gone home and found a memory card for his camera that he thought he had lost. It had slipped into the crease of his camera bag. He had snapped some redshanks and lapwings on the marshes, hoping they were on the card.

Photography was more than a hobby for him. It served as an escape, a way to capture moments of beauty and stillness in a world that was becoming ever more chaotic, damaged, and unpredictable. Each photo he took was a fragment of time and beauty—the world preserved just as he saw it.

Colin started up his laptop computer and inserted the memory card into the slot on the side. The card mounted on his desktop, and he browsed through the images he had taken. The number of good shots he had surprised him. He'd taken several of the redshanks on the mudflats, with their distinctive red legs, and a few of the lapwings, with their crests in clear focus. Those were his favourites. Perhaps nothing he could enter a competition, but the camera club might like to see them.

He leaned back in his chair, sipping hot chocolate as he scrolled through the photos. The rich, chocolaty warmth spread through him, offering a brief respite from the persistent chill that seemed to seep into his bones. The images brought a smile to his face, each bird caught in mid-movement, each scene a moment of quiet beauty of the marshes.

The last images he found were older ones he hadn't cleared from the card, taken around New Year. They were wide shots of the marshes and the views over Fishbourne Channel. One of the photographs struck him. He wondered if he'd taken it by mistake. The shot was across the water, with Chichester Cathedral in the background. In the foreground were a man and a woman walking together hand-in-hand. He wore a warm jacket and scarf and had blond hair escaping beneath a blue cap. She was slender, with long blonde hair caught by the wind and blowing behind her. Colin remembered they had walked into the shot and ruined it. But the photograph made him feel strange. It was her—the woman he had found in the creek. Her face had burned into his memory. He yanked out the memory card, making the computer complain. He'd had an awful night last night thinking of her and didn't want another. But what should he do with the photograph? She was walking with a man he didn't recognise. Would the police want to see it? He stared at the small plastic device in his palm and considered his options. Then he reinserted it into his computer, right-clicked on the drive's icon, and clicked *Format*.

Chapter Fifteen

Wednesday

Summers was still getting dressed when Dinescu knocked on her front door. She pulled open her bedroom curtains to look out onto the road below and saw his car. The sun was rising, and a sheen of frost was over the rooftops and across the green. She wrapped her long dressing gown around her and made herself decent. Rushing out of her front door, she caught her toe on the threshold and swore. She took the rest of the journey down the steps more slowly. Pulling the main door open, she didn't hide her surprise at seeing him.

"God, am I late for something?" she said.

Dinescu smiled. "Not at all. I'm sorry to call on you so early. I wanted to catch you before you had breakfast. I want to treat you."

"Sir?"

"It's about time we caught up."

"Oh. Okay, but you could have rung."

"That's what Lisa said. Sorry, but it only occurred to me this morning."

"Do you want to wait inside?"

Dinescu declined. "I'm not sure what your neighbours would think if they saw me leaving your flat this morning. I'll wait in the car. There's no rush."

Flustered at first, Summers wondered if she had done something wrong. She calmed herself. This was out of her control, and it wasn't her fault he'd come early. She hoped he wouldn't be making a habit of it in the future. She shook her head, dispelling the lingering anxiety that had crept into her mind. She flung off her dressing gown and finished getting dressed, moving back into the hallway to grab her coat and shoes.

As she slipped them on, she noticed the small tear in the seam of her skirt, something she had been meaning to fix for weeks. She made a mental note to do it this weekend. Grabbing her handbag from the table, she gave herself one last look in the mirror, checking her makeup—it would have to do. She did a quick mental inventory. She had everything, so she headed outside into the crisp morning air.

Feeling a bit more awake, she greeted Dinescu with a smile and got into his car.

"You're going to treat me?" she asked.

"I am," Dinescu replied.

He drove out of the city with the rising sun in his mirrors and along the Old Broyle Road.

Summers glanced at Dinescu, who seemed quite at ease this morning. "I'm intrigued," she said, holding her finger to her lips. "You know it's not my birthday?"

"Isn't it?" Dinescu pretended to gasp in shock. "I'll turn around then."

Summers was confused. It wasn't usual for him to be jokey with her. She had only known his style of humour to be on the dry side. It crossed her mind he was having a mental health episode and abducting her. He was a powerful man, and there wouldn't be much she could do to stop him. Then she wondered when she had become so cynical about men doing nice things for her. She shook her head, laughing to herself. Perhaps she had been working too hard.

"Where are we going?" she said.

"Not far."

He turned towards West Stoke, pointing towards the hills of Kingley Vale, and after half a mile, pulled into some farm buildings and stables.

"We're here. Wellies—my favourite place for breakfast."

He led Summers to a farm building converted into a tearoom. A friendly blonde waitress in glasses, who knew Dinescu by his first name, greeted them, and he introduced Summers to her as a colleague. Summers had turned the heads of the workmen who had come in for an early breakfast.

"This is nice," she said. She took in the rustic flint and brick walls and the counter loaded with tempting cake slices and flapjack. The rich aroma of freshly brewed coffee and sizzling bacon filled the air.

Dinescu was already reading from the menu, so Summers thought she had better do the same. They both ordered coffee with a full English breakfast. Dinescu's conversation with the waitress was light and friendly. She asked him about Lisa and Sophia, and he gave her an unspecific update. Once the waitress had left them, he replaced the menu in the holder and looked at Summers.

Summers stared into his blue eyes. "Okay, sir. What have I done?"

"We're not on duty yet, so you don't have to call me sir. I'm catching up with you, and perhaps you can help me, too."

"Okay?" Summers rested her head in her curled hands with

her elbows on the table. The warmth of the tearoom seeped in, making her feel more relaxed.

"I'm concerned about you. I don't know anyone who's worked as hard as you to succeed in your role. You've managed to win the respect of your colleagues, too. That's some achievement, Emily." He paused, looking through the window into the distance. "Any SIO would be lucky to have you. You could easily run an investigation on your own." Dinescu looked like he was going to say something else, but pulled back.

"Thank you, but there's a *but* coming," said Summers.

Dinescu shifted in his seat as if he were changing tack. "Yes. But... we are all human beings, and we have needs like everyone else. All I ever see you do is work, go home to sleep, and then come back to work again. I see no play in your life. No fun."

"That's my choice. I'm happy with that."

"I know it's your choice. I'm just concerned that you'll burn out yourself."

"It's *burn yourself out*," Summers said. "Like a candle with no more wax."

"Is that how you say it?"

"Yes. But I didn't think I was burning myself out."

"To be successful in this job, you must be a full person. A whole person. You must find time to play, too."

"Is this some sort of wellbeing chat you have to do?"

Dinescu shook his head. "Not at all. I care about you, Emily. And there's something else."

"Go on."

"You said something to me the other evening that worried me. You weren't sure if Lisa was happy with you when it didn't work out with Kieran. Lisa loves him but understands you've just come out of a controlling relationship. Kieran knows this, too."

"Why are you worried?"

"We all need our friends. Apart from your mother, I don't

see you having anyone else. Lisa would like to reach out to you. Kieran appreciates you, too. And Sophia—she's practically in love with you. There are no hard feelings anywhere."

Summers felt the prickle of tears in her eyes. "Thank you."

"I hope I don't sound too much like your father." Dinescu smiled.

"My father left us when I was young, so I wouldn't know what a father should sound like."

"I'm sorry to hear that."

"That's nothing compared with your history." Summers smiled, putting her menu back in the holder. "Look, Kieran is lovely. He makes me laugh. God, he's so funny! I didn't have that for a long time. But I'm not sure I'm ready for another relationship yet."

"No one is saying that you should be romantically involved with Kieran. That's not where I'm coming from. None of my business. Make yourself open to friendships outside of work, Emily. I'm your friend, but also your boss. Kieran would be a good friend to you. You get along well together. You laugh at the same things—things I don't understand at all. They are way over my head."

Summers laughed. "I'm not saying it wouldn't work out with Kieran, but the timing was awful. You're right. I just needed a friend."

"He knows that."

"Is that what this is all about? I thought I was in trouble."

"No," said Dinescu. "Your coffee-making skills need some work, but other than that..." He grinned and unwrapped his knife and fork, tied up with a napkin and string. "I just want you to consider having something else in your life other than work. But I know that's your choice."

"Thank you. I'll bear it in mind. Honestly, I will."

"Good." He looked away and nodded as if he had ticked that subject off. "And there's one last thing, I promise."

"I'm all ears," she said.

He told Summers about Sophia and the trouble she'd had with Charlie.

"I'd have smacked him," said Summers. "How dare he treat her like that?"

"I know. Poor Sophia was heartbroken. Boys can be so thoughtless."

"You're telling me! I was, let's say, a *large* girl at school."

"I can't imagine that," said Dinescu.

"Why, thank you, sir," Summers laughed.

"Lisa and I are not having any more children, but Sophia needs a big sister."

She came right back at him. "I'll be her big sister!"

Dinescu smiled. "That's what I was hoping you'd say."

"I'll fight her corner anytime."

"Thank you. I'm not asking you to move in or anything."

"Good!" Summers laughed again. "Because that really would be weird. No, I understand completely. And I've never had a sister, either."

The breakfast arrived, and the nerves had left Summers. She was hungry.

Dinescu began tucking in. "I don't want you to feel that you have to, with me being your boss and everything."

"I'd love to," she said. "I can keep the two sides of my life separate." She looked up with a glint in her eye. "And it's not like I have anything else to do."

Chapter Sixteen

Sarah Burgess lifted her braided hair and turned her coat collar against the chill wind. As she crouched, she could smell the musty sweetness of earth and rotting leaves. The morning shadows in the churchyard had crept around her. How long had she been there? She had to get back to the office.

She stared at the polished marble slab, her eyes wet with tears. Draped over the engraved name of *Corporal Niles Burgess* was a length of weather-worn, purple tinsel placed there by Rosie just before Christmas. She had attached a silver bauble to the end, but that had gone now. Rosie had made it for her father but had no memories of him. She only knew him from her mother's stories and the photographs she had shown her.

"What am I supposed to do, Niles?" said Sarah. "It's been three years."

A noisy line of rooks jeered and mocked her from the church roof before flying off towards the city over the fields.

Sarah brought out a tissue, dried her eyes, and stuffed it into her pocket. She removed the tinsel from the grave and ran her fingertip over the letters of his name, caressing the curves of the chiselled grooves.

"I miss you."

Drawing a sharp breath, she stood, blew a kiss, and turned away. As she walked back along the shingled churchyard path, her mobile phone rang. It was Summers. She couldn't ignore it as she was supposed to be working.

Sarah cleared her throat and counted to three. "Sarge?"

"Sarah," said Summers. "The boss and I will be a few minutes late this morning. He's treated me to breakfast."

"Very nice. I hope you chose a big one."

"I did. Can you tell Gareth we'll have a briefing first thing? I don't want him going off anywhere."

Sarah did her best to engage her brain. "Okay, Sarge."

"Are you in the office?"

"No, I've popped out. We needed more milk. CID stole it. Just to warn you, the office is freezing this morning."

Summers paused. "Is everything okay? You sound…"

Sarah composed herself. "I'm good, Sarge. All good."

"Ah, okay. See you back at the ranch."

Sarah ended the call and sighed.

"I'm such a terrible liar."

The briefing for the Major Crimes core team started in a cold office. All the windows were wide open, and the detectives wore their coats. They had traced the decaying stench that had permeated the entire office to a forgotten king prawn salad left in a drawer in CID over the weekend. It was a major cake penalty for the detective involved.

Dinescu saw someone slip in and stand at the back. He recognised her as DI Daisy Irving, the woman who had attended the briefing the day before.

"Can I help you?" he asked her.

"So sorry to interrupt, sir," she said. She had a subtle Scottish accent. "I'm DI Irving, based at Centenary House. I've been asked to follow the Operation Brook investigation. I tried to get here sooner to speak to you before the meeting started, but the traffic was terrible."

"Can you come closer? I don't want to shout across the room."

DI Irving blushed and held up her warrant card to Dinescu for him to check. Dinescu's suspicion faded into a smile. "And who asked you?"

"Detective Chief Superintendent Faraday, sir," said Irving. "He said he'd let you know. He obviously hasn't."

"No. I still don't understand your reason for being here."

"I'm preparing for my PIP level three SIO assessment, ready to become a temporary DCI. I'm observing for my own development."

"I see. Perhaps we can catch up later. Sit with us, Daisy. My team is reporting back on some of their investigations."

"Thank you, sir."

Dinescu turned to Burgess. "Sarah, tell us about your enquiries yesterday."

Burgess recounted her meeting in the charity shop and the mysterious visit from Lily's friend with a suitcase on Friday. She held up the Jack London novel she had borrowed.

"Have we spoken to this friend of Lily's?" asked Dinescu.

"The friend's name is Heather. No, sir," said Burgess. "We don't know who she is yet."

"We're still going through Lily's Facebook account," said Summers. "Her friend may be on there. Lily was only on Facebook occasionally—happy birthday messages and a few of her paintings. She last used it back in June last year."

"Anything else?" Dinescu asked.

"Yes, boss. I spoke to Gillian Murphy, who hosts the Chich-

117

ester Landscape Art Society. She owns a converted barn in South-bourne. Lily was a regular there, sharing her landscape paintings of the marshes, and was also into ink sketches and calligraphy. She told me that not everyone at the club liked Lily, but there was nothing substantial to follow up on. It was all based on jealousy of her talent and looks. It's an avenue we could explore if we're running short of leads."

"Agreed," said Dinescu. "Thank you."

Summers turned to Booker. "I thought you were heading to the incident room this morning."

"I wish I were, Sarge," he said. "It's warmer than this place." He smiled at Irving, who had her chin buried in her coat. "It's not usually like this, ma'am. Can't we close the windows yet?"

"You really wouldn't like that, Gareth," said Summers. "The smell is awful."

"Anyway," said Booker, "the DS from Worthing relieved me early with one of his officers so I could attend the briefing. I gathered some useful information during my time there yesterday. Colin Jackman came to see me about something he'd missed in his statement." Booker recounted Jackman's account of seeing a man with a beard, followed by the comments from the woman Booker and Burgess had met on the footpath. "So, that's two similar descriptions. The man they saw was tall, with a grey beard, wearing a camouflaged jacket, khaki trousers, and a hat. He appeared to be in his fifties or early sixties."

"He could be a local," Burgess suggested. "I'll ask around the Fishbourne Centre to see if anyone knows him."

"We should check the pubs along the main road," Summers added. "Talk to the local PCSOs, too. They're a good source of local intelligence."

"One moment," Dinescu interjected. "We must be careful not to stir up a witch hunt. Don't forget to reassure people we meet.

There's enough speculation already. He's a potential witness— that's all they need to know. Keep it low-key."

"Will you bring in a forensic psychologist, sir?" asked Irving. "For profiling, perhaps, considering the strange way the killer left the victim?"

"Not at the moment, Daisy," said Dinescu. "We must consider the cost, too."

Irving frowned, pursing her lips. "You seem reticent to pursue this man wandering the marshes. He seems to me to be a key witness, maybe even a suspect."

Dinescu wondered if she was trying to make a point of crossing him. "I'm speaking from experience. I will pursue no one until I have grounds to do so. He is a potential witness, unless you have information that says otherwise?"

Irving shook her head.

"There's something else Jackman told me, boss," Booker continued, breaking the tension. "What do you know about PC Wallace?"

Dinescu shrugged and looked at Summers, who shook her head.

"Jackman mentioned a police officer was murdered at the same spot on the marshes in 2004. Could that be related? It seems like quite a coincidence, being in the same place."

Burgess shook her head. "Twenty years ago. It's unlikely."

"Is he sure about that?" Summers asked. "We can check with HQ."

"I'm checking on the police memorial site now," Booker said as he typed on his computer. After a few seconds, he leaned forward with his face near the screen. "Here we are. It looks like Jackman's right, Sarge. January 11th, 2004—almost exactly twenty years ago. *PC Roger Wallace, 35, was found with a head wound and drowned in Fishbourne Creek. He was working under-cover, investigating drug smugglers. A local man, Joseph McKin-*

ley, was found guilty of manslaughter by reason of diminished responsibility."

"I can't see how that has any connection with our victim," Summers said.

"Neither can I," Dinescu replied, though he knew this would now nag at him. "We'll keep it in mind."

"Thank you, Gareth," said Summers.

"I was out of the office yesterday," Dinescu said. "Lily's post-mortem revealed she had scratches on her forearms caused by thorns. I wondered how she'd got them." He detailed how he had found the piece of torn material with blood marks on it in the brambles by the pillbox. "The cloth fragment is with Forensics now."

"We should ask Yolanda if she recognises the pattern," Summers said.

"Yes, I was going to ask you to do that. I have a photograph of it. If we can prove she was wearing it when she left her house, it could help us understand what she was doing that day."

"Was she running from someone?" Booker suggested. "Maybe the killer dragged her back to the bridge."

"Or she was hiding something," said Burgess. "Could she have put something inside the pillbox?"

"Possibly," said Dinescu, "but the entrance is blocked off. Let's see if we can identify the material as Lily's first." He looked at Summers. "Emily, tell us about the forensic results."

"Thanks, sir." She checked the notes she had taken from the email. "The lab confirmed Lily's DNA on the watch and noted damage to the strap, suggesting it came off during a struggle. The blood they found on the footbridge was likely from Lily's head wound. As expected, the footprints at the scene were unusable. Finally, Digital Forensics will send us a copy of any saved messages on the answering machine later."

Dinescu caught Irving watching Summers after she had given

her report, and it unsettled him. He passed a dry marker pen to Booker and asked him to write up the description of the man Jackman saw on the whiteboard. "These are our next priorities. Gareth, write these down." Booker wrote a list as Dinescu spoke. "We must locate Lily's car, find this Bosham art dealer, Justin, and get hold of Lily's medical records. Doctor Dufour mentioned Lily had a caesarean scar."

"She was a mother?" Burgess said, surprised. "Did Mellor know?"

"Apparently not," Dinescu replied. "We don't know anything about the child or when she had it, but it may be important."

"Could you look into that, Sarah?" Summers asked.

"I will," said Burgess. "Now that we've confirmed her identity, I can contact her GP."

Summers's mobile rang, and she took the call.

"Let's outline our hypotheses so far," Dinescu said. "I'm certain someone Lily knew murdered her. That was always the most likely scenario. Number one—Yolanda Mellor. She admitted to arguing with Lily before she left the house. Perhaps she was jealous. It could be her feelings for Lily were stronger than she's making out to us."

"That could explain the slap injury to Lily's face," Booker said.

Dinescu agreed. "But it doesn't explain the burglary. No one forced an entry or even attempted to fake one. Why?"

"The murderer must have had Lily's door key," said Burgess.

"Or Yolanda simply forgot to break a window," Booker said.

"Hypothesis number two," Dinescu continued. "The art shop owner from Bosham—"

"Sir," Summers interrupted. "I've had a call from Digital Forensics. They were able to pull off that last message for us immediately. The others will take a couple of days. They emailed me the audio file."

"Go ahead," Dinescu said.

She turned up the volume on her computer and pressed play.

"Lily, it's me... Justin. I tried calling your mobile, but it's switched off. I've thought about what you said... I won't be there tomorrow. You know what I wanted more than anything, but now you're going to betray me. You've broken my heart, Lily. Broken my heart. I won't let it go unpunished. I promise you that."

"Justin," Summers said. "The art shop owner from Bosham."

"Can we get the phone records for the landline?" Booker asked.

"He withheld his number," replied Summers.

"That was a threat," said Dinescu. "So that's our priority. Find Justin."

"Can't be that hard," said Booker.

"Off you go then, Gareth," said Summers. "Justin from Bosham is hypothesis two. Do we have any others?"

Dinescu shook his head. "We must step up the search for Lily's car. I don't understand where it's gone."

"There's nothing on ANPR, sir," Booker said. "We've got people looking for it. It has to be somewhere. I've asked for reports of anything matching a burnt-out Mini. Nothing received yet."

"I'll talk to Lily's GP about her baby," said Burgess. "Then I'll head to the Fishbourne Centre. I've heard that one of Lily's friends works there. That should keep me busy. We could use Chester and Ross back here, boss."

"I know," said Dinescu. "I've heard Ross is untouchable." Irving dropped her pen, interrupting Dinescu's flow. He picked it up for her. "There may be some negotiating room for Chester. I'm working on it."

"If we're done, boss," said Summers, "I'd like to crack on."

"Absolutely," said Dinescu. The meeting broke up, leaving

Summers, Dinescu, and Irving. "I'm not free to talk right now, Daisy. Perhaps another time."

Irving smiled. "Of course, sir. No problem. Thanks for letting me sit in."

Dinescu felt Summers watching him as he watched Irving leave the office.

"Sir?" said Summers. "She's very... sweet. What's going on? Was she trying to distract you?"

"I'm not entirely sure, Emily. Chewed-up toffee's sweet, too. If she comes back to the office when I'm not here, let me know. I will tell you my thoughts soon, but not yet. There's nothing to worry about. Not for now."

Chapter Seventeen

Booker parked in the Bosham car park and looked up at the overcast sky, wishing he'd brought his coat. He heard the wind on the halyards *clink-clink* a steady rhythm against the masts of the boats stored there. It was the sound of his childhood, growing up by the sea on Hayling Island.

Walking into Bosham Lane, he checked his mobile phone. He had searched for art shops in Bosham and found two. One was a gallery, and the other sold art supplies in the craft centre.

Hadley Media Arts Gallery was only a few yards from where he stood. With its sleek lines, the pastel grey shopfront showed modern style and sophistication. He stepped closer and peered through the large window. The display showcased a mix of black-and-white photographs and watercolour paintings, all by local artists.

In the centre of the display was a large watercolour landscape. It captured the Fishbourne Marshes, with a ray of sunlight breaking through a thunderous sky, illuminating the reedbeds below. He read the card on the picture frame—by local artist *Lily Watson*.

"This must be it," Booker said to himself.

When he pushed open the door, an electronic chime announced his entrance. The first thing Booker noticed was the polished oak floor gleaming under the warm lights. Inviting scents of vanilla and jasmine filled the air, creating an atmosphere of comfort and sophistication. Gentle classical music played through speakers on a desk, a soothing string quartet. He knew little about classical music, but he enjoyed the calming melody.

As he took in the surroundings, a blond man in his thirties, dressed in a smart blue waistcoat, emerged from the back of the shop.

"Good afternoon. Was there anything you were looking for?" His voice was soft and well-spoken, quite different from the message on Yolanda's answering machine.

Booker held up his police warrant card. "I'm Detective Constable Booker from Major Crimes in Chichester."

The man's eyes widened. "Oh, can I help?"

"Can you tell me your name, sir?"

"I'm Justin Hadley, the proprietor."

"Mr Hadley, I'm here to talk to you about Lily Watson. Do you know her?"

Hadley's face dropped as if a mask had fallen off.

"Yes, she was a local artist and a friend. There's a landscape of hers in the window. Is this about the news?"

"You've heard Miss Watson was murdered in Fishbourne yesterday afternoon?"

He brought his hands to his face. "My partner told me about it, then I saw the news report. I only spoke to Lily on Saturday night."

"Is that the last time you spoke to her?"

He nodded. "It was. All of this is a terrible shock." He wrapped his arms around his shoulders as if he was hugging himself. "Lily was a kind, gentle soul. Do you know who killed her?"

Booker ignored the question. "Did you leave a message for Lily on Sunday evening on her answering machine?"

"No."

"Someone left a message for her on Sunday at 21:35, and the caller said his name was Justin. A friend of hers identified the caller as a man from Bosham who owns an art shop."

"It wasn't me, constable. I spoke to her at about seven on Saturday evening. I let her know she had made a sale. I never left any message."

"Does she know anyone else called Justin?"

"I don't know. And why would anyone pretend they were me?"

Booker shrugged and asked, "Were you in a relationship with Miss Watson?"

"Goodness, no! I already have a partner."

Booker took a moment to assess Hadley's demeanour. He seemed sincere, but Booker knew better than to take things at face value. He looked at the notes on his mobile phone and puzzled over them. "Would you be happy to attend a voluntary interview? It's just that we have conflicting information. We are trying to ascertain Lily's whereabouts on Sunday night, and someone told us you had arranged to go on a date with her."

"Definitely not me, constable!" A look of horror crossed his face. "I think there's been a mix-up. I'm happy to come to Chichester Police Station now, if you want."

"That would be very helpful. It shouldn't take long. You'll be interviewed under caution, but you won't be under arrest."

"Thank God for that! Give me five minutes to lock up, and I'll meet you there."

Raymond Collier ran his fingers through his thinning hair as he paced the room in front of the TV. His clothes were crumpled and stained. He was hungry, unwashed, and suffering from lack of sleep. He looked up when he heard the report start. The scene by the Bull's Head pub was on the screen again, with the reporter standing before the police mobile incident room. *"The local community is in shock after the body of a forty-year-old woman was found on Fishbourne Marshes yesterday,"* the reporter announced. *"This afternoon, the police released the woman's identity as Lily Watson, an artist from Chichester. They will be holding a press conference later this—"*

Ray turned off the TV and swore to himself. He wanted a drink but needed to keep a clear head. There were now two potential problems he must deal with. One of them was McKinley—this had to be his doing.

"What did I leave behind?" He tapped his fist against his forehead. "Come on, man!" He had to think. Should he act first, talk to the senior investigating officer and offer his help? "No!" It would put him in the spotlight. He should stay away—wait in the shadows and prepare for the knock on the door.

"Why the hell am I panicking? God, Heather! Why do this to me now, woman?"

He ran his finger down the long, weeping scratch on his forearm, wincing at the sting. Those nails he'd paid for had done their damage. He picked up the letter from the table. Nothing about it seemed familiar. He had no memory of writing it, and yet... Was he going senile? Should he destroy it? But it was evidence. Evidence that would either save him or break him.

The phone rang, and Ray sighed at the interruption. He went into the hallway and answered it. "Hello?"

"Oh, hi Ray, it's Tony at the club here. Can I have a word with Heather, please?"

Tony, Heather's boss. Heather called him a nice guy. Always ready to listen, she said. Nice-Guy Tony.

"She's not here."

"Oh. It's just that we were expecting her to be in this afternoon and yesterday, too. Is everything okay? We're all worried about her. And she was a friend of that woman who—"

"Ah, she didn't tell you."

"Tell me what, Ray?"

"Heather had to go away. A death in the family. Sudden. She probably didn't get the time to let you know."

"I see. I'm sorry to hear that. She's lost two people close to her then. Do you know how long she'll be away? I need to organise cover."

"Sorry, Tony, I don't. I'll get her to call you."

"Is her mobile working? I've been trying to call, but it's unobtainable."

"She's switched it off. It's a difficult time. Obviously."

"I see."

"I'll let her know. Bye for now."

Tony tried to ask another question, but Ray ended the call.

Heather smiled at him from the photograph on the mantelpiece, and Ray sighed, heavy-hearted. Where was she? She hadn't touched their savings, so she must be using her mother's money. She wasn't smart enough to pull this one off on her own. Maybe McKinley helped her. He found his revenge.

"Pull yourself together, Ray," he said to his haggard reflection in the mirror. His face was pale, almost ghostly—a shadow of the man he used to be. "She'll be back. You know she will."

Booker and Justin Hadley were facing each other in the interview room. Hadley's body language was relaxed at first, almost nonchalant. While Booker sorted out the notes for the interview, Hadley looked around with an amused expression.

Booker kept it light and friendly, a technique he sometimes used to soften the suspects and lull them into a false sense of security. He acknowledged his bias against the pretentious middle classes, and he considered Hadley to be one of them. He tried to manage this bias, though he wasn't always successful.

Hadley had declined a solicitor. "No need," he'd said with a dismissive wave, telling Booker it wasn't necessary as he had nothing to hide.

Booker went ahead with the required introduction, telling him he wasn't under arrest, and then the police caution. When he reached the words *you later rely on in court*, he noticed Hadley stiffen as if he had only just realised this wasn't a friendly chat.

"Justin, we're here today to talk about the murder of Lily Watson. We believe someone murdered Lily on Monday, somewhere between two and eight o'clock in the morning. Do you understand that?"

"Yes, of course, and I want to help in any way I can."

"Thank you. I must ask you, did you meet with Lily on Monday morning and kill her either accidentally or intentionally?"

Hadley laughed in shock. "What! Am I suddenly a suspect now?"

"I need to ask you, Justin. Can you answer the question, please?"

"No, I bloody didn't!"

"Okay. Let's go back to the beginning. How did you know Lily Watson?"

"We were friends in business. She's an... was an artist, and I sell art. I met her at an exhibition my partner put on. Lily was a local, and I thought it would be good to include her artwork in my catalogue."

"How long had you known her?" asked Booker.

"Three years or so."

"And when was the last time you saw her?"

"Before Christmas, about a month ago. But I spoke to her on the phone on Saturday. I was in London with my partner, and someone was interested in one of Lily's pieces."

"Were you ever in a romantic, sexual relationship with Lily?"

"As I said in the gallery, I'm quite happy with my current partner, thank you." Hadley shook his head and tutted. "These questions!"

"All necessary, Justin," said Booker. "Do you know of anyone who would harm her? Anyone who had a grudge against her for any reason, no matter how trivial."

"Not at all. She was lovely." Hadley swallowed as if he were struggling to hold something back. He sat forward and put his elbows on the table. "The local art community had huge respect for her. If anyone had issues with her, it would be her housemate, Yolanda."

"Tell me about that."

"Yolanda was very possessive over her time with Lily and always wanted to know where she was."

Booker made a note on his notepad. "Did Lily tell you that?"

"Yes, more than once."

"So, Lily felt able to talk to you about personal matters."

Hadley blinked. "Well, sometimes, yes. Usually, when she was a bit frazzled or something like that. Any personal information was always unsolicited, I can assure you. I try not to get involved with my artists' problems. I don't have the time or the interest, for that matter."

"Where were you from Sunday, the 7th of January to Monday, the 8th?"

"That's easy. I was in London, staying with my partner in a

Premier Inn hotel. She was in and out of meetings, but the hotel will have a record of my stay."

"Which part of London was that?"

"Holborn. We were attending an exhibition nearby from Saturday to Sunday. We checked out on Monday morning around ten. I had a few pieces for sale there."

"You know I'm going to be checking this," said Booker.

"Of course! The reservation was in my name."

"Was it a successful exhibition?"

Hadley looked blank for a moment. "Successful?" He swallowed. "It was okay, I suppose. Could have been better."

"How many pieces did you sell?"

"Why do you need to know that?"

Booker raised his eyebrows and waited for the answer.

"Three. And I won't tell you how much for, so don't ask."

Booker smiled and took a sip of water from a paper cup. "Did Lily ever talk to you about her children?"

Hadley looked astonished. "Children! What children?"

"We don't know for certain. We're trying to find out, but we know she had a child at some point."

"News to me. These are bizarre questions, constable."

"On Sunday, someone left a message on Lily's answering machine. The caller said his name was Justin. Was that you?"

"No."

"Did you leave a message and try to disguise your voice?"

Hadley scoffed. "Don't be bloody ridiculous. No!"

"Have you ever felt let down or betrayed by Lily?"

"Not at all."

Booker read through his notes and looked up. "I think we're done, Justin. Thank you. I'll check with the hotel in Holborn, but that's about it."

"Fill your boots," said Hadley, now with a deep frown. "I have nothing to hide."

"Do you have anything you'd like to clarify with me?"

"No. I want to leave. But…" He looked up and hesitated. "Just to add, you said someone murdered her between two and eight in the morning. Lily wouldn't have been near the marshes before sunrise. She only went there to paint. Anyway, she told me once she thought the place was haunted. No, she wouldn't have been there in the dark."

"That's helpful. Thank you." Booker made a note. "If there's nothing else?"

Justin shook his head.

"Interview terminated." Booker stopped the recording.

Swanage wasn't as Heather remembered, but this was winter, and out-of-season holiday towns have a particular bleakness about them at this time of year. Maybe it was her mood that was at fault rather than the town.

The drive there was dismal, with the spray on the roads forcing her to drive slowly and concentrate. But once she had got off the Sandbanks Ferry and saw the Studland sand, the weight lifted from her shoulders and the tension eased in her neck.

The view from her room was of a grey, rolling sea. The scent of saltwater mixed with the distant roar of crashing white breakers tumbling onto the beach. She'd watched the sea all morning, mesmerised by its motion and the changing tide. Daring to go out, she took lunch at a local restaurant on the seafront, one of only four customers seated, and still returned with a heavy heart.

Heather knew she had burned her bridges. She'd left Ray in a storm of abuse. Confused and terrified, he denied any knowledge of the letter. In a vile tirade, he called her a fantasist and accused her of having an affair. He continued lying to her about the letter, even as she slammed the front door in his face. She'd loaded the car before she told him, and everything she had left behind was nothing she would ever need again. He'd tried to stop her, but she'd made it to her car before he could. Her best move was to hide his car keys in his sock drawer. He must have been so livid. She could imagine his face.

A tap on the door. "Room service!"

Heather opened the door to a pleasant young man in a black waistcoat and tie, who placed a tray of sandwiches and tea on the coffee table.

"Do you have everything you need, Mrs Collier?" he asked. "We've got a storm coming in tomorrow night. Not nice for your break."

"I'm good, thank you," she replied. "That's okay. A change is as good as a rest, they say. I'll hunker down in my lovely room, read a book, and watch TV."

"I don't blame you, Mrs Collier." He smiled. "Enjoy your tea."

The young man left, and Heather was alone again. She wasn't sure if she was hungry, but she was desperate for a cup of tea. The worry had affected her appetite, and her stomach was still in knots.

She had to make plans. That was her priority. She needed a property to rent until she found a place to buy. Her choice was between Swanage and Corfe Castle. They were her dream locations. She loved both towns, enjoying wonderful memories of them as a child, and she could afford to live in either, thanks to her mother's money. Money that Ray had tried several times to get his hands on. But her mother knew what he was like, and there was nothing he could do about it.

Divorcing him was going to be hard. He wouldn't let her go easily. She'd already decided she wanted no part of the house. It would make things so much easier. But then all of that could be academic once Lily did what she'd promised to do.

Swanage was a place she and Ray came to in their early years. He'd have forgotten it by now. He was more into his golfing holidays. The tedium she had to endure while he sat at the bar with his police buddies. She wondered if that was when her resentment began. She watched the other wives drink themselves into a stupor, feeling a mix of pity and fear at the prospect of sharing their fate.

Her stomach turned. Here she was, thinking about Ray again. Would he always haunt her now? She needed Lily to bring him down. She looked at her new mobile phone and wanted to call her. What was her plan? Heather found Lily's number, ready to call, but the courage wasn't there. Not yet.

She sipped her tea and looked out at the sea once more. The seafront road had emptied of cars, avoiding the incoming storm. She half wondered if Lily would come and join her. She would have appreciated her company right then.

When Heather switched on her TV to catch the news about the storm, she imagined she had caught a glimpse of Lily's face. But then, a tall, bald detective was speaking to reporters, asking for witnesses, and talking about the murder of Lily Watson.

Chapter Eighteen

A wave of weariness fell over Dinescu. Strangers surrounded him in a noisy hall in Fishbourne, where chairs were being put away and people stood around with drinks from the bar. He had just finished a community update about Lily Watson's murder. Earlier, he'd ploughed through media appeals to various news networks. Having done this several times before, he knew how to word his responses with care.

He stood and leaned on his chair to stretch his aching back, noticing a queue of curious individuals wanting to discuss local crime issues. But he wasn't there for that and didn't have the time. A local neighbourhood sergeant stepped in to rescue him, allowing Dinescu to head for the exit, pretending to be on his mobile to avoid more questions. He felt a slight twinge of guilt, but the exhaustion and the weight of the day's events left him with little choice.

He stepped outside into the chilled darkness, the lull before the forecasted storm. He sighed, his breath forming clouds of vapour. Hungry and late off, he still had to brief the team at the station before heading home. In the quiet, he took a moment to check messages from Lisa. All was okay at home, and Sophia's day had gone well. No more emotional traumas—apart from the one he'd left behind on the kitchen table that morning. He had left early to take Summers out for breakfast, placing the letter from HQ under a note for Lisa to read. *I don't know what to do*, was all he wrote.

Dinescu got into his car and drove to the station, his mind running over how Lisa might have taken the news. He imagined her various reactions and how he would respond. She hadn't let on in her messages, leaving him concerned about what would greet him.

Ten minutes later, he arrived at the Major Crimes Office, finding the core team gathered around the whiteboard. He felt they had made little progress today and hoped the appeal would yield more information.

"I saw you on the TV, sir," said Booker. "It's already triggered the armchair experts on social media. Perhaps we should hand the investigation over to them."

Dinescu rolled his eyes. "I always ignore them."

Summers took out a notepad. "It's late. Updates please. Gareth, your interview with Justin Hadley."

"Yes, Sarge. Mr Hadley runs a gallery on Bosham Lane," Booker began, running through the main points of his interview. "He said he didn't leave a message on the answering machine on Sunday night. To be honest, Sarge, his voice sounds nothing like the voice on the message."

"Did you get the right Justin?" Burgess asked.

Booker laughed. "I'm sure of it. Someone called Tracey runs the other art shop in Bosham."

"When did he last see Lily?" asked Dinescu.

"He said he spoke to her over the phone on Saturday. He has an alibi for yesterday. He stayed at a Premier Inn Hotel in Holborn, London, from Saturday to Monday morning. He spent the weekend with his partner at an exhibition. I've checked it. He also said he didn't believe Lily would have been on the marshes in the dark. She told him she thought the place was haunted."

"What's going on?" Summers asked. "If it wasn't Justin Hadley who left that message on the answering machine, who was it?"

"This is perplexing," said Dinescu, rubbing the back of his neck. "Perhaps there's another Justin. Let's come back to this later."

"Okay, boss," said Summers. "Sarah, how did you get on with Lily Watson's GP?"

"The short answer is yes," said Burgess. "Lily Watson had a child in 2002, a boy, born by caesarean section. The child was healthy, with no further details about his health. Her GP thought Lily's mental health might be pertinent to our enquiries. She had several bouts of depression over the last twenty years and had been on antidepressants for a long time."

"Thanks, Sarah," said Summers. "I have something to add. Yesterday, I searched Lily's bedroom again and found some official paperwork in her drawer." She emptied some papers onto her desk. "I found her birth certificate, a few reports and certificates from school and college, and an empty diary. This morning, I found this tucked inside a document pouch." She held up a blank, white envelope.

"Something hidden?" said Booker.

Summers opened the envelope flap and pulled out a piece of paper. "It's a photocopy of another birth certificate," she said, reading it to the team. "Henry James Watson, born 15th March 2002, at St Richard's Hospital. Mother: Lily Watson, father… Joseph McKinley, land manager." Summers then read the handwritten text on the notepaper. "The note says Henry and a Brighton phone number."

"Sarge," said Booker, "what was the father's name again on the birth certificate?"

"Joseph McKinley."

Booker pulled up the memorial page for PC Wallace on his computer screen and looked at Dinescu. "Joseph McKinley. Boss, that's the name of the man convicted of the manslaughter of PC Roger Wallace. He was twenty-eight then, so he'll be forty-eight now."

Dinescu looked over Booker's shoulder. "Gareth, find out where Joseph McKinley is now. Is he still detained?"

"Will do, boss."

"And I'd like you to try that contact number for Henry." Dinescu wrote two names on the whiteboard. "Get some background on his relationship with Lily. If he is her son, why did Lily keep it quiet?"

"I'll see if he'll talk to me face-to-face," said Booker.

"Emily, let's dig into the background of PC Wallace's murder. The coincidence of the murders occurring in the same place intrigues me. It looks like Gareth's hunch was right. We know there is a connection through Joseph McKinley. I also want to consider this message from Justin."

"I'll request the files," said Summers. "We have a plan to go forward, sir." She turned to the rest of the team. "I need all reports updated before we go home. Let's crack on."

Emily Summers had a quick shower after work and headed out to Kieran's house. After a short walk, she arrived at the front door. Holding a bottle of wine in one hand and a box of chocolates under her arm, she rang the doorbell. The house was dark, but she knew that was normal.

The door opened as far as the chain allowed.

"It's me," said Emily.

"Hi!" The chain dropped, and the door opened wide. "Come in. I have no idea if the place is tidy or not. It smells okay, though."

"Can I turn a light on?"

"Oh, yes, go ahead."

Emily switched on the hall light and saw Kieran smiling before her in the spacious hallway. It was a massive relief for her. A yellow labrador was beside him, wagging its tail.

"I come with wine and chocolates," she said. "I'll put them here." She placed them on a ledge by the window.

"I hope they were expensive," said Kieran.

"Of course. They were the pound shop's finest."

"Naturally."

"Look, Kieran," said Emily, hesitating. "I'm sorry I stood you up the other day. That's why I didn't call ahead tonight... I didn't know if..."

He held out his hand for her to take. "Hey, it's okay. No worries. I know you're busy. I get it. Come on in. I'll get you a drink."

"Have you eaten?" she asked.

"No, but I think a curry would go well with the wine. Perhaps not so much the chocolate."

Emily smiled, recalling a similar thought she'd had a few nights ago. "Let me take you out for a treat. Save on the washing up."

"As long as you don't mind my furry girlfriend coming with us. She gets jealous."

Emily, Kieran, and Bella the labrador walked together into the city. East Street was empty, except for a handful of university students. They were starting their night out, their shrieks of laughter carrying the length of the street. Emily and Kieran were heading towards a restaurant at the far end of West Street, walking against a strengthening wind.

She looked at him, finding his quiet confidence attractive. She appreciated that he never tried to make her feel guilty or burden her with emotional baggage—so different from her past relationship.

"Have you been okay?" she asked.

"All good. Work's busy—a whole bunch of fresh cases, more veterans needing our help. The highlight of the week was finding where the cleaner moved the rubbish bin—all very exciting." He laughed with Emily. "It's great to go out in the evening. I don't do much in the winter, especially in this weather. The pavements are either too wet and slippery, or the cold makes my knees ache. God, I'm an old man all of a sudden! Has my hair gone grey?"

Emily laughed. "Not at all. And you're not an old man. We can share a dog-friendly taxi back." She pulled Kieran closer to her. "I'm sorry about not being ready for… what you wanted this to be. I didn't want to hurt you. You're such a lovely man."

"Lovely? Hang on a minute, I'm an ex-soldier. You can't call me lovely." He turned his face towards hers. "It's okay, Emily. I'm often told there are plenty of fish in the sea—mostly scaly, smelly ones that don't get my humour."

"It's not because of your disability. Do you know that?"

Kieran stopped walking. "The fact that you are here tonight, that's all I need."

"Thank you."

"Anyway, it's Bella who's got a thing for you, not me."

And as Emily laughed, Bella looked up, either at the sound of her name or just to let Emily know she agreed with her man.

Fourteen hours on duty wasn't an unfamiliar experience for Beniamin, but it didn't happen often nowadays. His uniformed colleagues were being asked to do that more and more, so he wouldn't complain.

When he hung his jacket in the hall, silence filled the house. The faint smell of lasagne lingered in the air. Beniamin loved Sophia's lasagne with extra cheese. In the kitchen, he found his dinner on a plate, covered in plastic film. He warmed it in the microwave and poured a cold beer into his favourite glass, which read "Best Daddy Ever" in a chunky font.

Entering the living room, he was surprised to find Lisa and Sophia asleep on the sofa. Sophia's head rested against her mother's shoulder, her walking frame propped up beside her. The light was low, and the fire was a dying glow in the grate. Beniamin sat in his armchair, placing his plate and drink on a tray, and watched them while he ate. Was he fussing over the extra two hours a day away from them if he took this job? But it wasn't just about the extra travel. It was about losing his team and being close to Sophia if she needed him. And she did need him—there was much for her to navigate as a child with cerebral palsy. All those Charlies out there, for a start. Could he do that? He felt a pinch in his gut, knowing this wasn't right. He was already happy where he was, and so were those he loved.

Sophia stirred first, her head jerking up. "Oh, hi, Dad! You're back late. Is everything okay?"

Then Lisa woke up, bleary-eyed. "Ben. You must be so tired."

"I'm okay," he said, looking at his empty plate. "The lasagne was really tasty. Thank you." He put down his knife and fork. "It's been a long and hard day."

"I'm sorry. We stayed up for you," said Lisa. "We wanted to talk to you about the letter."

"But you're half asleep. And Sophia has school—"

141

"Be quiet and listen." Lisa sat up and leaned forward. "We know how important your work is to you."

"But it's not as important as you two are to me."

"We're not moving, are we?" asked Sophia. There was more than a hint of anxiety in her voice.

"No," he said. "This is about me making Guildford my base. It's just over an hour away, but it would mean more responsibility with a promotion. Longer hours, too."

"Then I have one question for you." Lisa took her feet off the sofa and sat forward. "Would working from Guildford and a promotion to superintendent make you happy? Would it make you feel more fulfilled?"

He didn't need to think about his response. "No. It would make me miserable. It would be harder to get back to Sophia if she needed me, and I would be further away from doing the job I enjoy most of all, with the people I enjoy being with."

"Then you've answered your question," said Sophia.

"Yes, I know," he said. "I just need to explain that to DCS Faraday. I can't believe they want to restructure the team. It works so well and has proven results. I tried to talk to Emily about it during our breakfast together, but it was too hard."

"Break up your team! What does he know?" Lisa said. "Take him on, Ben. Don't give in—fight for your team. They're like an extended family to you."

Beniamin nodded. "I have more than a feeling that he's already lined up someone to take over my position."

"Really?" said Lisa. "Who?"

"A younger officer—a DI from Worthing. She's on her way to becoming a DCI. Her name's Daisy Irving. She turned up at a couple of briefings this week, sizing us up."

"I'll have a word with her!" said Sophia.

"I'm sure you would." And he felt the weight lifting off his shoulders. "I won't give in if you're sure."

"We are," Sophia said. "Do we need the extra money? It's not as if I'm asking you to buy me a real donkey or anything."

Beniamin laughed. "The extra money would be nice, but we don't need it."

"Then that settles it," said Lisa. "Turn the job down and stand your ground. Fight to keep your team, Ben."

Chapter Nineteen

Thursday

Gareth Booker stood in front of the Brighton i360 Tower. Its shining glass viewing pod, which looked like a ring doughnut on a stick, reflected the morning light. The attraction was closed today. Opposite him were the creamy-white buildings of Regency Square and the South African war memorial with its dark bronze bugler. The cold, bright day and the calm blue sea were a welcome change from the recent run of grey days, giving him a positive vibe. He was glad to be out of the office, with the crisp sea air invigorating him and offering a fresh perspective on the challenges of becoming a first-time father.

He had left early to arrive on time, leaving Chloe, his fiancée, in bed with morning sickness. In fact, Chloe suffered from all-day sickness, and no one had warned them how horrible it could be.

Booker checked his watch, feeling on edge. It was 10:40, and Henry Watson was already ten minutes late. Henry had mentioned needing to start work at a local pub in an hour. He checked his mobile—no messages. He looked up and saw a young man wearing a long grey coat nearby. The man was tall and thickset, with dark red hair and a full matching beard. He glanced over at Booker several times. He matched the description Henry had given of himself over the phone.

"Henry Watson?" Booker asked.

"Rushton," said the young man. "My mother's name is Watson. You're the police officer?"

"DC Booker from Chichester Major Crimes." He held out his lanyard.

"What's this about? Has this got something to do with my mother? Nobody else knows my birth name."

"It does, Henry," said Booker. "Can I buy you a coffee?"

The two men crossed the road and entered a Kings Road café. They sat by the window, the sunlight pouring in. They removed their coats, and Booker brought over two coffees and sat opposite Rushton.

"Henry, thanks for meeting me at short notice," said Booker.

"It sounded important. I'm a bit worried, to be honest."

"I assume you haven't seen the local news. I have something difficult to tell you. On Monday, your mother, Lily Watson, was found dead on Fishbourne Marshes. I regret to say we believe she was murdered. She was discovered drowned in the creek."

Rushton stared at his coffee, watching the demerara sugar sink into the thick foam. He remained expressionless for a moment, then shook his head.

"I'm sorry, Henry," Booker said. "There was no easy way to tell you. We issued a press release yesterday, giving your mother's name. We wouldn't have done that without informing you, but we only just found out about you."

"That's okay. Who did this?" Rushton's eyes were cold and distant.

"We don't know yet. Our enquiries are ongoing."

"We'd only just found each other. I can't believe it." Rushton turned away, rubbing his eyes with the back of his hands. They both looked outside as a flurry of seagulls squabbled over a bread crust. "We were looking for each other. I put in a request to find her. I wasn't going to, but something inside me wanted to know. Then, I found her on Facebook last year. A family in Brighton adopted me when I was two. Lily said she had to give me up after a breakdown. She told me my real father had left and couldn't be there for us."

"This must be very hard for you. When did you last see Lily?"

"I saw her last month, just before Christmas. She came to my flat. She kept saying she wanted to make amends for everything. She wanted to help me clear my student debt and shit like that. I didn't care, but I suppose she felt guilty. I totally get why she let me go, and I had okay parents growing up. I last heard from her on Sunday, which is spooky now that I think about it. She said she'd found a way to help me pay back my student debt. She asked to see me this weekend. She wanted to transfer some money to me."

"Did she say how she was going to do that?"

"No real detail," said Rushton. "Just that someone owed her some money."

Rushton looked out across the road towards where the old West Pier used to be.

"Can you think of anyone who would want to harm Lily?"

"I didn't know her well enough. The only thing she was worried about was my father. She said she had some news about him. She wanted me to meet him. To introduce him to me."

"Did she tell you where he is?"

"No, he's living in Chichester."

"Really? Where?"

"Not sure. I got the impression she had something to do first before she could bring him over. To be honest, I think she was scared of him. She said he'd been violent in the past. I didn't care if I saw him or not."

"How did she seem when you spoke to her on Sunday?"

"Fine. She was chatty and told me about her painting and some strange people in her art club."

"Do you know if she was in a relationship with anyone?"

"Not that I know of. Only that she'd got back in contact with my father, but I don't think they were back together again. She lived with a woman called Yolanda. She said she was controlling, always wanting to know where and who she was with. Lily thought she was into her. My mother wasn't like that. She was straight and told her she wasn't interested."

"What were you doing two days ago—Monday morning?"

"Alone in my flat in the morning. I got up at about ten, put some music on, and played Football Manager for a bit. I was at work in the evening."

The two talked for another twenty minutes about football, Brighton and Hove, and their current season. Once Booker had all he needed, he handed Rushton his contact card.

"Call me if there is anything you remember that could be pertinent. I'm sorry for your loss, Henry."

"Yeah, thanks. It's a strange feeling, you know. She didn't feel like my mother. I'd only just got to know her. It's just... weird. It's my father you should be—"

Rushton looked out onto Kings Road and frowned as if he'd seen something. Booker noticed his expression change, his eyes widening, and the colour draining from his cheeks.

"Are you okay, Henry?" Booker asked.

Rushton licked his lips, giving a thin smile. "Yeah, fine. I have to go. Just remembered—work needs me early today." He stood and put on his coat. "We've got a delivery. I must run."

"That's okay."

Rushton was already away, looking out across the street again.

He left the café and ran around the corner towards the memorial. Within seconds, he was out of sight.

Booker saw nothing other than seagulls. He puzzled for a moment, then took out his mobile and looked up a few notes he had made earlier about Henry's adoptive parents. He dialled a number.

Rushton had run north along Preston Street. He had turned left onto Western Road, passing coffee shops and vape shops, hair-dressers—anywhere there were people. He looked for them in the reflections of the shop windows, but only saw the shadowy form of his own. No one was following him.

He wasn't built for running, and his sweat-drenched clothes clung to him. He undid the buttons on his coat and turned south, doubling back into more familiar territory. Slowing his pace, he caught his breath, and the feeling of tightness in his chest eased.

Walking up to a boarded-up house covered in scaffolding, he stopped. He wiped his face with his coat sleeve and sat on the step, closing his eyes. He tried to slow his heart, listening for foot-steps, the murmur of voices, anything that might signal danger.

"Taking a breather, H?" said a voice.

Rushton's eyes snapped open. Three of them blocked his exit. Two were wiry, skanky lads, and one of them, Jack, was glaring down at him.

"I told you, I'll get it to you next week, Jack."

"Did you?" Jack pushed his acne-ridden face closer. "Well, that's changed, H. I don't trust you. Who was that suit you were with just now?"

"No one."

"Looked like the filth to me, H. You telling tales on us?"

Rushton wanted to vomit. "It was a man from the council. Housing. They're kicking me out of the flat."

The other two men turned their backs on him, looking along the road. Rushton struggled to breathe. Jack pushed his knuckle into Henry's forehead. His ring dug in, piercing his skin. Rushton groaned with pain as Jack dragged his fist across Rushton's sweaty brow, the ring cutting a crooked line into his skin. Blood dripped into his eyes.

"Friday, by twelve, H. Not one minute later. Same place as usual. Don't be late, and don't try to run. We'll always find you wherever you go."

Rushton watched them leave, walking north. He waited, digging around his pocket for a tissue. He found a used serviette and wiped his forehead, leaving a red smear on the paper.

"Shit!"

He took out his mobile and sent a text. *I want more money. Cash again. Five this time. Don't piss me off, or I'll make good on my promise.*

From his office, Dinescu noticed DC Chester Kirby arriving before anyone else that morning. His short ginger hair was now accompanied by a trimmed, matching goatee. He came in to see Dinescu, telling him how he was grateful to be back in Chichester. Dinescu understood that. He wouldn't want to be anywhere else now, either.

"I'll get back to my desk, boss," said Kirby. "I can get up to speed with Operation Brook."

"Good to have you back, Chester," said Dinescu. "There's much to do."

When Summers and Burgess arrived a short while later,

Dinescu could hear the traditional sarcastic greetings to help Kirby feel at home.

"We were wondering where you'd gone," said Burgess, dropping her bag on her desk. "I heard Crawley had found someone else to make the coffee."

Kirby smiled. "Funny, Sarah. And, yes, please—plenty of milk, no sugar."

"And what's that fluff on your chin?" said Summers.

"Something my wife enjoys, Sarge. Good to see you, too."

Dinescu came out of his office to join Summers as she outlined the current state of the case to Kirby.

"I thought something sounded familiar," said Kirby, reading Colin Jackman's last statement. "I remember the stories about the PC murdered on the marshes years ago."

"McKinley murdered PC Roger Wallace in the same place as Lily," said Summers.

Kirby was about to respond when Gareth Booker entered the office, looking flushed. Removing his coat, he sat with the team and then produced his notes from Brighton. He saw Kirby was with them, raised his hand, and high-fived him. "Welcome back, mate. Nice beard."

Dinescu, with a coffee in hand, perched on the corner of Summers's desk. Booker's apparent excitement intrigued him.

"So," said Booker, catching his breath. "Lily's mental health fell apart after the court put McKinley away for manslaughter. A couple from Brighton fostered and later adopted Henry. His adoptive parents gave him the surname Rushton." Booker checked his notes. "Henry is known to the police. He has a caution for shoplifting, possession of class B times two, and an arrest, but no conviction for ABH. Despite that, he's not anti-police. He told me his birth father was in Chichester. So, I did some checks. They released Joseph McKinley from the secure hospital into a rehabilitation unit in Chichester in August last year. The mental health tribunal deemed him no longer a danger to society."

"Where is he?" said Summers.

"He's a resident of Dean Court."

"That's off North Street."

"Indeed, Sarge. Henry told me Lily was trying to arrange a meeting with McKinley. I don't know if this is connected, but she had told Henry she wanted to help him clear off his student debt. They were due to meet up this weekend. He never heard from her after that."

"So Lily died the same way as Wallace," said Kirby. "A blow to the head and drowning in the creek. McKinley?"

"This has got to be the same murderer, surely," said Burgess. "Is McKinley the man people have seen on the marshes?"

"Just so you know, Sarge," said Booker, "McKinley was ex-army. He served in Bosnia until they invalided him out with PTSD and psychosis. I don't know the details, but it might explain him wearing the camouflage jacket."

"That gives a better background to his mental health problems," said Dinescu. "Bosnia of all places."

"I found the phone number for Henry's adoptive parents. They're in Norwich now. His mother, Eileen Rushton, said they want nothing more to do with Henry. It's got to do with the trouble he got into a few years ago. She said he stole from them and had been violent. She said they never reported it."

"Violent?" said Summers. "You said he was arrested for ABH, but no conviction."

"That's right, Sarge. The guy seems to have his life in order now. He was okay to talk to—has a flat and a regular job."

"And he's in Brighton," said Summers. "Some way from Chichester."

"Yes, Sarge," said Booker. "Henry shared some memories of

Lily and her visits to Brighton. She'd told him Yolanda was controlling. She wanted to know where she was and who she was with. Henry implied that Yolanda may have wanted to be in a relationship with Lily, but his mother wasn't having it."

"Unrequited love," said Kirby.

"Yolanda never said anything about having feelings for Lily," said Summers. "But maybe she wouldn't tell us. As Yolanda described it, I sensed a hint of control in their argument."

Dinescu remained silent. He was listening but focusing on the whiteboard.

"Sir?" said Booker. "What do you think?"

Dinescu shook his head. "I don't know yet. So, they released McKinley last year. It's all very convenient to blame him. We must speak to McKinley, of course. Did he have a motive to kill Lily, and did she know he was back?"

"Likely she did," said Burgess.

"Agreed," said Dinescu. "I want to see those case files for Wallace's murder. Who was going to look those out?"

"Me," said Summers. She checked the time on her mobile. "They're being delivered to us anytime now."

"Good. Can we speak to McKinley's support workers?"

"I can do that, boss," said Booker. "It would be good to get an update of McKinley's description, too."

"Okay," Summers said to Booker, looking up from her computer. "I want to go with you." She pointed at Kirby. "Chester, now you're back, I'll give you something more up your street. We must work out Lily's movements after she stormed out of her house on Sunday evening. It's a job Gareth has started, but you're more methodical than him. No offence, Gareth."

"Cheers, Sarge," said Booker. "I'll try not to take it personally. Nice to have you back, Chester."

"I'm going to get my hands dirty, too," said Dinescu. "Sarah, you and I will do a little reading around the subject." Dinescu pointed to the entrance to the office with his eyes. Two police staff wheeled in sack trolleys piled with case files in cardboard boxes. "The Wallace case files are here."

Chapter Twenty

"Where's she gone, Ray?" asked Craig, leaning the garden fork against his fence.

"No idea," said Collier. "I think it's the change. She's been so emotional lately and dithering."

"Mine dithers too," said Craig, rolling his eyes. "We go to the shops, and she can't choose between this skirt or that skirt. Three shops later, we're back at the first one she saw."

Collier sat on the garden chair, the seat damp from the overnight rain. "I've not had a decent meal since Sunday."

"You must let Irene cook you something," said Craig, sitting beside him.

"I don't want to be a bother."

"You're no bother."

"I wish she'd come to her senses. She's got a home and a husband who cares for her."

Craig picked at the plaster on his thumb. "You know, Ray. We couldn't help but hear what happened on Sunday. I hope you don't mind me prying, but it was a hefty old row you had. I mean, most of the effing came from Heather, of course, but we heard banging too."

Collier turned towards him. "It was a huge row. She lost her temper and smashed my old bookcase. Luckily, we had a new one on the way." He hung his head. "The truth is—and keep this to yourself—she's had affairs."

"No!" Craig's hands went to his mouth. "Your Heather's had it away?"

"Yep. Don't you tell Irene, either. Otherwise, the world and his wife will know."

"My lips are sealed. Who was it?"

"I know one of them for sure." Collier looked around him. "An ex-copper—a few years back."

Craig leaned in. "Who?"

"No names. Then there were others. Not all men, either."

"God, Ray! You think she was a…"

"Possibly. One of them, this woman, broke it off with her. She was all arty."

Craig nodded, pursing his lips. "That's definitely the type."

"I know. Well, she ended up dead at the weekend."

Craig slapped his hand against his chest. "This is the stuff of Channel Four! You must be devastated."

"I am. The worrying thing is—and you mustn't tell Irene—Heather was with this woman before she died."

"That's sick. You're not saying… Are you?"

Collier shrugged. "Maybe I am, maybe I'm not. You'd have heard of it on the TV."

"Not that woman on the marshes!"

Collier nodded.

"And now Heather's gone?"

"As I said, don't tell Irene. I don't want it getting out."

"I won't, Ray. Your Heather. Who'd have believed it? Have you been to the police?"

"I am the police, remember?"

"Oh, yes!"

"I spoke to them. They may come over soon to talk to me. If you see them knocking at my door, don't tell Irene what it's about."

"No, I won't."

Collier glanced at his watch. "Thanks for the cuppa. Much appreciated." He stood and looked at the line of spades and forks against the fence. "I'd put those away if I were you. Looks like rain's coming again."

Collier turned and left through Craig's front door, stepping over the short privet hedge to his driveway. As he put his key in the lock, he smiled to himself and nodded.

Summers and Booker walked through the automatic doors of Dean Court into an empty reception. A phone rang in an office behind the front desk, and the detectives exchanged glances.

"No security here," said Booker.

The air was thick with the smell of antiseptic, and a wet floor warning sign stood before them.

Summers looked around for a call button to press, but there was no need. A tall, slim woman in jeans and a grey roll-neck jumper appeared from a door.

"Hi," she said. "Can I help you?"

They produced their warrant cards. "Good afternoon. I'm DS Summers, and this is DC Booker from Major Crimes in Chich-ester. We need to speak to someone overseeing the stay of one of your residents."

"Which resident?" asked the woman. She unclipped a badge from her jeans pocket. "I'm Doctor Val Stiles, senior manager. I'm happy to talk to you, but I can't discuss our patients' medical issues without a court order. I'm a stickler for that."

"I understand, Doctor Stiles," said Summers. "This is about Joseph McKinley. Do you know where he was last Sunday night and Monday morning?"

"He's free to come and go as he pleases. He was medically discharged, and this place isn't a secure facility. It's about reintroducing people into society. You can ask him yourself or talk to one of his support workers."

"The medical tribunal released him to you in August," said Booker. "Has he settled in well since then? Any problems?"

"I've already told you I can't talk about that," the doctor replied, folding her arms. "Joseph is in the common room if you want to talk to him yourself. But to warn you, he's not a fan of the police." The doctor tilted her head and looked at Summers. "Has he done anything wrong?"

"I'm sorry, Doctor Stiles," said Summers. "I'm not at liberty to tell you that."

"So it works both ways," said Stiles.

"Where's the common room?"

Stiles flashed a smile. "Follow me."

She led them through the door and down a corridor. The smell of stewing cabbage hung in the air, reminding Summers of the school from the last murder case she'd worked on. They entered a large room with high-backed chairs, coffee tables, and a big TV on the wall. Summers noticed cigarette smoke drifting in from an open patio door.

A man in a red checked shirt sat in a chair, reading a newspaper. Two cups and an opened packet of biscuits were on the table in front of him.

"Jeff, where's Joseph gone?" asked the doctor.

He looked around the room and shrugged. "He was here a few minutes ago. Maybe he's gone out. You must have just missed him."

"Do you know where?" asked Summers.

"Sorry, who are you?" Jeff asked.

"Police officers. We'd like to speak with him."

"Police? What do you want with Joseph?"

"As I said, we'd like to talk to him about something."

"I don't know where he's gone. Into the city, probably. He likes to walk in the open air. He could be anywhere."

"Can you describe him?"

"He's tall, well-built, and has a thick beard."

"What's he wearing?"

Jeff put down his newspaper. "Green trousers and an army-style coat."

"Look," said Summers, "he's not in trouble, but we must talk to him urgently. Can you give him my card so he can call me?"

The doctor took the card. "I'll let him know. You must excuse me. Joseph's made some genuine progress, and I'm quite protective of him."

"That's understood," said Summers.

Doctor Stiles saw them out and promised to give McKinley the card.

Summers and Booker did a cursory search of the area, but he was nowhere to be seen. They returned to their car, and Summers thought about what to do.

"Why is she so protective of him?" she asked.

"Quite maternal, I thought," said Booker.

"We'll continue looking for him, but I've got a feeling we won't find him."

The new front door lock felt stiff, so Yolanda wanted to try the new keys before leaving the house for the morning. She still couldn't believe she had to change the locks. The burglary was no coincidence, she knew that. But what was he looking for? He'd trashed the place but stolen nothing. Were her portraits worth something to him?

She zipped up her coat and put on her woollen hat, bracing against the biting wind despite the shining sun. She'd seen the weather forecast warning of a storm coming later, though Yolanda didn't believe it. She lifted her chin as she stepped outside, feeling undefeated and that everything would work out.

As she reached her front gate, a large, bearded man appeared, blocking her way. She yelped in surprise, her mind racing with suspicion.

"What do you want?" she asked.

He didn't reply at first. He screwed up his face, deepening the creases around his eyes and cheeks. He stumbled over his words like he was gnawing on something.

"*I said, what do you want?* I have my finger on an emergency button on my phone. The police know me!"

"Are you Yolanda?"

"Why should I tell you?"

"I was a friend of Lily—"

"I very much doubt that!"

"Think what you like, but I was. I'm sorry she's gone. Devastated, to be honest."

Yolanda tilted her head, trying to determine if the dishevelled man was a friend or foe.

"Who are you?"

"Joseph McKinley."

She shrugged.

"Can I have a quiet word?" Joseph glanced at the front door.

"I'm not letting you inside, Mr McKinley. I've had my fill of unwanted visitors recently. Was it you who ransacked my house?"

Joseph frowned. "I don't know what you're talking about. I need to talk to you about Lily."

"You can stay behind the gate and don't move an inch closer. I don't have long. I have to be somewhere."

He growled under his breath, looking left and right. "A long time ago, Lily and I had a... disagreement. I let her down badly. But we found each other again recently, and I believed she'd forgiven me. She said she had something for me, and I thought she was going to help me. But at the last minute, she let me down."

Yolanda noticed the man was getting agitated. "I don't have a clue what you're talking about." She took two steps back, keeping her hand on the phone button in her pocket.

"She said she would help me, Yolanda. She promised. She had something that proved I was innocent."

"Innocent of what? What did she have?"

"Evidence of some kind, she said. I'm not sure exactly what it was."

"If you can't tell me, how can I help you?"

"Let me look through the stuff she had with her when she died. Maybe in her room."

"Absolutely not! The police have already been through it."

"Have they? What did they find?"

"Nothing. Her phone's gone, if that's what you want. Someone stole it."

"I don't want her bloody phone!" he snapped. "It must be something else, maybe something written in a book."

"A book?"

"What about in her room?"

"There's nothing there. Just clothes and some personal papers. That's all I'm going to tell you."

"Oh." He stepped back, deflated. "Well, thank you. I know

who killed her—I just need to prove it. I need that evidence, whatever it is."

Yolanda was breathless, her knees trembling. "I can't help you."

Joseph didn't answer. He turned and walked away with his head hung low.

Chapter Twenty-One

Despite the large quantity of paperwork, Dinescu and Burgess had located the pertinent files. They had taken over a meeting room, arranging the documentation in order of interview transcripts, statements, and evidence.

Summers and Booker found them immersed in their work.

Dinescu looked up when he saw Summers. "McKinley?"

"He magically disappeared when we arrived," Summers said, flopping into a chair and scowling. "We searched for him. He could be anywhere."

"Was he tipped off?" he asked.

"I don't know, sir. We'll have to go back for him another time. The staff weren't very helpful. I think McKinley's anti-police."

"That's not unusual," said Burgess, "but he shouldn't be at Dean Court if he is still a threat to the public."

"Never mind that for now," said Dinescu. "I'm sure he'll turn up soon."

"That didn't take you long to go through," said Summers, looking at the pile of statements. Her frown eased.

"I've worked on many cold cases," said Dinescu. "Fortunately, this case summary is thorough."

When Summers's phone rang, she took the call and walked to the window.

"What was the key evidence against McKinley?" Booker asked, taking the chair Summers vacated.

Burgess answered, "DS Raymond Collier caught him holding Wallace in the water. He was Wallace's sergeant. Forensics found McKinley's DNA on Wallace's jacket, and a gold neck chain belonging to Wallace was in McKinley's pocket. Collier knew McKinley from previous dealings with him."

"There was a drugs surveillance operation going on," continued Dinescu. "Collier and Wallace were watching for small boats from France dropping drug packages in the marshes. Collier suspected McKinley of picking up these heroin packages and distributing them. Collier hid among the reeds, spying on the boats and waiting for McKinley. They had identified that he often waited inside the old pillbox." Dinescu sipped his coffee, listening to Summers's side of her call.

"Sounds like McKinley got himself involved way too deep," said Booker.

Dinescu agreed. "Wallace was on his way to take over from DS Collier, but something happened at the creek. They assumed Wallace confronted McKinley. Collier testified that he heard shouting in the distance, but didn't register it at first. Something made him check, and he found McKinley holding Wallace under the water in the creek."

"What was McKinley's defence?"

"He said he was trying to lift Wallace out." Dinescu glanced at Summers, who was pacing the room. "However, there were contradictions in his account. Wallace had a head injury that had knocked him unconscious, and McKinley appeared to be under the influence at the time."

Booker shook his head, sceptical. "Lily Watson was also struck on the head."

Burgess added, "Collier said McKinley tried to flee the scene when challenged, implying guilt."

"Finally, there was this." Dinescu held up a photograph showing a pole with a metal hook on the end. The measuring ruler photographed alongside it gave a length of five feet. Summers, still on her call, came over and looked at the photograph with them. "The end had traces of Wallace's blood on it. It matched the injury to his head. McKinley's fingerprints and DNA were all over it. It was McKinley's pole. Previous surveillance showed him using it to fish out packages from the marshes."

"Where did they find it?" Booker asked.

"In the reeds near the footbridge," said Dinescu.

Booker frowned. "What, just thrown in there?"

"That's what the prosecution alleged," said Dinescu. "McKinley denied everything. He said Wallace was in the water when he found him. He claimed he kept the hook in the pillbox, and someone else must have taken it."

Booker nodded. "Why did he run?"

Dinescu stood to stretch his back. "Because he believed Collier was trying to frame him for Wallace's murder. He said he was terrified."

"Circumstantial, most of it," said Burgess.

"But Wallace's blood was on the pole," said Booker.

"I agree with Sarah," said Dinescu. "The defence argued that McKinley's state of mind at the time meant he didn't always remember what he was doing. Years of cannabis use had left him with psychosis."

"And that was his defence?" said Booker.

Dinescu nodded. "The defence solicitors thought no jury would believe his account, so that was his best chance."

"And the jury convicted him of manslaughter," said Burgess, "due to diminished responsibility."

Summers returned to the table. "I just had Yolanda Mellor on the phone. She said McKinley was at her door, wanting to look for something in Lily's room. She recognised his voice on the answering machine message, calling himself Justin."

"But why was he using the name Justin?" Booker asked.

"God knows," said Summers.

"He may be the only one who does," said Dinescu, frowning. "We have enough to arrest McKinley on suspicion of murder. He was around when Colin Jackman found Lily Watson's body, and now there's the threatening message."

"I've given McKinley's description to the response team sergeants," said Summers. "They've added him to their briefing. I'll get a couple of uniformed officers to search around Dean Court."

"Emily," said Dinescu. "We should visit Raymond Collier and get his views on McKinley. It was a long time ago, but I'm sure the recent news would have stirred up memories. Are you free to come now?"

"I am, sir."

Kirby put his head around the door. "I may have something, Sarge. I need to go into the city later to check some CCTV. I may be late off tonight."

"What have you got?"

"I don't want to say just yet in case I'm wrong, but I don't think I am. I'll update you soon."

Kirby's head disappeared, leaving Summers bemused.

Summers got into the car, and Dinescu entered Raymond Collier's address into the satnav. He lived on Brandy Hole Lane, a narrow road by a copse north of Chichester city centre. Dinescu took a route through the city. He heard Summers's tired sigh. "Are you okay?"

"Yes, sir," she said, staring out of her window. "It's been a full-on day. Hopefully, this case will become clearer soon."

"It will. I can feel it," said Dinescu.

"But where is Lily's car?"

Dinescu shook his head. "The killer's hidden it somewhere. Maybe it's in a car park."

"Or torched. That takes a lot of desperation or confidence. Overconfidence often screws these offenders. They think they're untouchable."

Dinescu nodded. "When I first came to England, I went to a school in Harrow. One teacher took a dislike to me. I was young and couldn't speak English. He secretly hit me, pushed me, and pinched me. He did other unpleasant things too."

"Shit!" Summers's jaw dropped. "That's horrible!"

"I told my parents, and they went to the headmaster. One day, the headmaster caught him trying to push my head through the wall. The police were called, and he eventually went to prison. He thought he was clever and could always get away with it. I use that experience to remind me that even the most devious people will make mistakes."

"I can't imagine you ever being a boy, sir. In my mind, you were always a giant. How tall are you? Six-two, six-four?"

"It depends if I'm sitting or standing."

Summers rolled her eyes and laughed. "Well, it was appalling for you."

"The detectives involved were first-class and very patient with me. They left me with a positive impression of the police. It was one of the things that led me to join up."

"You always manage to turn your bad experiences around somehow."

Dinescu smiled. "It's the only way to win, Emily."

After driving around the north of Chichester, Dinescu took the road towards Midhurst and turned left onto Brandy Hole Lane.

Collier's house was behind a tall hedge, with a new blue Range Rover on the driveway.

"Someone's got a good retirement package," said Summers.

When they got out of the car, a dishevelled man in his sixties opened the door. He was overweight, unshaven, and had popped his shirt button over his stomach. He studied the two detectives, especially Dinescu.

"Yes," he said, folding his arms across his chest.

Dinescu took the lead. "This is DS Summers, and I'm DCI Dinescu from Major Crimes in Chichester. Are you Raymond Collier?"

Collier scowled. "Yes."

"May we come in? We want to discuss a previous case—a man you put away twenty years ago."

"Really? Twenty years is a long time. Come in. I'll give it a go."

Dinescu turned to see two figures standing in the window next door, trying to catch what was going on.

Collier led the detectives into a lounge. A log burner crackled in a brick fireplace. The room was dark and smoky. Empty coffee cups lined an occasional table next to an armchair with a pizza box on it.

"Sit," said Collier, gesturing to a sofa.

"Thank you," said Summers, moving a pile of newspapers onto the floor.

"A bloody DCI venturing out of the nick?" said Collier. "What's the world coming to?"

Dinescu wasn't sure if he was being humorous or sarcastic, so he ignored the comment. "We'd like to talk to you about Joseph McKinley."

Collier laughed. "With an accent like that, I guess you're not from around here."

"No, I'm from Bracklesham Bay." Dinescu took an instant

dislike to him. Something in his manner reminded him of the old-school officers he used to work with in the Met. "And I'm Romanian."

"I suppose we were all foreigners once. Our ancestors, I mean."

"Can you help us?" Summers asked.

"You want to talk about Joseph McKinley? Yes, I remember him, even from twenty years ago. He's a scum cop killer. We should have the death penalty for those. Have you heard he's out on licence?"

"I can't comment on that, Mr Collier," said Dinescu.

Dinescu saw photographs on the mantelpiece. Raymond Collier was in each one with a dark-haired woman, always standing behind his right shoulder, giving a thin, loyal smile to the camera.

Collier caught him looking at the photos. "That's the wife—Heather. Married for thirty-five years this year. No kids—I never wanted them." He looked away, stopping himself from saying more. "I saw you on the news. Didn't you think of linking Roger's death to Lily Watson's?"

"PC Wallace's murder was way before my time in Sussex. Lily Watson's murder must have brought back memories for you."

"Of course it bloody did." Collier's eyes flickered. He sat back in his armchair and pushed his comb-over back into place. "Thanks for reminding me."

"Is it right that you witnessed McKinley drowning PC Wallace?" asked Summers.

"Read my statements, lady." A frown fell over his face. "Yes. I saw him. He was a lowlife. He screwed his brain with drugs when he was young, and he was a wreck. Gangs on the coast manipulated him. They made him pick up drug packages from the boats and drop them at prearranged locations. He was violent and would do anything not to get caught."

"I read in the unused material," said Dinescu, "that McKinley was getting help with his addiction. His psychologist stated McKinley appeared to be trying to sort his life out. He also had a newborn son to come to terms with."

"That was the rosy picture the defence tried to put forward." Collier scowled at Dinescu.

"I'm merely stating there were contradictory views about McKinley's motivation."

"He was involved with distributing drugs coming in from abroad. That was a proven fact. Roger caught him on the marshes and stupidly challenged him. McKinley's masters would have killed him if they thought he'd blown their operation. So he killed Roger, thinking he'd get away with it."

"What did you make of his relationship with Lily Watson?"

"I didn't make anything of it. He left her to bring up that kid on her own. I doubt there was any love lost after that."

"Can you remember there being any sense of betrayal or disloyalty from Lily towards McKinley?"

"You're looking for a revenge motive," said Collier, smirking. "It's possible. Her breakdown caused their son to be taken away. Perhaps he blamed her for it."

"Only speculation, then."

"It was a long time ago. It's not something I think about every day."

"You already know McKinley is out on licence," said Summers. "Have you seen him recently?"

"No," said Collier. "I hope for his sake I don't. If he comes anywhere near me, I'll have him locked up before the piss dries in his pants."

"How about Lily Watson? Have you come across her in the last month or so?"

"No. Haven't seen her for years. I doubt we move in the same circles." He glanced at the window. "Now, if you don't mind, I'm busy, and it's getting dark."

Collier led Summers and Dinescu to the front door, where Dinescu saw several unopened letters on the windowsill. He noticed all the coats hanging up in the hallway were men's.

"How's retirement going?" Summers asked as he opened the door.

"It's not all it's cracked up to be, sergeant. You get to know who your real friends are."

Dinescu and Summers didn't speak as they drove away into the long shadows alongside the copse. Summers drummed her fingers on her armrest.

"Did he bother you?" asked Dinescu.

"Is it that obvious, sir?"

"Me too. Something's wrong in that house."

"It looks like she's not there," said Summers. "The place is untidy. It's a nice house, but dirty cups are everywhere. Did you see the unopened letters to Mrs H. Collier?"

"I saw those." Dinescu looked up at the trees, shaken by the wind. "Most of the evidence against McKinley was circumstantial."

"And the jury believed the word of a police officer against that of a petty thief and cannabis user."

"Let's keep ourselves focused on the case at hand. McKinley has some questions to answer, sooner rather than later."

Summers agreed. "When we get back, I'll head over to Dean Court to see if he's returned. Gareth and Sarah can search his room."

Chapter Twenty-Two

Summers waited for the uniformed police officers to exit their car before entering Dean Court. This time, a woman was behind the reception desk.

"Can I help you?" she said.

Summers showed her warrant card. "Is Joseph McKinley here?"

"Joseph?" said the woman. "I haven't seen him since this morning. Do you want to talk to Doctor Stiles?"

"Can you check if he's here for us?"

"I'm not sure. I have to talk to Doctor Stiles first." The receptionist was already on the phone. She looked up. "She's just coming."

A cold rush of air blew in as the automatic doors opened, revealing a tall figure. McKinley entered, glaring at the police officers as the doors closed behind him.

Summers stepped closer. "Joseph McKinley?"

"What do you want?" McKinley said, his voice growling.

Doctor Stiles appeared, looking alarmed. "What's going on?" She tried to push past Summers.

"Just wait," Summers said.

"I'm not letting you take him anywhere. He's under medical supervision."

"You told me yourself he's been discharged. Stay where you are." Summers glared at Stiles, pulling her back. "Back away now, or I'll arrest you for obstruction."

The two police officers stepped forward. One unclipped his taser.

"I haven't done anything," said McKinley. He moved forward.

"Turn around and put your hands behind your back," said the officer. "I don't want to fight you."

McKinley huffed. "For God's sake! Why?"

"Do as the officer says," said Summers, "and I'll explain." The officer handcuffed McKinley. "Joseph, I'm arresting you on suspicion of murder—"

"What? I didn't kill anyone!"

"You do not have to say anything, but it may harm your defence if you do not mention, when questioned, something that you later rely on in court—"

"You know it was Collier who framed me!" McKinley was shaking.

"Anything you do say may be given in evidence. Your arrest is necessary to prevent physical harm to another and for prompt and effective investigation of the offence and your conduct through interview."

Summers updated the officers, who led McKinley away just as Burgess and Booker rushed into Dean Court.

"You okay, Sarge?" Burgess asked.

"Yes, I'm fine."

"Joseph isn't violent," said Doctor Stiles from behind them. "You had no right to come crashing in like that!"

"Ah, yes. I did. Now Joseph is under arrest, my boss will authorise a search of his room. So, please, Doctor Stiles, stop trying to obstruct me and let us get on with our jobs."

Summers turned to Booker and Burgess. "Once that Section Eighteen authorisation is given, get straight into McKinley's room. I'm heading back to the station."

Booker and Summers stood outside Interview Room One, while for Summers juggled her notes. "We found nothing of interest in McKinley's room, Sarge. We've seized some muddy boots that he could have worn down the marshes."

"Okay, Gareth," said Summers. "Let's get in there and see what he says."

The detectives sat opposite Joseph McKinley and his duty solicitor. McKinley seemed to fill his side of the table, and the solicitor looked tiny against him.

Booker tapped the record button. "This interview is being recorded on video in an interview room at Chichester Custody."

McKinley looked up at the video camera and smiled. Summers knew her boss was watching the interview from his desk. Booker got everyone to introduce themselves for the recording and gave McKinley the police caution.

"You've given me limited disclosure, DS Summers," said the solicitor. "There's nothing to support this baseless allegation of murder."

"We'll continue with what we've given you," said Summers.

"It seems this is the police sweeping up the usual suspects. A lazy broom, in my opinion. In that case, my client would like to say the following." The solicitor read from a prepared statement. "*I did not murder my friend, Lily Watson. I was on and around Fishbourne Marshes on Monday, the 8th of January, as this is my usual walk to pass the time. I saw no one other than a male on the footbridge wearing a blue anorak. I heard the male call for help, but he was on his mobile phone when I got to him.*

Not wanting to get involved, I walked away again. I did not know Lily was in the water at that time. This is my client's statement about the matter, and he will answer no further questions."

"Thank you for that," said Summers. "Joseph, did you kill Lily Watson on Monday, the 8th of January?"

"No comment," said McKinley, his voice low and gruff.

"You heard my client's statement," said the solicitor.

Summers continued. "You said in your statement Lily was a friend of yours. Tell me about that."

"No comment."

"We have located a birth certificate for Henry Watson, who now goes by another name. The certificate names you and Lily as his parents. Tell me about your relationship with Lily and Henry."

"No comment," said McKinley, inspecting his nails.

"How often do you go to Fishbourne Marshes?"

"No comment."

"It's about two miles from Dean Court. You have quite a walk to get there every day. Why Fishbourne Marshes? Wouldn't it be easier to walk inland?"

"No comment."

"What time did you arrive on the marshes on that Monday?"

"No comment."

"The male you describe seeing had just discovered Lily's body. That's why he was calling for help. Why didn't you help him?"

"No comment."

"Is it because you already knew who was in the water?"

McKinley's breathing grew louder, but he didn't answer. He shuffled in his chair as if unable to make himself comfortable.

Summers waited, but no answer came. "Lily's killer struck her on the side of her head and held her underneath the water. This is *exactly* what you did to PC Wallace twenty years ago. And exactly—and I mean *exactly*—the same location. Can you see how this looks to us, Mr McKinley?"

"DS Summers!" the solicitor interjected, "you are trying to prejudice the case against my client by bringing up past convictions. I'm not going to allow—"

"Look, I understand your concerns," replied Summers, cutting across the duty solicitor. "But I'm not here to dredge up the past for the sake of it. The line of questioning I'm pursuing is well within the framework of the law, specifically under the provisions set out by the Criminal Justice Act." She slowed her speech for emphasis. "It's crucial for us to consider certain aspects of Mr McKinley's history. The nature of this case bears striking similarities to his previous conviction. It's *not* about prejudgment."

McKinley shook his head, and his eyes flashed with rage.

"Joseph?" said Summers. "What is it?"

"Can't you see what he's done?" burst McKinley. "Don't you know?"

"Forgive my ignorance," said Summers. "Tell me." She leaned forward and made eye contact, wanting to connect with him.

"He made it look like it was me. He's done it all over again, and because he's a copper, he's going to get away with it *again*."

"Mr McKinley," said the solicitor. "I strongly advise you not to—"

"Shut up a minute!" said McKinley, holding his hand up to the solicitor. "We need to talk about it."

"Carry on, Joseph," said Summers. "What do you want to say?"

"I didn't kill that police officer. I was set up, and the man who did kill him has made it look like I killed Lily."

"Who would do that to you?"

"DS Collier, Raymond Collier. He's the one I saw drowning that police officer twenty years ago. He asked me for help to get Wallace out of the water."

"Did you see Mr Collier with Lily on Monday morning?"

"No."

The solicitor leaned away as if he had given up on McKinley.

"To clarify, you are saying you hadn't gone to the marshes to harm Lily," said Summers.

"No."

"I'm going to play you an excerpt from an answering machine message left for Lily Watson at some time on the day before she was killed. This is a copy of the message made by Digital Forensics, produced as GH/02."

Summers opened up a laptop. It was ready to play. McKinley listened to the recording, nodding his head. The solicitor scribbled down some notes.

"*Lily, it's me... Justin. I tried calling your mobile, but it's switched off. I've thought about what you said... I won't be there tomorrow. You know what I wanted more than anything, but now you're going to betray me. You've broken my heart, Lily. Broken my heart. I won't let it go unpunished. I promise you that.*"

"That was me," said McKinley. "That's what you're going to ask me."

"It was, Joseph. Tell me about why you left the message."

"I'd like some time with my client," said the solicitor.

"Okay. Interview suspended at 17:45."

Booker took McKinley and his solicitor to a separate room, and Dinescu came and joined Summers.

"I'm guessing McKinley wants to talk to us," Summers said to Dinescu. She leaned against the wall, arching her back to avoid the alarm strip.

"The solicitor has picked up on the veiled threat in the message," said Dinescu.

"We have nothing else on him, so this isn't going very far unless he suddenly confesses. The CPS won't run with it without evidence."

Dinescu rubbed the back of his neck. "He said on the answering machine message that he felt betrayed and wouldn't be there tomorrow. We need his explanation for this."

"And Yolanda told us McKinley believed Lily had evidence that would prove his innocence," said Summers.

"It would need compelling evidence to reopen the Roger Wallace case," said Dinescu. "It's not easy to overturn a verdict on an appeal."

They heard the solicitor calling out in the corridor.

"I'll get them."

"You're doing well," said Dinescu. "I'll catch you afterwards."

"Okay, boss."

"I believe he's telling the truth, and if I were a member of the jury for his trial, I'd have found plenty of room for reasonable doubt."

Dinescu left, and Summers brought back McKinley and the solicitor.

"Interview resumed at 18:07," said Summers. "The same people are in the room. Joseph, you are still under caution. You have spoken again to your solicitor. Is there anything you want to change or add to your statement?"

"My client has chosen, *against* my advice," said the solicitor, "to speak openly and frankly with you. I will still be here to offer advice when needed."

Summers nodded. She was going to be extra understanding. "Joseph, we want to get to the truth. We're not looking to trip you up or put you away again. We want to know what happened to Lily Watson on Monday, the 8th of January, and what you know about it."

McKinley composed himself. "Lily called me on Sunday afternoon, and we arranged to meet on Fishbourne Marshes on Monday morning. She said she had something to give me that would prove Ray Collier killed Roger Wallace. But there was something she wanted to do first." McKinley looked away. "She was going to blackmail Collier. She said Henry needed fifteen grand to help pay off his university fees, and she would give me ten grand to help me start a new life, maybe rent a flat."

"Explain to me the message you left on the answering machine."

"I had time to think about what she said, and I didn't like it. I called her in the evening, sometime before ten, but couldn't reach her on the mobile. I needed to talk to her urgently. I didn't want that nosy cow, Yolanda, to know it was me. I knew Lily was seeing someone called Justin, so I pretended to be him. Stupid, now I think of it, but I didn't want my real name on the recording. I told her I wouldn't go with her to meet Collier. I didn't want the bloody money. I only wanted the truth to come out. I thought she was stringing me along." McKinley pointed at Summers. "She knew how important it was to me, but she put money first."

"What about the threat you made?" asked Summers. "You said you wouldn't let it go unpunished."

McKinley kept his eyes on Summers. "I was talking about Collier framing me. I wanted to bring him to justice. I wanted justice! I wasn't threatening Lily. It was a promise about Collier."

Summers looked at her notes. "To summarise, Lily was going to give you something that proved you didn't kill Roger Wallace. But she'd planned to blackmail Raymond Collier with some information."

"Yes."

"She was going to split the blackmail money, giving your son, Henry, fifteen thousand pounds and you ten thousand. That makes a total of twenty-five thousand pounds."

"I don't know if it was in cash or not. She asked me to help her meet with Collier at about 9.30. She thought it wouldn't be busy then. She needed me to protect her from him if he got nasty."

"It's all a bit vague, Joseph. What was she going to give you, and what was she blackmailing Collier with?"

"I don't know what she had for me, and I didn't want to get involved with any blackmail. When I said I wasn't going, I thought she wouldn't do it on her own. But late Sunday night, I couldn't sleep. I still couldn't get through to her. I was worried she would meet with Collier despite me not being there. So I got to the marshes after nine on Monday—just before the time we agreed to meet—but I didn't see her, so I waited."

"What route did you take from Dean Court to Fishbourne?"

"North Street, West Street, and Westgate. Then over the bridge to Fishbourne Road East and through the underpass."

"Was she due to be meeting Collier on the footbridge?"

"Yes, and it was his suggestion. I thought even then the bastard was trying to wind me up—meeting up where he'd killed Wallace. She wasn't there when I arrived, so I waited on the foot-bridge. Nothing. When she didn't appear, I thought she'd changed her mind. I couldn't check with her as her phone was still off." McKinley shrugged, staring at the wall. "So, I went to get some lunch and returned to the marshes later to think things through. I sat by the old pillbox, and that's when I heard that fella shout for help. I immediately knew what had happened when I saw him climbing out of the creek. I knew Collier had done it again."

"What do you think, sir?" Summers asked Dinescu. He had joined her at her desk. The only other person in the office was Kirby, who was putting his coat on.

"We can easily check McKinley's movements through the city on Monday," said Dinescu. "And he knows that."

"I'm sure you're right, sir," said Summers. "But what about his account that Lily had something for him, and the blackmail story? The way McKinley was—he sounded credible enough."

Dinescu rubbed his temples. "We have no evidence to prove any of that. But we can look into his whereabouts. He can stay over tonight, and we'll get someone to check his movements in the morning. Think about it, Emily, if he were waiting on the foot-bridge for Lily…"

Emily grimaced. "She would only have been a few feet below him. That's horrible."

"And if he is telling the truth, then we have nothing to hold him. Was someone trying to set him up?"

"You mean Raymond Collier, boss?"

"According to McKinley, meeting on the footbridge was Collier's suggestion."

Summers yawned, her eyes glazed over.

"Time you were off home," said Dinescu. "Are you busy tonight?"

"I'm going to see a friend. A catch-up is overdue."

"And you?"

"I have to go to Worthing to meet with DCS Faraday."

Summers looked at her watch. "What, now?"

Dinescu nodded. "It was the only time he had free. I'm not going to be there long. I've got to get back to help Sophia with her maths homework." He looked over at Kirby's desk and saw his car keys. "Why is Chester still here?"

"He's got a bee in his bonnet about something on CCTV. He said he'll update us tomorrow."

"I hope he remembers to go home."

Chapter Twenty-Three

Dinescu walked through the long corridor of Centenary House at Worthing Durrington Police Station. To him, the building epitomised 1960s concrete and glass, an architectural eyesore. He navigated the open-plan offices directly to where DCS Faraday was holding court with the Proactive Crime Team.

Faraday was younger than Dinescu, fast-tracked in his career with minimal real-world experience. He was unlike the seasoned commanders Dinescu had known in the Met.

When Faraday saw him, he raised his hand, signalling for Dinescu to wait as he finished telling a joke. Faraday then approached, flashing a slick smile and nodding at him.

"Good evening, Ben," Faraday said, smiling. "You managed to find my only available slot today. I guess you have an answer for me."

"Yes, sir," Dinescu nodded.

Faraday led him to his office, tucked out of sight, with blinds and tinted windows overlooking the road and a small roundabout. The office was sparse, reflecting either Faraday's transient nature or his vacuous personality. A single bookshelf stood against the wall, filled with procedural manuals and dusty books on leadership. An organised pile of paperwork on the desk hinted at a man who liked control, in contrast to the person engaged in lively banter outside. Dinescu waited until Faraday invited him to sit, then he straightened his tie and jacket.

"Go on, Ben," Faraday said with a glint in his eye. "I can only imagine you're going to bite my hand off for that position in Surrey."

"I would like to decline the opportunity at this time, sir," Dinescu replied.

Faraday's smile vanished, replaced by genuine surprise. "I don't understand. Are you saying you're not interested in the job?"

"No, sir. I'm happy where I am, and so is my family. The Chichester Major Crimes Team is working effectively under my management, and I'm happy there."

Faraday appeared to gather his thoughts. "You sound very serious, Ben. Lighten up! Look, I have no doubt your team is effective, but this is about pooling resources when money is tight. You know that. Yes, the Chichester team is under review—my letter made that clear. But we could use your skills better else-where, not on a rural crime team."

"But you're not considering breaking up the team. You already have someone else in mind to take over. You're using this as a threat to coerce me into leaving. Reassigning my team would be a mistake. They work well together. You won't find a better team of detectives in Sussex or Surrey."

"Are you accusing me of lying, Ben?"

"Daisy Irving. She is very keen. You never told me she was coming, sir."

Faraday's frustration broke through. "This isn't your decision to make!" He sat back and folded his arms.

"Who is really pushing for this change?" Dinescu asked, already knowing the answer.

"Senior management. We've all agreed your skills would be better served in Surrey with the joint Major Incident Team. And there's a chance for promotion—temporary superintendent for a year, then a substantial—"

"With respect, I don't have to take the position or apply for the promotion."

Faraday frowned again, with a pout forming. Dinescu had seen this before when Faraday didn't get his way.

"We're not giving you that choice," Faraday said. "We want you to relocate to Guildford within the next three months, so you may as well go for the promotion!"

"It would be too great a change for my daughter, sir. She needs me around more, not less."

Faraday sighed, exasperated. "Some officers would give their right arm for this opportunity!"

"I'm not one of them."

Faraday's face reddened. "Clearly."

"You're trying to move me out of the way for someone else. Have you already promised my role in Chichester to Daisy Irving?"

"Is that what you think? I'm very disappointed, Ben. Very disappointed. I will have to discuss this with senior management. I hope your decision doesn't affect any future opportunities for you." Faraday's tension was evident in the subtle twitch of his jaw and the grip on the desk until his knuckles turned white. "You haven't thought this through. I'm giving you more time to decide. Think about how this will affect your career path. We'll meet again."

"I've already made up my mind."

"We'll see."

"If I must return, I'll have a Federation rep with me."

"That will be all, Ben. Thank you for coming over." Faraday looked away at his computer screen. "Close the door after you."

DC Chester Kirby walked over the railway crossing and headed north. It was dark now, and the roads were busy with Friday commuters heading home. As he continued, he noticed the wind had increased, recalling the office chatter about an approaching storm. The wind pushed through his coat, prompting him to pull up the collar against the chill on his neck. Despite the discomfort, he felt the satisfaction and purpose that came with a new lead.

Kirby was glad to be back in Chichester, working with his team. The familiar streets brought him comfort and routine, a stark contrast to the chaotic nature of his last role. Best of all, it meant he wouldn't be home so late.

He knew Summers was right about his knack for systematic analysis and sifting through CCTV footage. He loved the detail, but not everyone had the concentration for it. He had been trawling through hours of video footage with other detectives. They had found Lily's Mini passing the Avenue de Chartres car park cameras and turning left onto South Street. He saw her again, going into Cawley Priory Car Park. The video footage was clear enough. They had Lily in a dark coat, leaving the Mini on her own, heading towards South Street on foot.

Kirby worked through the possibilities as he followed her path in his thoughts. The South Street cameras weren't working, which meant some footwork to visit the pubs and restaurants. He turned right, passing the Methodist church, and arrived at the car park. Standing where Lily had parked, he looked up at the CCTV camera.

"Come on, Lily," he muttered to himself, "let's see if we can find you."

He walked down Theatre Lane, a narrow, one-way road, and onto South Street. People were streaming past on their way home. The nearest pub, a good place to start, was opposite him, so he went inside and spoke to the manager, who was preparing for a busy evening.

The manager took Kirby into a back office and brought up CCTV footage of the main doors on Sunday night. Fortunately, it wasn't very busy.

"She was in her early forties," Kirby told the manager. "Long, blonde hair. Dark coat. She left the car park at 21:34 and headed onto South Street. She may have met someone here—I'm not sure." He pulled a photograph of Lily Watson from his jacket pocket.

The manager scratched his head and punched in the time from 21:30. He played the video at double speed until someone appeared, then slowed it down.

"There!" said Kirby. "That's her."

"She doesn't come in," said the manager. "Is she that murdered woman?"

Kirby nodded. Adrenaline surged through his veins. It felt like they were staring at a ghost. "Her name is Lily. Have you seen her before?"

"Maybe. I'm not sure."

Kirby leaned closer to the screen. "I wonder what she's doing?"

"Waiting for someone, by the looks of it," said the manager.

They watched her wait outside for ten minutes, each passing minute becoming more tense. A silver Audi appeared in front of the pub. A man in a smart suit stepped out of the car and spoke to Lily.

"Looks like they're arguing," said the manager.

"Pause it there," said Kirby. He noted the car's registration number and took a photo of the screen with his mobile phone.

The video played on. Lily and the man embraced, and the manager laughed. "And now they've made up."

"Well, well," said Kirby. His mind was already turning over

this new information. A few moments later, the video showed Lily getting into the Audi, and the car drove away.

~

"I won't be much longer, honestly. Tell me all about it when I get home. Love you."

DC Ross Taylor ended the call with Bill and stared at his computer screen. The long hours were taking a toll on him, and his husband wasn't thrilled about him being late home again.

In front of Taylor was a list of possible suspects for a trafficking case he was working on. He had traced their movements, their meetings, the ANPR cameras they had passed, and the locations where their phones had pinged. The work was in-depth, and he was fed up with it. He longed to rejoin his team in Chichester.

As he had this thought, he looked up and saw someone familiar walking past his office. It was DCI Dinescu. By the time he left his chair, Dinescu was already heading out of the building. He looked tired and angry, and Taylor didn't blame him. Coming from the direction of Faraday's office, he must have been in a meeting with him.

No one in the section liked Faraday. He pretended to be one of them, meeting them for coffee and sharing the banter, but he was a total bastard—a creepy one, too. Taylor had heard the rumours about the student officers whom Faraday had *supported*. Always female. Always young and pretty, with a lot to offer. Then there was his latest acquisition. She had been Taylor's DI for the last few months. His colleagues considered her a catch: single, tall, and slim with a *nice arse*—their words, not his. A flirt, even with junior officers, but her charms had no effect on Taylor.

He stroked his grey beard stubble. Seeing Dinescu, one of the best bosses he'd had, stirred everything up again. Taylor had information on Faraday but didn't know what to do with it. He had sat on it for too long.

Taylor had seen Faraday's tactics before, pushing aside people in his way. Faraday knew nothing about real policing, having been fast-tracked from nowhere. He was a charlatan. But Taylor wondered what he could do. He couldn't go to his DI. His colleagues in Special Ops would stick together to protect themselves. They couldn't risk being moved by Faraday. Taylor had heard of one officer being threatened with redeployment to Hastings, of all places.

He checked his watch. Dinescu would be driving home now. Taking out his mobile, Taylor decided it wasn't safe to text him. His knowledge of surveillance had taught him this. Instead, he pulled up Booker's number and, after a quick search on Google, sent him a cryptic message. Booker wouldn't understand it, but perhaps Dinescu would.

Chapter Twenty-Four

Friday

The winds had died down, and the overnight storm had brought flooding to the coast. All the team had made it to the station on time except for Kirby, who called in to say he was battling through a flooded A27 near Arundel.

Burgess returned to her desk with the morning coffee and noticed a large, shiny purple bar with her name on it and a thank-you message. Chocolate. She smiled.

"It was the biggest one I could find," said Booker from behind her.

"You're forgiven," she said, picking up the bar to dance with it for a moment.

Dinescu and Summers came out of his office and caught the last few seconds.

"Very nice," said Dinescu, laughing. "Let's have a catch-up."

While the team gathered around, Dinescu updated the whiteboard. Some detectives who had worked with Kirby also listened in from further back.

Dinescu's phone pinged with a message from Lisa. *You've got this, Ben.* He and Lisa had spoken for hours about his meeting with Faraday yesterday. She told him she smelled a rat, and he agreed. The whole thing seemed to be controlled by Faraday alone. But he had to put that aside. His team was counting on him to lead this investigation. He stepped forward, leaving his concerns behind.

"Joseph McKinley gave us his account in his interview yesterday evening. I've tasked some officers with checking his movements on CCTV."

Chester Kirby arrived in the office looking flushed but pleased with himself. He joined the others and sat next to Burgess.

"Chester," said Summers. "Glad you could make it. We're catching up on what we have. We'll get to you in a moment."

"We have no other suspects apart from McKinley," said Booker. "Have we spoken to everyone Lily knew?"

"There's Justin Hadley," said Kirby, straightening his tie.

"It wasn't Justin on the answering machine message," said Booker. "It was McKinley. Hadley had an alibi for Sunday night."

"He's lying," said Kirby.

"No, he's not. I checked with the hotel where he was staying in London. He booked out on Monday morning. Prove me wrong, and I'll take a cake penalty."

"I hope you've got your wallet today, Gareth, because he was definitely lying. He was on South Street with Lily Watson at 21:55 on Sunday, and she went off in his car. I have them on CCTV. They were having an affair if their kiss was anything to go by."

"Chester!" said Summers. "You clever man. Do you have the CCTV?"

"I do. That's why I was late off last night."

Booker rolled his eyes. "How did he book himself out of the hotel on Monday?"

"I don't know, Gareth. But you're the detective buying cakes for everyone."

"Don't worry about it, Gareth," said Dinescu. "I'd like to see that footage. Is it clear that it's Lily?"

"Yes, boss. The cameras caught her Mini going into the Cawley Priory Car Park and then her walking onto South Street. She waited outside the pub for Hadley for ten minutes. They had a disagreement, kissed, and then she left in Hadley's car. I need to check ANPR for Hadley's movements now."

"Is Lily's car still in the car park?" asked Burgess.

"Sadly not," said Chester. "That would have been too easy."

One of the senior front office staff came in. "DS Summers," he said. "Someone has walked in claiming they know who killed Lily Watson. I assumed you would like to speak with her. I used to work with her husband, DS Ray Collier."

"Bloody hell!" said Booker. "Suspects are like buses around here. First, you have none, and then they come in all at once."

"That's such an old man thing to say, Gareth," said Summers.

"Suspects are like buses?" said Dinescu. "I don't understand this saying. Never mind. Perhaps you and I will speak to this woman, Emily."

"Yes, sir. Chester and Gareth—arrest Justin Hadley on suspicion of murder. Sarah can interview him."

"Heather Collier is Lily's friend, sir," said Burgess, offering a piece of chocolate. "She's the one who brought the books into Lily's shop."

Dinescu declined Burgess's offer. "A friend of Lily's? This should be interesting."

As Summers slipped a large square of chocolate into her mouth, he watched Booker reach into his jacket pocket and pull out his wallet. "Cakes it is then, sir." His eyes lit up. "Ah, boss! I've just remembered. Ross texted me last night. Part of the message is for you, but I don't have a clue what it means."

Dinescu went over to Booker, who lifted his phone towards him. He read the message. "Forward it to me, please, Gareth. I'll read it later." But he was almost sure he knew what it meant already.

～

Summers escorted Heather Collier from Reception to a statement room. Despite her designer clothes and chic appearance, her red, puffy eyes and the scrunched tissue in her hand gave her away. Dinescu stood to greet her, and she returned a nervous smile. The two detectives sat down, with Dinescu leaning back to let Summers take the lead. Summers introduced herself and helped Heather settle down, putting her at ease.

"Did your husband ask you to speak to us?" asked Summers.

"I'm here for Lily," replied Heather. "Not that excuse for a man. I guess you've already spoken to him."

"Briefly," said Summers. "Are you still living with him?"

"I walked out on Sunday afternoon. I had to prepare everything, but I did it. All those years of marriage, finished." She looked around the room, dabbing her eyes. "He'd hate that I'm here. But I saw the report on the news." She looked at Dinescu. "It was you, I think. I had to come back. I wouldn't be here if it weren't for dear Lily."

"How did you know Lily Watson?" asked Summers.

"We were close friends. I bet Ray didn't tell you that. I worked at the social club in Fishbourne. Lily used to come in, and we got to know each other. She needed somewhere to stay, so I introduced her to my friend Yolanda, and they became friends. But she didn't share private things with Yolanda as she did with me. We were honest with each other."

"Did Lily know it was your husband who convicted her partner?"

"She did, eventually. I don't know when. It took us both a while to open up. When we did, I thought things would be difficult between us, but she was okay about it."

"Was she angry with your husband for putting him away?"

"She was, but there was something she didn't know that changed everything. Roger and I...do you know who Roger is?"

"We do," said Summers. "PC Wallace."

Heather nodded. "Roger and I had an affair. Lily didn't judge me when I told her, but she didn't like me talking about it either. I think the connection to her partner upset her."

"Tell us about your relationship with Roger Wallace."

"We met at one of the police Christmas dinners. Ray was drunk, touching the arse of anyone in a skirt who passed by. Roger sat next to me to keep me company. He felt sorry for me. He didn't want me to feel awkward. Someone made a complaint about Ray's behaviour, so Ray's buddies took him home, and Roger drove me back. But something happened. I don't understand how, but it did. We ended up having sex in the back of his car. We were mad for each other ever since."

"Did your husband discover the affair?"

"He did, although I found out after Roger was murdered. We were always careful. I never saw Roger the week he died. I never got to say goodbye to him. Ray finished everything for me."

"You're implying your husband murdered Roger Wallace. Is that right?"

"I'm telling you he did! And he fitted up poor Joseph McKinley. He needed someone to blame, and McKinley was an easy target. He had mental problems, and he'd been in trouble before for theft and violence. He was a druggy."

"Why are you telling us now?"

"Because I think he also killed Lily in the same way. He's robbed me of my best friend. And it's..." Heather swallowed hard, struggling to speak.

"Heather?"

"And it's my fault."

"Why?"

"Being married to a police officer for all those years, I knew I needed evidence to prove my husband was a murderer. But I didn't have anything on him. Not until two months ago. I was cleaning out the attic. Some things we'd stored up there had got damp and were covered in mildew. Lily was helping me. We found a diary hidden beneath some mouldy old police folders. Ray must have forgotten it was there."

"A year diary or a journal?" Summers asked.

"A year diary—appointments for 2004. Lily found it and was passing it to me when something fell out of the back. I would've missed it if she hadn't told me. A piece of lined paper with a handwritten letter from Ray to me. It was Ray's writing— different from today, but definitely his. I started reading it, but I had to stop. It was a confession. I was shaking so much. I had to hide it from Lily—there was something on there she couldn't see."

"So you didn't show Lily the letter at that time?" Summers asked.

"Not then," said Heather. "She could see it had upset me, but I said I'd show her later."

Summers made a note on her pad. "Do you have the letter?"

"I'll get to that, DS Summers. As I said, Ray wrote it as a confession to me. I don't know why, but that's what it was. Maybe he was thinking of ending it all or something. He confessed to killing Roger. He'd discovered our affair and drowned him in the creek. Worse still, he framed McKinley. He said he regretted it, but McKinley was a waste of space, anyway."

"You're certain Raymond wrote this?" asked Dinescu.

"It's his writing. He dated it, too. May 2004. He admitted it all in the letter and signed it at the bottom."

"What did Lily say when you told her?" Summers asked.

"I called her. She was horrified. Lily knew this confession letter was the last straw for me, so she came up with a plan." Heather rubbed her palms on her face, sighing deeply. "I had to keep it all from Ray—God knows what he would have done if he'd found out. I hid the letter in the diary and placed it under some books Ray's father had left him. I put everything into an old suitcase and took it to Lily in her charity shop."

Dinescu moved his chair forward. "Why not just give Lily the letter?"

Summers glanced at Dinescu with a hint of a smirk.

Heather stared back. "When Ray found out I was friends with Lily and that she had been to the house, he forbade me from seeing her again. I couldn't get the letter to her."

Summers frowned. "He forbade you? How could he do that?"

"You don't know Ray. He used to check on everyone I met and everywhere I went. I just followed Lily's plan, as it was the safest way. She said it was part of a bigger plan to bring Ray down and exonerate Joseph, but she could only do it once I'd left him."

"What was that plan?"

"I don't know. She wouldn't tell me, just in case Ray questioned me."

"An officer found one of the books in Lily's charity shop," said Summers.

"That's good," said Heather, looking pleased with herself. "Lily must have done something with the letter. Those bloody books—he was always on about them. The most valuable thing Ray's father left him sits forgotten at the bottom of Ray's wardrobe, never to see the light of day again. Idiot."

"Did Lily mention anything about blackmailing Ray with this letter?" asked Summers.

"Blackmail?" said Heather. She looked down, blinking as she

considered the idea. "No. I don't think she had it in her to black-mail anyone. Besides, Ray wouldn't have stood for it. She said she would bring him down. And I believed her."

"Did Lily speak to you after that?" Dinescu asked.

"No. I'd turned off my phone and thrown away the SIM card. I didn't want Ray to follow me. I told her I'd contact her in a few days. But then... I saw the report on TV. It's all my fault."

"Is the letter in Lily's shop, or did she take it home?" asked Summers.

Heather shrugged. "Who knows? I don't know where it is now."

"Did you talk to your husband about the letter?"

"Lily said, whatever was written in the letter, I should confront Ray about it. So, I did, just before I left him. He went mad. He said he didn't remember writing a letter. But he was lying. He's always been a bloody liar. Affairs, gambling. But Ray's a scheming bastard. I know him so well! He killed the one person in this world who ever really loved me—Roger. So, I told him. I told him I'd given his bloody confession to a charity shop hidden in a book. You should have seen his face. I said someone would find it, and he'd never know when they might pass it on to the police. He was in pieces. Kept saying he didn't remember. But I'd won."

"You won?" said Dinescu, frustrated. "You should have gone to the police with it, not played these silly games! Instead, you let your friend Lily decide what to do with the letter. She may have paid the price for it, Heather."

"How dare you! It wasn't a silly game! You don't know Ray. You don't know what he's like."

Dinescu shook his head. "Either way, without that letter, there is nothing we can do."

Chapter Twenty-Five

The aftermath of last night's storm meant a lot of spray was kicking up off the roads. Kirby sat with Booker as they pushed through heavy traffic. Booker was driving and made use of his blue light permit, pressing the triple-nine button on the centre of the dashboard. The blue lights in the car's grille lit up, and he tapped the horn button, starting the siren. They slipped through the parting traffic, heading towards Justin Hadley's home.

"Pick a lane!" Booker shouted at the van blocking his path. Kirby noticed Booker's tight grip on the steering wheel, his knuckles white.

Kirby wondered why Booker was so edgy. "People panic when they hear sirens behind them. Turns their brains to mush. It's hardly a grade one, Gareth." He knew that wouldn't go down well.

"Hadley lied to us, Chester." Booker gritted his teeth, glancing at Kirby. He killed the blues.

"I know. But it's you who has to justify your driving, and you'll lose your permit."

Booker nodded. Kirby felt the tension in Booker and realised Hadley had dented his pride, with Kirby delivering the blow.

At the next roundabout, they took the Fishbourne turning and headed towards Southbourne.

Booker took a breath. "Are you glad to be back?"

"I am. It was hard to face every day. I worked with children who were broken before their lives began. Some of their stories were heartbreaking. No wonder they ran away."

"A load of kids absconding from children's homes," said Booker with a wry smile. "Just plain old murder now, then."

Kirby frowned. "Kids used by county lines gangs, you mean? They're vulnerable, not naughty, Gareth."

They pushed onwards at speed, overtaking a line of traffic.

"Hadley seemed genuine when I spoke to him," said Booker. "Are you sure it was him on the CCTV? You haven't seen him before."

"It was him," Kirby replied with a hint of irritation.

"I'm just checking."

"The car was his, and he matches *your* description on the log. Stop taking this so personally, Gareth!"

"I'm not!"

Kirby looked away. "And why are you taking the piss out of my time in Crawley? Right at the big church—the roundabout."

Booker took the right a little too fast and headed north. He turned onto a single-track road leading to a large house in the distance.

"Sarah's been here before recently," said Kirby, reading through the case logs. "It's the barn where Lily's art club meets. She spoke to a woman called Gillian. She's Hadley's partner. Didn't you ask him her name?"

"Obviously not."

They pulled up by a barn and went to the house next door. They saw people moving inside through the windows and heard laughter. In front of the barn were several expensive cars. Kirby took an interest in one of them.

"That's the car on the CCTV," said Kirby, pointing to an Audi parked in front of a garage.

"It looks like he's having some kind of party," said Booker. "We're going to spoil the fun."

"We'll ask him out here."

"Why? I don't care if we embarrass him in front of his guests."

"Dignity, Gareth. And we want him to cooperate, not put his back up." Kirby squeezed Booker's shoulder. "Come on, mate! What's wrong with you?"

Booker looked away. "I ballsed up."

"So? We cover each other. We're here now. Let's nick him."

Kirby found a knocker and rapped on the door.

Justin Hadley appeared. He looked puzzled for a moment. "DC Booker, I'm afraid now isn't a good time."

"Can you step out here for a moment?" said Kirby.

"Why? I'm clearly busy. I have clients with me for lunch."

Kirby glanced at Booker. "Fair enough, Mr Hadley. You match the description of someone seen with Lily Watson on the evening of Sunday, the 7th of January, in South Street, Chichester. We also believe you gave a false statement to the police regarding your whereabouts at that time."

A woman with red hair came out to join Hadley. "Who is it, Justin?"

"The police," Hadley replied. "Go back inside, Gill. I'll sort it." He turned to the detectives. "Can't we talk about this later? I've got some five-figure deals going on inside."

Kirby nodded to Booker.

"No," said Booker. "Mr Hadley, I'm arresting you on suspicion of the murder of Lily Watson and attempting to pervert the course of justice."

"What? That's ridiculous! You don't have to arrest me, for God's sake. Let's talk."

Booker gave him the police caution and explained the necessity for the arrest. "We're taking you to Chichester Custody. Anything you have with you will be booked in." Hadley picked up his mobile phone from inside the door.

With Hadley handcuffed, Kirby put him into the back of the police car. Several people were at the door by then, shouting abuse at the detectives. One of the guests was on the phone, videoing them.

"See what you've done?" said Hadley, as Kirby put the seatbelt around him. "You guys are going to seriously regret this! I'm going to make it very painful for you."

Kirby smiled and sat beside him. "Remember you're under caution, Mr Hadley." He pointed to a black box clipped to his pocket. "And everything you're saying is being recorded on video."

PC Daniels turned right onto Crossbush Lane, enjoying the drive as the lane opened onto fields on either side. She put on a local eighties radio station, turned it up, and sang along to Billy Ocean, hoping no one would see her or, for that matter, hear her. It felt good to let loose, even if just for a moment.

She reached the junction of a no-through road that wound northwards and stopped the car to check the message on her mobile. The incident report said it was halfway along this road. Continuing along, the carriageway became a single track with passing places. After only a few minutes, she found what she was looking for dumped at the entrance of a ploughed field. She tucked the police car into the gap and turned on her rear reds.

The burnt-out shell stank. She peered inside and was relieved to see nothing that looked like human remains. The charred interior was a mess, with the seats reduced to skeletal frames and the dashboard deformed by intense heat. Pieces of shattered glass from the windows were strewn across the floor, glinting in the sunlight. The acrid smell of burnt rubber and plastic lingered in the air, sharp and nauseating, making her wrinkle her nose in disgust.

"Control from Alpha-Whisky-Two-Zero," PC Daniels said into her radio.

"Go ahead, Two-Zero," came the reply.

"I'm with the burnt-out car. It's dumped in a field off Clay Lane in Crossbush. No visible plates on the vehicle. The doors are open. Looks like it's been stolen and torched. It's a BMW Mini." She looked at the corner of the windscreen, but saw only a melted mass of plastic and glass. "Can you tell me where to find the VINs on these cars? The number on the windscreen is unreadable."

"Two-Zero, I'll get a traffic officer to call your mobile."

"Thanks, control."

Daniels saw a woman approaching her with a black labrador.

"Bloody hooligans!" the woman said.

"Did you report this?" Daniels asked.

"Yes, on Tuesday and again yesterday. Didn't think you were coming."

Daniels's mobile rang. "PC Daniels speaking."

"It's Sergeant Smart from Roads Policing. You have a burnt-out Mini?"

"Thanks for calling back, Sarge. I'm not good with cars. Where do I find the VIN on this thing?"

"If you can't read the one on the windscreen, try the driver's side door pillar. Have a look."

Daniels put on her blue gloves and rubbed her finger across the bottom of the door pillar. She found a blackened plate with a vehicle identification number stamped into it. She read it out over the phone.

"Let me do a search," said the sergeant. Daniels kept the phone to her ear.

"Are you going to tow it away?" asked the woman.

"I can arrange for Highways to remove it."

"Major Crimes has flagged the vehicle," said the sergeant.

"What does that mean?" Daniels asked.

"We need to get it forensically recovered ASAP. It's part of a murder investigation. I'll text you the crime number."

"Thanks, Sarge. I'll update control."

Daniels ended the call and turned to the woman. "You said you saw it here on Tuesday morning."

"I did. It was still smouldering."

"Did you notice anyone acting suspiciously?"

"Not at all."

"Someone's coming to pick it up now. It's been involved in a serious incident."

"I don't care, as long as it's gone." The woman turned around and walked away.

"No need to thank me," said Daniels to herself. "Just part of the service."

Chapter Twenty-Six

Dinescu was rewatching the interview with Joseph McKinley. On his desk was a document from the Roger Wallace murder case—an impact statement from Wallace's sister, Penny.

McKinley had told them that Lily had blackmailed Collier over Wallace's death. That confession letter Heather mentioned would have been a good tool for that. The idea disturbed him. It kept going around his mind like a needle stuck on a record. Why would Collier write it unless he planned to take his own life?

Dinescu wanted a more personal conversation about Roger and the day he was murdered. After retrieving Penny Wallace's details from the database, he called her and then texted Summers. Picking up the keys for the silver Focus, Dinescu headed out into the late afternoon traffic.

A flood on the fast road to Portsmouth forced him to take the back roads—the scenic route. Even these roads were busy with diverted traffic, so he used the time to mull over the case and the story of the woman he was going to see. Penny Wallace, Roger's eldest sister, was more than willing to discuss the day Roger died.

As he navigated the winding country roads, Dinescu couldn't help but think about the weight of the case. Each detail led to more questions than answers, a frustrating pattern that gnawed at him. Lily's murder was a near-perfect copy of Roger's. Was there a connection between the two murders they hadn't seen, other than Joseph McKinley?

He rejoined the A27 and exited at Cosham. The traffic was still heavy, but his mind was too preoccupied to notice.

Before long, he found himself in Portchester, passing under a railway bridge and turning onto a large estate on a hill. Within minutes, he was standing outside Penny Wallace's front door, hearing a dog barking behind it. The door opened, and a brown cocker spaniel jumped up at him, trying to lick him.

He held out his warrant card. "I'm DCI Dinescu, Chichester Major Crimes. Ms Wallace?"

She stepped back and invited him in.

"You said your sister might be coming over?"

"Yes. Jeanette is here, too."

Penny was in her forties, short, with a large build and dyed blonde hair. Her sister entered the hall, looking similar to Penny, but a few years younger and wearing glasses.

Walking through the house, Dinescu noticed the photographs lining the walls. Everything was about family—memories of happier times, family gatherings, and holidays.

Penny led him into a lounge diner. The kitchen area had a large central island with a black marble-effect worktop. She guided him to the dining area, with the dog prancing around his feet, wagging its tail.

"Stop it, Toby!" said Penny. "Get in your bed." The dog lowered its head and went into the lounge.

They sat together. Jeanette smiled at Dinescu, waiting for him to speak. Penny looked more serious.

"Thank you for allowing me to visit you at such short notice," said Dinescu.

"Where are you from?" asked Jeanette. "I love your accent."

Dinescu smiled. "I'm Romanian. I came to this country when I was a boy."

"When you were a boy? It's still very.., Romanian."

He laughed. "I spent a lot of time with the Romanian community in London. My adoptive parents encouraged it."

"It's been nearly twenty years to the day since Roger died," said Penny. "We never forget him." She pointed to a photograph hanging on the wall. It showed a handsome young man with thick black hair and large eyes. He was wearing a full-dress police uniform, displaying his warrant card to the camera. "That was taken at his attestation," said Penny. "I was there."

"Your family must have been very proud."

"We were." She pointed to the opposite wall. The photograph showed Roger with his arm around a younger Penny. He was grinning at the camera, and Penny was laughing. "He'd just passed his detective exams. Dad took that the day before Roger died. We'd just been out for dinner, and Dad made a big thing about giving him his watch. That's the one in the photograph. I'd bought him a gold chain he liked. That bastard McKinley stole it from him."

Dinescu stood to inspect the photograph more closely. He could see the excitement in Roger's eyes, and it chilled him to think he would be dead the very next day. "Such a devastating time for you as a family."

"Dad passed away ten years ago and joined Mum. She died of a broken heart a year after Roger. It never leaves you, even after all these years."

"I'm truly sorry," said Dinescu, sitting once more. "I'm investigating another case, and there appears to be a link to Roger's death. I'd like to ask you some questions about your memories of the investigation into Roger's murder. I understand this is not easy for you."

"Go on," said Jeanette. "We want to help."

"Thank you. You would have been informed that the medical

tribunal released Joseph McKinley on licence last year, subject to evaluation."

"Yes," said Penny, looking down at her feet. "It made me feel sick to my stomach. McKinley is magically better now and can continue with his life, yet we live with losing Roger every day."

"How confident were you in the investigation into your brother's death?"

"Confident?" Penny frowned, considering Dinescu's question. "It was cut and dried. The detective sergeant was there when... Roger died. He saw McKinley."

"Dad wasn't so sure, though," said Jeanette. "He was ex-police, too. A DCI like you, but at Portsmouth Central. He didn't like DS Collier. He thought he was a bit of a dodgy copper. But in the end, he got the job done."

"Was there anything in particular your father found dodgy?"

"How quick the whole thing was," said Penny. "But what more did they need? They caught McKinley in the act."

Dinescu nodded. "What was Roger's mood like the morning he was killed? He was living at home, I believe."

"Yes, we were all still at home," said Penny. "Mum and Dad couldn't get rid of us, but they loved having us there. We were very close. Roger was in a funny mood that morning. He said he had a call from Collier about a job on the Fishbourne Marshes. I didn't have a clue where that was. Roger seemed distracted and worried about something. He was going into CID on secondment before officially becoming a DC. He had his best suit on and everything. He looked so handsome. He had that call at the last minute, and then he was desperately trying to find his welly boots."

"Why do you think Roger seemed distracted?"

"You're the first person to ask that. We all wondered why." Penny and Jeanette looked at each other. "We think he'd met someone. He used to go out at odd times, but he'd never say who it was. We used to tease him, but he got touchy about it. Something wasn't right. And he didn't like that DS Collier. He found him brash and unprofessional. Dad must have listened to him."

"Dad kept going back to the marshes," said Jeanette.

Penny agreed. "Yes. He was trying to make sense of it all. He was always looking for something down there."

"I think he was looking for some part of Roger," said Jeanette.

"How is Roger connected to the case you're investigating, DCI Dinescu?" asked Penny.

"This isn't something I haven't already shared with the press. The victim drowned in the same place Roger drowned, and it's also a murder."

"Oh God!" said Penny, putting her hand to her mouth. "Is this what's been on the news? I didn't realise it was the same place. Was it near the footbridge?"

"Yes. Very."

The two women held each other's hands. "Then you know who did it! Bloody McKinley's on the loose again."

Dinescu gave nothing away, but he could see their anxiety rising. "We will get to the bottom of this, I promise. But you need to prepare yourselves—I fear it may reopen old wounds."

"Have you arrested him?" Penny asked. "Surely you've arrested him?"

"Penny, I understand your concerns, but I'm not at liberty to discuss our ongoing enquiries. All I can say is we've arrested a forty-eight-year-old male and released him under investigation."

"Wait a minute. Do you think there's some doubt about McKinley's conviction?"

Dinescu looked down. "We will do everything in our power to get to the truth, no matter how hard that is."

Dinescu re-parked the Focus in its usual spot near the workshops behind the police station. It would be dark soon, and he could almost taste the sour smell of diesel from the nearby fuel pumps. The return journey along the back roads had been frustrating, stuck behind a convoy of tractors. He hesitated, wondering if he was about to do something he would regret. He took out his mobile and read the message Booker had forwarded earlier. Most of it was for Booker—vague and generic. The last part, though, was for Dinescu: *Tell the boss: call Bill's soţ cod 0.*

Ross Taylor was working indirectly for DCS Faraday. Sending a message via Booker showed Taylor's concern about being discovered. He'd even used the cedilla on the letter T. Two of the words were in Romanian, making the message read: *Tell the boss: call Bill's husband code 0.* Bill was Ross's husband, and code zero meant it was an emergency.

Dinescu called Ross using WhatsApp.

"Just a moment," Ross replied. He was finding somewhere to talk. "Sir, thanks for calling back."

"Very ingenious, Ross," said Dinescu. "Is everything okay?"

"Not really. I can't be long. It's DCS Faraday. He wants to move you out of Chichester so his lover can take your job. DI Irving, sir. She's my line manager. She's sleeping with Faraday for favours. And I don't mean sleeping."

"I'd guessed something was going on. But I need evidence before I can challenge him."

"It shouldn't be hard to find, sir. I even caught them in the act, in the bloody toilets of all places. It was ridiculous. They hid in the cubicle until I'd gone. Rumours are going around here, too. To move you on, Faraday has had to forge something, and I'm sure of it. Irving's been boasting to the team about moving to Major Crimes soon. It makes me sick to my stomach. Faraday has no right being in the job."

"I agree."

"No one is questioning anything he says. No one would cast suspicion on him. But all it would take is someone to request the paperwork from HR. Examining the signatures will prove it. I'll testify to catching them in the act. I'm sure others would do the same if they thought it was safe."

"Ross, I am very grateful."

"No worries, boss. I can't have this information and do nothing."

"I appreciate your integrity. Leave it with me."

"That's good, sir. I hope to be back soon. Did you like my Romanian? I had to use Google Translate."

"It was perfect. I'm looking forward to seeing you again."

"Got to go! Speak soon."

The call ended.

Dinescu knew what he had to do. There was a briefing to attend, but afterwards, he had a call to make to an old friend. This friend was someone he had first known in the Met, but who had later transferred to Sussex for a promotion.

Dinescu didn't want his anger to affect his team or cloud his judgement. He counted, slowed his breathing, and thought about how grateful he was for Taylor's kindness.

Chapter Twenty-Seven

Burgess escorted Justin Hadley from his cell. After three hours of waiting, he looked dishevelled. He flattened his hair and followed Burgess into the interview room, sitting at the desk.

He picked up a beaker of water and took a sip. "Why did you have to arrest me in front of my clients? That was bad form."

"It wasn't me who arrested you, Mr Hadley," said Burgess, smiling and tilting her head. "Where's your solicitor?"

"I sent him away. I didn't want him."

"Why?"

"He's a friend of Gill's brother. This will get back to Gill. I can't have that."

"You are entitled to free and independent legal advice while you are at the police station. Do you want us to find another?"

"No. I don't think I'm going to need it."

"You've been arrested on suspicion of murder."

"I believe I can clear this up quickly."

"Okay. Have you had lunch and something to drink?"

"Lunch? So that's what it was. I did wonder."

Burgess nodded sympathetically. "Our regulars say they enjoy it. Let's get started." She pressed the record button on the machine, which played a long tone. "This interview is being video recorded and is taking place in interview room three at Chichester Custody. I'm Detective Constable Burgess, warrant number NB 5101. Please state your full name and date of birth."

"Justin Bartholomew Hadley, 4th December, 1980."

"Can you confirm no one else is in the room, and you have declined a solicitor?"

He looked around and under the table. "I can."

Burgess continued the interview process, watching Hadley's body language while she explained the police caution. He sank into his chair, rubbed the stubble on his chin, and fidgeted with his hands. "Mr Hadley, you were arrested today on suspicion of the murder of Lily Watson on Monday, the 8th of January."

Hadley put his head in his hands. "Yes."

"Did you kill Lily Watson?"

"No."

Burgess leaned forward. "Two days ago, you gave a voluntary interview with my colleague, DC Booker. You told him you were in London from Saturday the 6th to Monday the 8th of January, checking into a hotel in Holborn. You then said that you left London on Monday morning. Is that correct?"

"Yes."

"Do you think you might be mistaken?"

"I should know."

"I want to show you a video recording, exhibit CK/02." Burgess opened her laptop, and a still image taken above a doorway on the street appeared on the screen. "This is the CCTV camera covering the door of the Norfolk Arms in South Street, Chichester." Hadley gave a defeated sigh. "That's the time and date in the left corner. For the recording, it says 21:54 on Sunday, the 7th of January. Do you recognise the woman in the shot, Mr Hadley?"

"Yes. It's Lily."

"We know it's Lily Watson because we followed her car on CCTV. I'm going to press the play button. What's this video going to show me?"

He looked down at his hands. "You already know."

Burgess clicked a button, and the scene played out with Hadley arriving, arguing with Lily and then embracing. It ended with Lily Watson stepping into Hadley's car.

"Who is that male Lily is arguing with and then kissing?"

"Father Christmas."

"That's your car, isn't it? That's your registration plate. Is that you, Mr Hadley?"

"Of course it's bloody me!"

"We've seized your mobile phone and will examine your phone records, including messages and calls. We will also look at your cell site data to determine your location on Sunday and Monday. What will that data tell us about your whereabouts on Sunday evening and Monday morning, the 8th of January?"

"That I was in Tangmere on Sunday evening, staying at the Bader Hotel."

"So, you weren't in London, as you previously stated."

"Not if I was in Tangmere."

"What time did you check in there?"

"Just after 3 p.m."

"When did you check out?"

A line of sweat had formed on Hadley's top lip. "Monday morning, sometime after 11 a.m."

"Did Lily stay with you overnight on Sunday?"

"Yes, she did. I picked her up from outside the pub and then dropped her off in the car park so she could pick up her car. She then followed me to the Bader Hotel."

"What time did she leave you?"

"She left about seven-fifteen on Monday morning. She said she had to meet someone at eight in Fishbourne."

Burgess made a note. "We both know this is easy for us to check. Who did she have to meet?"

"She didn't say."

"Why did you lie to us about seeing Lily?"

"I didn't think it was any of your business!" Hadley sat back in his chair, tears filling his eyes. "I told Gill I had to meet a client on Sunday, and she was happy to check me out when she left. I'm heartbroken Lily is dead. I'm broken, and I can't tell anyone or show anyone how I feel. We loved each other. I was going to leave Gill, and Lily was going to leave that controlling bitch she lived with. But we couldn't let them know. Not yet. Lily wanted to make peace with her son first. So, I had to wait."

"I've met Gillian," said Burgess. "She never told me she knew about you and Lily."

Hadley stiffened, his eyes wide. "You told Gill!"

"No, but she never mentioned Lily having an affair with you. Did Lily threaten to tell her at all?"

He eased back into his chair. "No. She'd never have done that. She was a decent human being. Talented, too."

"We'll check with the Bader Hotel about your stay there."

"Fine."

"Where did you go after you left the hotel on Monday?"

"I dropped my bags off at home, made it look like I'd slept there, and then went to work. I spoke to a few friends at the art centre if you want to check."

"Thank you, and as I said, we'll check your mobile data. Did you visit the Fishbourne Marshes on Monday?"

"No."

"Do you know why she went there?"

"Not a clue."

"Did you pay anyone else to harm Lily?"

"No!"

"Going back to Sunday night, the CCTV from outside the

Norfolk Arms shows you and Lily arguing. What were you arguing about?"

"It wasn't an argument. I was worried. She was supposed to meet me at the hotel at five. But she didn't turn up. I was annoyed because she didn't let me know."

"How did you find where she was? She didn't have her personal mobile on her."

"She had a secret phone—you'd call it a burner phone—hidden in her car. We used it to talk to each other, to keep our affair from Yolanda. Anyway, she called me in tears. She said she needed time to work things out and had some calls to make about something important. Then she'd had an argument with her housemate about our affair. I told her to meet me at the pub."

"What was this important matter?"

"I don't know."

"Is her burner phone number stored on your mobile?"

"Yes. Under Mr Marsh."

"That's helpful, Mr Hadley."

Burgess summarised Hadley's account, and Hadley agreed. "Is there anything you think I've misunderstood or anything you want to add?"

"No. I want to go home now."

"I'm afraid we can't release you just yet. We have some checks to do first. We can only keep you here for twenty-four hours, Mr Hadley. We'll release you as soon as we verify your account. Otherwise, there will be more questions to answer."

Summers entered the office, carrying a tray of coffee and a plate of doughnuts. A small cheer went up as Dinescu followed her in, hanging up the car keys.

"Glad you're back, boss," she said. "The goodies are from Gareth. The cake penalty he promised us."

Dinescu laughed.

"Well done, Gareth," said Kirby, picking up a doughnut. "You're a good man for taking it on the chin."

Booker and Kirby joined Burgess, who had just finished updating the case files after her interview with Hadley.

Summers scanned Burgess's update. "We should be able to confirm Hadley's new alibi with the hotel. Get onto that as soon as you can, Sarah."

"I've already tasked one of the Worthing detectives to go to the hotel," said Burgess. "I'm waiting to hear back."

"Great job."

Summers bit into a doughnut and walked over to the whiteboard. She wrote the four suspects' names in large red letters and underlined them: Joseph McKinley, Justin Hadley, Raymond Collier, and Yolanda Mellor. She could sense Dinescu was now standing behind her.

"I have doubts about two of those names, Emily," he said. "And we're still missing Lily's car and clothing."

She turned to face him. "The toxicology results are back, and the pathologist has adjusted Lily's time of death to between 07:00 and 09:00. That's with a high probability now."

"Okay," he said, taking off his coat, "that's much better for us to work with."

"McKinley being on the marshes when Colin Jackman found Lily doesn't prove he murdered her. CCTV from the city confirms he couldn't have arrived before 09:00. We can eliminate him."

"I agree," said Dinescu. "We have nothing that directly connects him to Lily's murder."

Summers rubbed McKinley's name off the whiteboard with one hand while holding a sugary doughnut in the other. "This so-called confession letter Heather gave to Lily. That must be what Lily had promised McKinley to prove his innocence."

"Useful to blackmail Raymond Collier with, too. But we only have Heather's word for the existence of this letter."

"Sarge, I have something else," said Burgess.

Summers stopped chewing her doughnut and waited while Burgess flicked through her interview notes.

"Keep us in suspense, why don't you," said Booker.

Burgess found the note and continued. "Lily kept a secret mobile phone in her car. She used it when calling Hadley to stop Yolanda finding out about their affair. We can trace it, but I have to get the number from Hadley's phone."

"A mobile in her car!" said Summers with excitement. "That's a breakthrough! We may be able to track its movements. Gareth, can you get Hadley's mobile from Custody? Take it to Hadley and access it in his presence. Get the number for Lily's burner phone."

"Yes, Sarge." Kirby licked his fingers and dried them on a paper towel. "Is he cooperating now, Sarah?"

Burgess nodded. "Yes, once he'd seen the CCTV footage."

Summers picked up a call from her desk phone. Her face flushed as she heard the message.

When she put down the receiver, she smiled at Dinescu.

"Boss, they've found Lily Watson's car. An Arun PC located it burnt out down a lane in Crossbush near Arundel. The VIN was still readable."

"What was it doing there?" asked Dinescu. "That suggests two cars and, therefore, at least two people."

Summers agreed. "One to drive them away from the dumped car."

"Did you say Crossbush?" Dinescu walked over to Summers's desk. "Show me on a map where they found it." She opened the incident log and retrieved the location information for him.

"Look. It's only a twenty-minute walk to the railway station. It still could have been one person. When was the car left there?"

"Monday," said Summers. "The woman who reported it wasn't certain what time."

"ANPR didn't pick the car up?"

"No, sir. The officer said it may have had the number plates removed."

"If we could just get a time."

Burgess interrupted. "I've just spoken to the detective checking Hadley's alibi at the Bader Hotel, and he confirmed that Hadley stayed there with Lily on Sunday night. They have CCTV of Lily leaving the hotel at 07:18 on Monday. Hadley stays until about 11:10. His car remains in view of their cameras until he leaves. Lily doesn't return."

"So that excludes Hadley as a suspect, too," said Summers.

"It does," said Dinescu. "Get onto Digital Forensics regarding Lily's burner phone. Let's find out where it's been."

"I'll expedite the request," said Summers.

"Shall I get Hadley released under investigation, boss?" Burgess asked.

"Yes," said Dinescu.

"And what about Raymond Collier, sir?" said Summers.

Dinescu checked his watch. "We need to arrest him to ask about the letter and Lily blackmailing him. It's late. Collier can come in on Monday morning. If we arrest him now, he'll still be here tomorrow. The team needs a weekend rest. There's already a lot to process this evening, and I'd like to get the story straight about where Lily's car's been. Everyone here has been exceptional."

"Thanks, sir," said Summers. She noticed Dinescu had something on his mind. His eyes were far away. "Is everything okay, boss?"

"It will be soon. I have a call to make."

Dinescu went into his office and closed the door. Sitting at his computer, he knew he had to deal with Faraday and the information from Ross Taylor. Placing his mobile on the desk, he scrolled through his contacts until he found the name he needed. His thumb hovered over the call button. Was he overreacting? Had he overstepped the mark? Wrestling with his doubts, he ignored the team's waves goodbye and pressed the button.

A gruff voice with a Midlands accent answered. "Tom McBride speaking."

"Sir, it's Beniamin Dinescu."

"Ah, Ben! Good to hear from you. How are things?"

"I need to speak with you urgently. Are you available?"

McBride paused. "I'm in a meeting with the PCC at the moment, Ben. Can I call you at home later?"

"I'd really appreciate that, sir."

"Okay. It sounds important. I promise I'll call. Give my regards to your wife."

"Thank you, sir."

Dinescu hung up and stared at his phone. Rubbing his left temple, he traced the line of the burn scar on his cheek. He had given so much for this job; he wasn't about to give in now.

Chapter Twenty-Eight

Saturday

Beniamin couldn't settle. He kept replaying his phone call from last night. Sophia was with Lisa's parents for the day, something she did on alternate Saturdays, and Lisa was marking work. She didn't want to be interrupted, except for neck massages and cups of coffee.

"I can see something's bothering you," she said, cradling her coffee cup. "Is it DCS Faraday?"

"Partly, but there's nothing I can do about that now."

"Is there something else?"

"It's that pillbox on Fishbourne Marshes," he said, standing by her office door. "I think something's hidden inside."

"Is that why you were tossing and turning last night?"

"Possibly."

"Not one of those dreams?"

"No. I'd tell you if they were back. I was wide awake, rerunning the options in my head."

"Why don't you go in?" Lisa suggested. "Sophia's with Mum

and Dad, and I'm busy. Go on, before I find something for you to do around the house. We can catch up later."

Beniamin nodded. "Just for a few hours. I want to take a look."

Still in casual clothes, he slipped on his lanyard. Driving from Bracklesham to Chichester, he made several hands-free calls. He didn't call Summers—she needed a weekend off—but he contacted the duty POLSA for advice on accessing the pillbox. By the time he reached the station, he had a plan.

Entering the office, he saw Summers's computer was on. He sighed, looking up as she walked in, her skinny jeans and red cashmere roll-neck jumper catching his eye. Her eyes widened when she saw him.

"Sir?"

"Emily."

"I was just sorting out…"

"Do we need to move your bed in here?"

"That's not fair. There's a lot to do. Updates to the database to check. And what are you doing here?"

He studied her face. Red suited her. "Since you're on duty, you can come with me. We're going to the marshes."

"Don't forget your wellies," said Summers.

The silver Ford Focus, freshly cleaned, was in its usual place. Summers had put on a fitted leather jacket and was waiting for him at the front of the station.

They drove to the Bull's Head car park, parking beside the mobile incident room.

"Has it been useful?" Dinescu asked, eyeing the converted camper van.

"It was for the first few days. It's a bit Q now."

"We'll keep it another week."

They left the car and walked along the muddy footpath towards the long footbridge.

"Are you angry with me?" Summers asked.

"Angry?" Dinescu replied. "No. Concerned."

"I had something on my mind. Something was bothering me."

He glanced at her as they walked. "Me too."

"What are you bothered about, sir?"

"The pillbox," said Dinescu. "Lily had scratches on her arm and we recovered a dress fragment that suggests she was beside it. I've been wondering why. I have a hunch she hid something inside."

"Is that what you're checking now?"

"Yes. What's bothering you?"

"Raymond Collier," she said. "The more I look at the case against McKinley, the more I don't like it. I can't put my finger on it."

"I feel the same, Emily. But we need something substantial if we suspect a miscarriage of justice."

They turned a corner and saw two police officers in black with tools. It was the police search advisor.

"You called a POLSA?" she asked.

"Yes. I didn't want to destroy any evidence."

The officers had cleared a space in front of the pillbox entrance and removed the brambles. Ivy had grown along the grooves of the prefabricated concrete panel, giving it a fairytale appearance.

"It's ugly," said Summers.

"Not designed for aesthetics," one officer said. "I'm Tim." He was muscular, bald, and had a beard and a broad smile for Summers.

"Thanks for coming out so quickly," said Dinescu to the officers.

"No worries, boss. We've found a metal grill covered by thick, mostly rotten plywood. We can get this off in no time. I've got some boarding material in my van to fix it up again."

"Thank you," said Dinescu. "I hope this wasn't a waste of time, but I need to know."

"But how would Lily or anyone hide something inside?" Summers asked.

"You could drop it through the loophole," said Tim. Summers looked at him quizzically. "It's the hole the gun poked out of."

Dinescu nodded, unsure if his hunch was crazy, but now that they were here, he had to follow it through. "Let's do it."

It was over in less than a minute. The crowbar attacked the rotten plywood, disintegrating it. Bolt cutters sliced off the galvanised grille, which was levered out of the hole.

Dinescu peered into the entrance as dank, heavy air spilled out, whispering its forgotten past. The interior was a gloomy cavern, the once-impenetrable concrete succumbing to decay from the marsh's seepage.

The floor was strewn with decaying debris: fragments of wood from the disintegrated cover, skeletal remains of small creatures, and a scattering of feathers and leaves blown in through the loopholes. A solitary, taped package beneath a loophole stood out.

Dinescu hesitated before going inside. The dark, enclosed space threatened him, so he took a deep breath.

"Let me go in, sir," said Tim. "I've got the right gear to look around. I'm guessing that's the package you're looking for. It looks new."

"Yes. I wasn't expecting it," said Dinescu. "But it seems to be why Lily was here."

"No worries, sir. I'll take a few photos and bag the package for you."

"Thank you."

Dinescu watched Tim dip his head and enter with an evidence bag. There were several flashes from a phone camera, then the sound of rustling plastic. Tim emerged moments later, filled out the details on the bag, and handed it to Dinescu.

"There's some writing on it," said Tim.

Dinescu moved the package, about the size of a shoebox, inside the evidence bag until he could read a label taped over with clear tape. He read the text. "To Joseph. I'm sorry. Lily."

"I'll get this to the lab," said Summers.

"Is that all, sir?" asked Tim.

Dinescu smiled and nodded. "I appreciate it, both of you."

Tim flashed a grin at Summers. "And if you ever need anything, sergeant, you know where I am."

Summers and Dinescu walked back while Tim and his colleague resealed the pillbox.

"Where is he from?" asked Summers.

"Tim? Bognor. He's the inspector responsible for search training."

"He's an inspector?" Emily's cheeks blushed as they walked into the wind. "Friendly."

Dinescu chuckled. "I hear he's very friendly, Emily."

Once back at the car, she placed the recovered package into the back seat and noticed a group of young people walking into the pub. "I don't suppose you fancy a quick drink?"

"As tempting as that sounds," said Dinescu, "I should get back."

They returned to the office and sat in front of the whiteboard, drinking coffee and passing the package between them.

"How did you know something was in there? Following the copper's nose?" Summers asked.

"It took me years to understand what that meant. But, yes— intuition. Why else was Lily there? I don't understand why she left a package for McKinley in the pillbox. Did she let him know it was there?"

"To protect it from someone, perhaps," she said. "Maybe she was killed before she had the chance to tell him. But, by all accounts, McKinley was always hanging around there."

"True. I want it examined before we tell McKinley about it."

"Yes, sir."

Satisfied he had scratched the itch that was bothering him, Dinescu looked at Summers. "Well, I'm going home. What are you doing?"

"Me too. I have some ironing to do. Then I'm out seeing a friend later."

"A friend?"

Summers laughed. "My business, sir. I'll book that package in."

"Thanks," said Dinescu, pulling on his fleece. "That red suits you, Emily."

Beniamin removed his lanyard and drove home to Bracklesham Bay, his mind shifting to thoughts of Lisa.

Chapter Twenty-Nine

Monday, 15th January

Frost covered the rooftops opposite the police station on the bright winter's morning. Dinescu, eager to start work early, needed to send an important email to Professional Standards. Staring out the office window, he sensed the case was concluding, but many troubling questions remained unanswered. Raymond Collier's involvement in Lily's death troubled him the most. He also doubted the safety of McKinley's conviction for manslaughter. It was clear everything revolved around Collier.

He heard the CID team arriving in the offices behind him. Turning, he saw one of them poking her head over the screens to see what was going on. Within a few minutes, the rest of the core team arrived.

"Good morning, boss," said Summers, smiling and looking relaxed. Her hair was different somehow.

"Good morning, Emily. How was the rest of your weekend?"

"Chilled, thanks. I did the ironing, went to the gym, and met a friend for drinks."

"So I heard," said Dinescu, and Summers blushed. "Kieran came for Sunday lunch. And your hair looks nice. What have you done?"

Summers laughed. "It's in a slide, boss, nothing special. But thanks for noticing." She posed with her hands on her hips.

Once the morning coffee arrived, Dinescu stood by the white-board. Several other detectives from CID entered and waited for the briefing to start.

Dinescu paused until the talking ceased. "Good morning, all. I will keep this short. Operation Brook has made several strides forward. Thank you all for your efforts with this case, including those persisting with the house-to-house enquiries in last week's rain. Those enquiries are as complete as they can be. Even though we've had no breakthroughs with them, they are always important."

"There is still one house on Mill Lane we need a result on, sir," said Summers. "The house with the CCTV. The neighbours said they were on holiday but were due back last night."

"Thank you, Emily." Dinescu pointed at the whiteboard. "We've eliminated two suspects from the investigation. One of them is Joseph McKinley." Some muttering came from the back. "Despite local rumours and some speculation from police officers, McKinley has an alibi for when Lily Watson was murdered. The toxicology results have refined the estimated time of death to be between 07:00 and 09:00 on the 8th. McKinley didn't arrive at the scene until later." Dinescu outlined further lines of enquiry but kept some of the latest details about Raymond Collier to himself. He didn't want those to be spread around. "We will be making a significant arrest soon, hopefully answering some of the big questions in this case. Thank you for your hard work. DS Summers will assign further tasks this morning."

The detectives and PCs returned to their computers to check their tasks while the core team stayed with Dinescu.

"Sir," said Booker. "I've just seen a note on the log. We have the outstanding CCTV from Mill Lane. The owners of the house went into the incident room this morning."

"Sounds promising," said Dinescu. "We should take a look."

"Gareth," said Summers. "You and I will go over there now."

"Okay, Sarge," said Booker. "I'll grab a car."

"You don't look so browbeaten today," Summers said to Booker as he drove them to Fishbourne, waiting for a gap in the traffic at the Fishbourne roundabout.

"Oh, come on!" Booker muttered. "People don't know how to use their indicators."

Summers laughed. "On second thoughts…"

"Yes, I'm feeling a bit better now, Sarge. Thanks."

Booker found a gap and lurched onto the roundabout, taking the first exit to Fishbourne.

"Good," Summers said, gripping the door handle as he took the bend.

"I've talked with Sarah. Baby stuff. I was getting the jitters, but I'll be okay."

"I can't help you with babies, I'm afraid. At least you don't have to go through the birth."

Booker sighed. "Nope."

"It would really mess up your hair."

They turned into Mill Lane and parked beside the mobile incident room in the Bull's Head car park. A civilian investigator sat at a desk as Summers walked in. He was in his sixties, a white-haired ex-DCI from Haywards Heath named Jim, whom Summers had met before.

"Hi, Jim. What have you got for us?"

"Ah, Emily," said Jim, leaning back in his chair. "Good to see you again—looking gorgeous as ever. Thanks for coming over. Mr and Mrs Robinson from Ardmore are back from a cruise around the Norwegian Fjords. Alright for some, eh?"

"I couldn't stand being stuck on a boat for two weeks," said Booker. "I'm getting seasick just thinking about it."

"Anyway," said Jim. "They've copied their CCTV footage from outside their house for Monday, the 8th. The camera captures a woman walking past at 08:05, heading towards the pub car park. She returns five minutes later with a full black plastic bag."

"Do you have it there?" Summers asked.

"Yes, I'll show you. I've uploaded it to the server. It took twenty minutes on this connection."

He ran video playback software on the laptop and inserted a USB stick. "This is a cropped version. The original is still on their computer." He pressed play.

The camera was high quality and in colour. The image showed a garden path to the front door, with the top third capturing the footpath along Mill Lane. After a few seconds, a woman in a brown coat walked past, glancing around.

"I think I know who that is," said Summers.

"You get a better shot of her in a few minutes," said Jim. He fast-forwarded four minutes. "Here."

Walking back the other way, the woman's face was unmistakable. She carried a black plastic bag with a large white address label stuck to the side.

"Yolanda Mellor," said Summers. "What's in the bag?"

"Clothes?" suggested Booker.

"I'll let the boss know. Find out what school she works at. We're bringing her in."

According to the sign Booker read, St Luke's Primary School would celebrate its centenary in six months. The building was an awkward mix of brick and dark blue aluminium panels with tinted glass, a design that didn't quite work, in his opinion.

The gates were locked, so Summers pressed the buzzer next to a keypad. As they waited, Booker glanced around. The school, in the north of the city, sat at the top of a long, sloping road and was surrounded by tall fencing. Children played outside in the cold, running and shouting, engaged in group games. At the back of his mind, he wondered if his child might attend this school. He and Chloe were just within the catchment area. Excitement bubbled inside him at the thought.

"Come on, Gareth," said Summers, already holding the gate open.

They followed the sign to the reception, where a manager with a convoluted job title greeted them. She was a petite, tidy woman with a small face and short hair.

"Do you have an appointment?" she asked Booker.

Summers responded by raising her lanyard. "I'm Detective Sergeant Summers, and this is Detective Constable Booker. We need to speak with Yolanda Mellor, please."

"Miss Mellor is about to take a class." The woman gave a narrow smile. "She won't be able to speak with you."

"You'd better find someone to cover for her. She's coming with us."

"That's not how this works," the woman said, scowling. "Miss Mellor is teaching. You'll have to come back later. I must ask you to leave."

"No, this is exactly how it works. Miss Mellor is coming with us. Find her now, or my colleague here will arrest you for obstruction, maybe even assisting an offender."

Booker turned away to hide a smirk.

"Oh." The woman stepped back, blushing. "I'll fetch her."

"Thank you. I'm glad I didn't have to set DC Booker on you."

The woman scampered away and, five minutes later, reappeared with a flustered-looking Yolanda Mellor.

"Can we talk privately, please?" asked Summers.

"Why?" Mellor replied. "I'm working. Can't this wait?"

Booker noticed Summers was still scowling after her run-in with the officious receptionist, so he stepped in.

"No, Yolanda, it can't." Booker closed the gap between them and lowered his voice. "You lied to us about where you were on Monday morning."

"I don't know what you mean."

"We need to question you about it. I'm arresting you on suspicion of the murder of Lily Watson."

"This isn't fair!" Mellor shrieked, as Booker cautioned her. "I'd never hurt Lily!"

"Calm down, Miss Mellor. Otherwise, you'll leave here in handcuffs."

Booker and three PCs from the specialist search team entered Mellor's house. It amused him how they only referred to Yolanda Mellor as the Detained Person—the DP.

Mellor had tidied up since his last visit. She'd had ample time to remove evidence if she wanted to.

"The video shows the DP with a black bin bag," said the lead PC, "possibly full of women's clothes. Any description of the clothes?"

"Not yet," replied Booker. "Maybe a blue, patterned dress. It's a long shot. We're also looking for a spare key for a Mini. Mellor may have moved the victim's car."

"On the DP's keyring?"

"It might have been," Booker said, holding up Mellor's keys. "But it's not now."

"I'm inclined to start with the outside bins," said the lead PC. "The council collects general waste every other Friday here, so it might still be there. Then we'll search any shed and storage, and finally the loft."

"You're the experts," said Booker.

"We are."

It didn't take long to find something. An officer recovered a black bin bag in the loft. He lowered it onto the landing, where Booker and the other officers had gathered. They photographed the bag, including a large white address label on the side with "lounge" written in black pen.

"They haven't long since moved in," said Booker. "Looks like the bag's from then."

They took care cutting away the knot at the top to preserve any DNA evidence. Inside, they found three rolled-up A1-sized canvases.

"Are you sure this is the bag on the CCTV?" asked the lead PC.

"Yes, I'm sure. This wasn't what I expected. Paintings of some sort."

"There aren't any other bags up there. But we found this in the DP's bedside drawer." He held up a car key in an evidence bag. "It has the Mini logo, so I guess that's it."

"Thank you," said Booker. "That's perfect." He took out one of the canvases with his gloved hand and unrolled it.

The painting depicted a fantasy version of Yolanda Mellor, naked and lying face-up on a bed draped in white sheets. One hand held her breast while the other ran through her hair. Sunlight poured through an open window, with white curtains blowing in the breeze. The painting was explicit: flushed cheeks, the curve of her thigh against the sheets.

"Well," said the lead PC, "I didn't expect that."

Booker frowned. "Quite."

He unrolled another painting, set in the same scene but more intimate and sexualised. He felt like a voyeur. He photographed the paintings and sent them to Summers.

"Blimey!" an officer said. "I bet she had sore thighs after posing for that."

Booker noticed something else at the bottom of the bag. He reached inside and pulled out a black plastic device with a tiny orange flashing LED. He held it up. "A tracker. So that's how she knew where the car was."

Chapter Thirty

Summers and Burgess sat opposite Yolanda Mellor in the interview room. The duty solicitor, a woman Summers had met before and got on well with, was present. Summers had disclosed only the CCTV evidence to her.

The interview began with Mellor in tears, her cheeks red and her eyelashes wet. She had already had some time to calm herself, but Summers couldn't wait any longer.

"Yolanda," Summers began, "I'm about to show you two CCTV recordings from a house on Mill Lane. They were recorded on the morning of Monday, the 8th of January, a week ago, between 08:05 and 08:10."

Mellor sobbed as Summers pressed play on her laptop, showing clips of Mellor on Mill Lane, including one of her returning with a black bag. Summers nodded to Burgess to continue.

Burgess's voice was calming. "Yolanda, you need to listen to our questions. You may have a perfectly valid explanation for us." Mellor looked up at her. "What were you doing there?"

"I had some things that belonged to me in the car. I wanted them back."

"What things?"

"Nothing to do with you," Mellor replied, folding her arms.

"Were Lily's clothes in that black bag you were carrying?"

"No. Not at all!"

"Were there paintings in the bag?" Burgess held her gaze.

Mellor looked away and shook her head.

"You shook your head. Was that a no, or are you refusing to answer?"

"I don't have to tell you," Mellor whispered.

"How did you know Lily's car would be in the Bull's Head car park at that time in the morning?"

"I can't say!" Mellor's breathing quickened.

Burgess placed a photograph in front of her. "Search officers found a black bin bag in your loft matching the one in the video footage. Here's a photograph from a still, exhibit reference GB/15." Mellor looked at the photograph as Burgess pointed at it. "Look, there's the white label. Is that the bag you were carrying from Lily's car?"

"Yes," Mellor admitted.

"Inside," Burgess continued, placing another photograph in front of her, "was this device—exhibit GB/06. What is it?"

Mellor shook her head. "I can't…"

"It's written on the side. It's a car tracker with a SIM card inside. You can get them on Amazon for thirty pounds. Did you plant it in Lily's car?"

"Yes."

"We also found some paintings in the bag. Tell me about them."

"I don't want to!"

"That's all we found. Were Lily's clothes in the bag at any time? The ones she was wearing when she died?"

"No! It was just the paintings. I thought Lily was on the marshes."

"Okay," said Burgess. "Tell me about the tracker. Why did you put it in Lily's car?"

"She kept turning off her mobile's location settings. So I bought the tracker and hid it under the car. It's magnetic. I have an app on my phone."

"And are you telling us Lily didn't know it was there?"

Mellor shrugged. "I guess she didn't."

"Did you use your phone app to locate Lily on Monday?"

"Yes. I have her spare car key at home. I saw her car in the pub car park. I took what was mine and removed the tracker. I'd had enough. I was scared Lily would show Justin my paintings."

"They are intimate paintings of you, Yolanda. Three of them. Did Lily paint them?"

"They were precious to me. We had a special time together last year. But after our argument, she took them back. She tried to punish me."

"Did they belong to you?" Summers asked.

"Yes. Lily painted them for me."

Summers leaned forward. "Were you in a sexual relationship with Lily?"

Mellor ran her fingers through her hair, curling a strand around her forefinger.

"Not really. Apart from one time—when she painted me. She was so tender. I was in love with her, but she couldn't…"

"She couldn't love you?" Summers finished.

"No. So, there you have it. Happy now?"

Summers glanced at Burgess. "Did you try to find Lily when you went to her car?"

"No. I saw her easel wasn't in the car, so I just assumed she'd gone onto the marshes to paint. It was early for her, but I didn't question it."

"I'm going to recap," said Summers. "Tell me if I've misunderstood anything. At some point before the day Lily was murdered, you placed the tracker on her car to follow her movements. On Monday morning, before you went to work, you found Lily's car using the tracker app on your phone. Correct?"

"Yes."

"You went to her car, located in the Bull's Head car park, took back intimate paintings of yourself, and removed the car tracker." Summers waited for Mellor to confirm.

"Yes. I didn't want her to show them to other people, least of all Justin." She frowned. "He'd try to sell them in his bloody shop. I thought he'd humiliate me."

"You didn't search for Lily, but you put the items from her car in the black sack seen on the CCTV footage. Then what?"

"I drove to work."

"Did you kill Lily? Either intentionally or unintentionally?"

"No! I loved her." Mellor thumped the table, and the solicitor whispered something in her ear, trying to calm her. "I'm sorry. I would never harm Lily."

Summers gave the solicitor a grateful nod before turning her attention back to Mellor. "You helped us identify Lily's body at the mortuary. The postmortem found a bruise on Lily's left cheek, likely caused by a hard slap. Did you slap Lily during your argument the night before?"

Mellor covered her face with her hands and nodded.

"Yolanda, you nodded. Can you answer my question for the recording, please?"

"Yes! I slapped her. Okay? She said horrible things. Called me a love-sick schoolgirl. Then she threw her phone at me."

Summers looked at Burgess, who shook her head. "We don't have any more questions, Yolanda. If there's anything you want to add or think we've misunderstood, now's the time."

Mellor shook her head. Her breathing slowed as she raised her head. "No, thank you."

"Here we are again," said Dinescu, closing the meeting room door behind him. He'd seen Faraday in the building earlier and didn't want him involved in the briefing.

Everyone was ready around the table. They were close to concluding this case. Dinescu began. "There have been important developments. Let's bring everything together. Emily, you can start."

"Yes, boss," said Summers. "We've released Yolanda Mellor under investigation. We checked with the school again about when she started work on Monday. The timing is all wrong for her to have killed Lily. The timestamps on the CCTV footage showed she wouldn't have had long enough to walk to the footbridge and drown her. If she had arrived earlier, it might have been different. Also, the tracker app data, stored online, confirmed Lily's movements. Even though the video of Mellor with the black bag appears damning, there were only paintings in there—not Lily's clothes."

"It would have been helpful if she told us she'd seen Lily's car," said Booker.

"Of course," said Dinescu. "But she was trying to protect herself. She was embarrassed by those paintings."

"I'm not surprised," said Booker.

"Meanwhile, Chester," said Summers, "you have some important news about the car for us."

Kirby sat up and cleared his throat. "I do, Sarge. We received the cell site analysis from Digital Forensics this morning. The phone data is tied to the individuals who own the phones, so I'll only use their names. We also have the location data from Lily Watson's secret phone—the one she hid in her car. Lily had left it switched on since she met with Justin Hadley on Sunday night.

We can track it to the Bader Hotel in Tangmere and then to Mill Lane in Fishbourne."

"Okay, Chester, give us what you have."

"Lily's car appeared on Mill Lane at 07:34 on Monday, the 8th. It left the area at 08:25."

"Mellor had missed seeing the car being driven away by fifteen minutes," said Burgess.

Kirby agreed. "Raymond Collier arrived in that area at 07:40. Then another phone appeared on Mill Lane at 07:45. It was Henry Rushton's."

"Henry!" said Booker. "What the hell was he doing there? He's lied about when he last saw his mother."

"Lily had met with her son. They were minutes apart."

"It didn't start getting light until about 07:35," said Burgess. "It was barely light when they met. This was a secret meeting."

Kirby continued reading from his list of times. "Raymond Collier left the area at 07:58, leaving Rushton behind, and Rushton left at the same time as Lily's car. Rushton stayed with the car until Crossbush, where they separated. He was next located at Arundel railway station, where he caught a train back to Fishbourne."

"So Henry Rushton dumped Lily's car and went back to Fishbourne by train to get his," said Summers.

"That's what the data suggests, Sarge. After that, he stayed around Chichester city centre for most of the day. He returned to Crossbush at 19:41, and shortly after that, the local phone masts lost Lily's car phone signal. Presumably, when he torched the car. Rushton then returned to Brighton."

They all sat in silence until Booker slapped his hand on the table.

"Bloody hell!" he said. "He's killed his mother."

"Either Collier or Rushton separately," said Dinescu, "or both together."

"Pretty compelling evidence either way," said Summers. "After removing Lily's clothes to get rid of DNA evidence, why didn't he think about turning his mobile off?"

"People don't think about the footprints mobile data leaves," said Burgess.

"There is much evidence to gather," said Dinescu. "In the morning, I will ask Brighton to arrest Henry Rushton and bring him to Chichester Custody. Chester, Sarah—go straight in afterwards on a Section 18 search. I'll authorise it straightaway."

"Emily, I appreciate you have a lot to do. Can you assign some officers to find out what Rushton was doing in Chichester city centre for so long on Monday?"

"Yes, boss," said Summers.

"Sarah, go now and arrest Raymond Collier on suspicion of murdering Lily, too. We have him at the location and at the relevant time, and there could be a motive for blackmail. You may want to grab some uniformed officers to help if he makes a fuss."

"Yes, boss," said Burgess.

"Gareth and Chester, you're going to search his house. I have a hunch that Collier could have that confession letter."

"Wouldn't he have destroyed it?" said Summers.

A tap on the door caught Dinescu's attention. DI Daisy Irving came in.

"Daisy?" said Dinescu.

"Can I have a word, sir?" said Irving. "I'd like to catch up with you. DCS Faraday wants to join us, too."

"Come to my office," said Dinescu. He glanced at Summers and smiled to reassure her.

Daisy Irving stood opposite Dinescu's desk, her hands fidgeting while she waited. Moments later, Faraday entered the office wearing his formal dress uniform: white shirt, black tie, and black tunic. Dinescu wondered if he'd attended a presentation. Irving flashed a knowing smile at Faraday, but he ignored her, focusing on Dinescu instead.

Faraday closed the office blinds and sat down, his expression cold and severe as he jutted his chin forward.

"I won't beat around the bush," he began. "Have you come to a decision, Ben?"

"I haven't changed my mind, sir," Dinescu replied, glancing at Irving. "This is a personal conversation. Without wishing to be disrespectful, why is she involved?"

Faraday's expression hardened. "Daisy will soon be promoted to Temporary DCI. She is here because she will be replacing you as the SIO in Chichester Major Crimes. You are being transferred to one of the major investigation teams in Surrey. You don't have a choice—it's happening. You'll receive formal notice in the post. Since you've declined the promotion, you will transfer as a DCI. I understand this might be difficult for you, Ben, but I hope it's clear."

"It's perfectly clear, sir," Dinescu said, his gaze flicking to the photograph of Lisa and Sophia on his desk before looking at his team's empty seats. They had gone to arrest Raymond Collier. He gave a heavy sigh and then looked between Faraday and Irving. "Why here?"

"What do you mean?" Faraday asked.

"What is it about this team you want? First, you told me we were under review. You threatened to break us up. Were you behind DCs Taylor and Kirby's secondments? Then that changed. It was just a threat to get me out of the way. Now you have a special interest in us. I wonder why."

"Senior management made the decision, Ben. That decision is final."

"Final? They never spoke to me."

"You have three months. Then you will transfer to Surrey."

Faraday stood beside Irving. His satisfaction at putting down Dinescu was obvious. Dinescu studied Irving's face. The whole situation reeked of dishonesty and sexual favours—two reliable ways for a police officer to lose their job.

"All of this so you can move in here," he said to her. "What have you sacrificed to achieve that?" He glared at Faraday. "And you've become overconfident, sir. You think you'll always get away with it. But you won't."

Faraday snapped. "Are you accusing me of something, DCI Dinescu? I won't stand for your insubordination! Three months—start making plans to leave!"

Dinescu didn't answer, turning away from them. Faraday, clearly rattled, ushered Irving out of Dinescu's office, and they left Major Crimes together.

Dinescu looked out of his window and saw Summers looking in. She had a question on her face. Should he tell her?

Chapter Thirty-One

Burgess rode in a marked police four-by-four with two uniformed officers, while Booker and Kirby followed in a CID car. They drove through the city, avoiding the railway gates, and then passed Chichester College.

"When I was a kid," said Kirby, "we would wave out of the back of the car at other motorists. Most people ignored us."

"Really?" said Booker. "You were one of those annoying little brats. They ignored you because they knew you'd give them the finger if they waved back."

"I was only six!"

"So?" said Booker.

"You and I must have had a very different upbringing."

Kirby was driving and kept glancing over at Booker. "Have I got something on my face?" said Booker.

Kirby smiled. "I was just trying to imagine you as a dad."

Booker rolled his eyes. "You think it's funny?"

"No. You'll be a great dad."

Booker looked back at him. "And what's the punchline, Chester?"

Kirby frowned. "There isn't one. You're lucky."

"Why?"

Kirby stopped for a pedestrian crossing. "Jenny and I can't have kids. We would have loved them. Just not meant to be."

Booker blinked. "Shit! I'm sorry, mate."

"No, it's okay." The lights turned green, and he sped up to catch up with the marked car. "We could've adopted, but life went in a different direction. I'm jealous. But not in a bad way. No, I'm happy for you. Do you understand?"

Booker nodded. "Yes, I do. I never really thought about not being able to have a child. It puts a different spin on things."

Kirby smiled. "Well, as I said, I think you'll be a brilliant dad."

"Thanks." Booker looked away as they turned into Brandy Hole Lane. "And you'll be a brilliant Uncle Chester."

They stopped outside Collier's house, taking up one side of the road. Burgess joined Booker and Kirby.

"I was so tempted to wave to you back then," she said to Booker.

Booker coughed. "You take him away, and we'll step in."

Burgess and one of the uniformed officers knocked on the front door and waited. Raymond Collier appeared, looking surprised.

"Raymond Collier?" said Burgess.

"What?" Collier grumbled.

"I'm DC Burgess from Chichester Major Crimes. We've had information relating to the death of Lily Watson that places you at the scene of the murder at the relevant time."

"What information?" Collier puffed himself up with indignation.

"I'm arresting you on suspicion of murder." Burgess cautioned him, and the uniformed officer pulled him out of the house to handcuff him.

Once Collier was in the back of the car with Burgess, Booker called Dinescu, who authorised the search of the house.

Kirby had brought out a search kit and switched on his body-worn video. The two detectives stood in the hallway, taking in the musty smell coming from the kitchen.

"Smells like our office," said Kirby.

"A letter," Booker said to Kirby. "It could be anywhere."

Kirby nodded. "I'll start with the lounge."

"And I'll go to the dining room."

When Booker entered the dining room, he found a broken cabinet on the floor, left in pieces. Next to it was a new, empty bookcase, with books piled beside it. The room was bright, with light streaming in from the conservatory. Scattered over a heavy, oak dining table were papers—bills, invoices, and a large brown envelope sitting on the top. Booker searched through the documents. Underneath the bills were old, yellowing newspaper cuttings about the trial of Joseph McKinley for murder.

Kirby came in and shrugged. "Nothing in the lounge apart from mouldy cups."

"Look at all this. He certainly had it in for McKinley." Booker photographed the pile on the table.

"What's in the envelope?"

"I haven't looked yet," said Booker.

Kirby tipped its contents onto the table, and a folded sheet of lined paper fell out. Kirby opened it and placed it on the table. "Bingo!"

14th May 2004

Heather,

243

If you're reading this, then I expect I'm dead. I never thought it would come to this, writing the darkest thing I've ever done. But here it is, in black and white. I have to let you know. I owe you that much, at least.

I found out about you and Roger. I knew everything and couldn't let it go on any longer. You were my world, Heather, and I wanted you to be mine and mine alone. That day in January, when we were working together on a job in Fishbourne, I confronted him on the bridge over the creek. Things got heated. I struck him hard. He was out cold and didn't even see it coming.

I looked at him lying there, and all I could think about was him sleeping with you. In a split second, I made a decision I couldn't take back. Something I've regretted over these last months. I dragged him into the creek and held him under the water. I watched him drown, and it felt good. It was over before I knew it.

I did it because of what he did with you, what he did to us. It's been eating me alive ever since. Every case I've solved, every criminal I've put away, doesn't change what I did. I'm no better than them. I framed Joseph McKinley for Roger's murder. He was an addict and a waste of space. But I told some terrible lies and got him convicted for something I did.

You need to know the truth, even if it's the last thing I do. I don't expect forgiveness. I just needed to get it off my chest.

Raymond.

"Well, that'll do it," said Booker. He photographed the A4 sheet and dropped it into an evidence bag.

"In May 2004, he was going to end it all," said Kirby, "but he obviously didn't. So, why keep the letter?"

"I'll let the sergeant know."

The light had faded, and another difficult day had passed for Dinescu. Faraday had made his position clear, expecting Dinescu to obey without question. While Dinescu would always follow a lawful order, this reeked of corruption. He had to trust his instincts and those who had promised to protect his interests. It was now out of his hands.

He stared out of the office window, holding a cup of coffee. His thoughts turned to Raymond Collier, wondering how he had become corrupt all those years ago.

"Sir?" said Summers behind him. Dinescu turned to see her holding a photograph of Collier's confession letter. "They found it in plain sight. They also seized handwritten notes for comparison and a pair of muddy boots."

"Have you sent it to Forensics?"

"Yes, sir."

Dinescu sipped his coffee, and a thought came to him. "What about items in the attic?"

"The attic?"

"Heather Collier said she found the letter under some mouldy police folders in the attic."

"Yes, I remember," Summers said. "I'll get Heather Collier to confirm it's the same letter she found with Lily."

"Well, we should get a SOCO to take mould samples from the folders. Forensic testing won't take long to prove whether Collier stored it there." He sighed. "Our forensics bill keeps going up."

"So I gather, sir."

"Didn't Sarah say Lily did calligraphy, too?"

"She did!" said Summers, pointing her finger. "Now, there's a thought."

Summers made a phone call, outlining what Dinescu had just suggested.

Dinescu finished his coffee and checked his mobile until Summers was off the phone. He'd had no reply to his message to Tom McBride.

"They're arranging a SOCO now, sir," she said. "The result won't be back until tomorrow afternoon at the earliest. We'll be cutting it fine with the custody clock."

"We'll get an extension if we have to," said Dinescu. "Continue with the interview now, Emily. I'll be watching. Don't let the man wind you up. Before you go, can you get me that old diary you found with Lily's paperwork?"

"Yes, sir. You know it was empty?"

"Yes, you said. But humour me. I want to look through it."

Summers returned with the diary, studying Dinescu's face. "This thing with Faraday's going to be okay, boss," she said. "It won't happen. Even if it did, I wouldn't stay here."

"Thanks, Emily. I don't want you to worry. Something good will come out of this."

Raymond Collier sat with his arms folded across his chest, staring at the floor. He was unshaven, wearing a scruffy T-shirt and jeans, and he reeked as if he hadn't washed for days.

Summers waited while Burgess went through the introductions and prerequisites for the interview. Collier's answers were terse, and his vacant, dead eyes shifted between them. He was cold and demeaning when he spoke, as if he knew the job better than they did. Summers focused on the task at hand and the points to prove.

His demeanour irritated his duty solicitor as well. She'd entered the interview room with a deep scowl, glancing at Summers as she shook her head.

Summers began the questions. "Raymond—"

"You can call me Mr Collier."

"Did you kill Lily Watson?"

"No, detective sergeant. I did not," he said, baring his yellow teeth.

"Did you arrange to meet Lily that Monday morning?"

"I'm guessing by now you've found the letter. Am I correct?"

"What letter is this?" the solicitor asked. "You haven't disclosed it to me."

"They wouldn't do that, my love," Collier said to the solicitor. "They wanted to bring it in later to discredit me."

Summers glanced at Burgess and sat back. "Mr Collier, we have evidence from your mobile phone's cell site data that you were in Mill Lane, Fishbourne, on Monday, 8th January, at about 07:40, leaving the area at 07:58."

"Well done, sergeant."

"Lily Watson's mobile phone arrived about six minutes before. Did you arrange to meet her?"

"Yes—obviously."

"Tell us about that meeting."

"We met on the Fishbourne Marshes, on the old footbridge where McKinley murdered Roger Wallace. McKinley was with her, wearing a scarf like a mask, carrying some kind of stick. The tosser thought I wouldn't recognise him." Collier laughed. "Lily had called me on Sunday. I don't know how she got my number— probably through Heather. She said she had something on me that proved I murdered Roger and wanted twenty-five grand to keep her from going to the police."

"She was blackmailing you. Why didn't you go to the police?"

"I was the police once, remember?" Collier flashed a grin at Summers. "I wanted to deal with it myself."

"And how did you deal with Lily?"

"Not the way you're implying. I knew she had nothing. Curiosity got the better of me, so I went to see what she had."

"You went out of curiosity, not guilt? Not out of fear of being exposed?"

"No. I didn't like being manipulated. I have no guilt, and there's nothing to expose." Collier smirked. "Good try, sergeant."

Summers pressed on. "Did you choose the location?"

"No, I imagine McKinley did."

Summers made a note. "What happened then?"

"I told her to show me this so-called important thing. It was barely light enough to see it. It was some bollocks confession letter I was supposed to have written. A forgery. She must have written it herself. So I snatched it from her and walked away. McKinley tried to fight me for it, but he doesn't move so well nowadays. I left and went home with the letter."

"Is this the letter?" Summers held up a photocopy. "This is a copy of what we found in your house, produced as exhibit GB/07."

Collier studied it for a few seconds. "Yes."

"Tell me if I've got this right. You're saying Lily forged this confession letter from you?"

"Yes, saying I killed Roger."

Summers nodded. "You are telling us that Lily forged a confession letter and demanded twenty-five thousand pounds from you? Otherwise, she would go to the police."

Collier rolled his eyes. "For God's sake! How many more times? Yes."

"And Joseph McKinley was with her, disguised?"

"Correct."

"Then you took the letter from Lily and went home."

"Correct again."

"How was Lily when you left her?"

"Pissed off, swearing, flapping her arms about. She was fine."

"Why did you keep the letter?" Burgess asked.

"I was going to bring it to you. But you did the job for me."

"Did you see McKinley kill Lily?" Summers asked.

"No. But he must have. He killed her in exactly the same way he killed Roger."

"Did he?" said Summers.

"Yes." Collier smiled, putting his hands behind his head and exposing his rancid-smelling armpits. "It's a bloody carbon copy."

"How do you know how she died?" Summers asked. "We never released those details."

Collier's grin vanished. "The reports say someone drowned her in the creek. So I assumed it was the same."

Summers pushed her chair back.

"Did you withdraw the twenty-five thousand from your bank account?"

Collier laughed. "Twenty-five grand! I don't have that money to throw away, and I couldn't take out that amount of cash that quickly. No one could. The woman was an amateur."

Summers glanced at Burgess, who had also sat back in her chair, away from the smell.

"How would you describe your marriage, Mr Collier?" Burgess asked.

"What's that got to do with anything?" Collier snapped back.

Burgess pressed on. "Are you having difficulties?"

"It's nothing to do with you."

"Heather knew about the letter," Burgess said, sitting forward. "She raised her concerns with us."

"Ah, she's already spoken to you. Stupid cow! She was best

buddies with Lily. What did you expect? Probably planned the whole thing with her."

"Did Heather know if you had the money to pay the blackmail request?"

"I can't answer for Heather."

"We will be checking your bank accounts," Summers said.

"I've nothing to hide."

Summers nodded at Burgess.

"We've spoken to Joseph McKinley," Burgess said, "and we can show he didn't get to the footbridge before nine that morning."

"I saw him! He was there."

"He couldn't be in two places at once, Mr Collier," Summers said. "He didn't get there before 9 a.m."

Collier looked indignant, turning to his solicitor. "Why aren't you saying anything? Somebody prove to me he wasn't there."

"That's not how evidence works, Mr Collier."

"Someone's lying here! And it isn't me."

Burgess nodded to Summers, who checked her watch.

"Okay," Summers said. "By my watch, it's now 18:45. We'll finish the interview there for this evening."

Chapter Thirty-Two

Tuesday

The day was reluctant to show itself, almost as if the sunrise wouldn't happen that morning. Seagulls cried their long calls from the Brighton rooftops, jostled by the stiff sea breeze.

Burgess and Kirby waited with uniformed officers in the rain outside Henry Rushton's flat, which had its own front door onto the street. They weren't sure he'd be in, but Henry Rushton came to the door in a hoodie and jogging bottoms, with a bemused look. It looked like he'd been sleeping in them. The police officers' body-worn video cameras beeped as they came on.

"What do you want?" His voice was low and croaky, and his hair uncombed. Burgess noticed a nasty cut on his forehead.

"Henry, I'm Detective Constable Burgess from Chichester Major Crimes. These officers are from Brighton. I need you to listen carefully: I'm arresting you on suspicion of murdering your mother, Lily Watson, on Monday, the 8th of January." As Burgess cautioned him, he tried to go back inside, but the uniformed officers took his arms and handcuffed him to the front. One of them had seen something. He put on blue gloves and reached behind the door. He retrieved a long pickaxe handle.

"Expecting someone?" asked the officer.

"These officers are taking you to Chichester Custody," said Burgess, as she put on gloves and searched him. "Do you have anything on you that's going to hurt me? Knives, needles?"

"No. I've got a spliff in my hoodie pocket. Nothing else."

Burgess took an evidence bag from Kirby and dropped the spliff inside.

"I thought I could smell it," Burgess said.

"Are you going to search my flat?"

"Yes, for anything connected to the offence we've arrested you for. Is there something in there we need to know about?"

Rushton nodded. "You're going to find it, anyway. There's a watch on my bed. Someone gave it to me. I didn't nick it."

"Valuable?"

"You could say that. You know I never meant to—"

"Hold that thought, Henry," said Burgess. "You're under caution. Best wait until you are in the interview."

Burgess pulled out a set of keys from his hoodie pocket. "Yours?"

"Yeah."

Burgess nodded to the officers, and Kirby gave them the arrest details. The uniformed Brighton officers put Rushton into the back of their police car and began their journey to Chichester.

The flat was cleaner than Burgess had expected, besides the sour-sweet smell of cannabis. An Xbox and TV were the focal points in the main living room. Rushton had a bookcase full of self-help and inspirational stories. The top of the bookcase displayed photos and a few small snooker trophies.

Burgess went straight into the bedroom. Sitting on top of the duvet was a Rolex watch in white and yellow gold with a white face.

Burgess turned towards the door. "Chester, come and look at this."

Kirby went straight to the watch, and his eyes lit up. He inspected it closely and turned it over. "Shit! This is a Rolex Submariner. Genuine."

"Must be a grand, at least," said Burgess. "What's he doing with it?"

Kirby shook his head. "No. I've seen one like this before. It's a vintage model in beautiful condition. I'd say more like thirty to thirty-five grand. This is very wrong."

Burgess agreed. "I'd better call the boss."

Dinescu received the email while he was in the middle of eating his lunch at his desk. He looked out of his office window and saw Summers look up. She must have just read it, too. She hurried into Dinescu's office.

"What do you think, sir?" she asked.

"Well, if the lab says it's a forgery, then it's a forgery."

"I don't understand. How does this change things?" She sat in the chair in front of his desk and straightened her ponytail, something she did when she was thinking.

"It means Raymond Collier didn't write that confession letter."

"Okay." Summers frowned. "And..."

"Lily was with Heather when she found the diary under the police folders."

"Yes, Lily found the diary. Heather said the letter dropped out when Lily passed it..." Summers's eyes widened. "Shit! Lily planted the letter! She planned the whole thing."

"It's likely," said Dinescu. "And the forgery was believable enough to convince Heather that her husband murdered Roger Wallace."

Summers rested her head in her hands and closed her eyes to help her think straight. Dinescu finished a sandwich while he waited for her.

"Lily believed Collier murdered Roger Wallace." Summers was thinking it through aloud. "But there was no concrete evidence to support it. So, she forged this letter and used it to convince Heather. But why? To get her to leave Ray? Push her to go to the police?"

"Possibly," said Dinescu. "This part is important, Emily. Raymond Collier didn't know what Lily had on him until he met her on the marshes. He then told us he'd snatched the letter and walked away. It doesn't make sense."

Summers leaned back in the chair. "You're right, boss. Why did he go to meet her? He said he was curious. But what if he actually thought she did have something on him? Why snatch the letter and keep it if it was a forgery?"

"Do we have any evidence he paid blackmail money to Lily?"

"Not according to his bank account," said Summers.

"The only thing we've proven is that Lily Watson tried to frame Collier for Roger Wallace's murder."

"And she tried to use Heather Collier, too."

Dinescu placed his palms together. "If we can show Raymond Collier made a blackmail payment to Lily, it would imply he thought she had something substantial on him. She could have got it right about Collier, but for the wrong reasons."

Summers nodded. "We have a custody extension granted. I'm going in with Collier now. If he wasn't going to let Lily blackmail him, why did he really meet with her? I don't buy this curiosity bullshit."

≈

Raymond Collier looked even more haggard and pale that afternoon. The custody sergeant gave Collier a chance to wash and get a clean T-shirt. He still smelled sweaty when he came into the interview room with the solicitor, but nowhere near as bad as he did. He was sipping from a beaker of water. He sat at the desk and tried to push his comb-over back into place with his fingers.

Summers interviewed Collier on her own, while Dinescu watched from the office. She avoided eye contact with him as she organised her paperwork, but noticed a long, inflamed scratch down his forearm. She began with the usual opening formalities. Collier looked like he was hiding a foul mood with a smug smile. If he was at all nervous, he wasn't showing it.

She ignored him, choosing to talk to his solicitor first. "Have you had a chance to read through our disclosure?"

"Yes, and thank you, DS Summers," said the solicitor. "I have nothing to add at this time."

"Very well." Summers turned her face towards Collier. "We kept you overnight as we were expecting test results to return, and I'm glad to say they have."

"Test results? What the hell are you testing?"

"We'll talk about it presently. First, Mr Collier, you have an infected scratch on your left arm. Our nurse should see to that before it gets worse. How did you get it?"

Collier groaned. "My wife. We argued before she left. I was breaking up an old book unit. She thought I was ignoring her, so she ran her nails down my arm in spite. She's a nasty bitch, sometimes."

"The custody clock is nearly up, DS Summers," said the solicitor. "Mr Collier has been here for twenty hours."

"That's true," said Summers, "so we requested an extension of up to thirty-six hours for further questioning."

"You must be bloody joking!" snapped Collier.

"Do I look like I'm joking, Mr Collier?"

"You're a bitch, too!"

"Excuse me?"

Collier turned his head away, folded his arms across his chest, and continued to swear under his breath.

Summers didn't flinch. "I want to talk about the alleged confession letter. We were able to rush through some testing on the paper. And your suspicions were correct. The letter is forged."

"Of course it is! Why would I keep a confession letter in the house?"

"Heather told us she was with Lily when she found the letter in the attic. It had fallen out of a diary covered by some old police folders. We went into the attic, seized those folders, and then had them tested. Mildew was present on the covers and inside pages, but no mildew was found on the letter. This indicates that the letter was never stored in the attic with those old folders. They ran some initial tests on the ink, too. The ink hasn't aged. It's new."

"You'd better release me then." Collier turned to his solicitor. "Come on, speak up. They have no evidence. They must release me."

Summers ignored him. "Then we checked your bank accounts. You certainly have the money to pay the twenty-five thousand Lily was demanding. But we see you didn't."

"I wasn't going to pay for something that was a fake. I didn't kill Roger!"

Someone knocked on the door, and Dinescu entered.

"Entering the room is…"

Dinescu stood over Summers. "DCI Dinescu, ND 3256." Summers looked up at him. "Could I have a word with you, DS Summers?" He smiled at the solicitor. "We will be resuming presently. An officer outside will be returning you to your cell, Mr Collier."

"Interview suspended at 13:14."

Chapter Thirty-Three

"I'm sorry to take you out of there, Emily," said Dinescu as they entered the office, "but we need to take stock of some new information." He could see she wasn't happy about ending the interview there. "I need you to trust my judgement on this."

The others had all returned from Brighton and were waiting by the whiteboard. Burgess stepped forward with a coffee and a smile for Summers, and an open packet of chocolate digestives.

"What new information?" Summers asked, taking the coffee and grabbing a biscuit.

Dinescu stood before them. "We're very close now." He wiped down the whiteboard and started afresh with a black dry marker pen. "Gareth and Chester have just returned from Henry Rushton's flat. He's in a cell and waiting for a solicitor. During the search, they came across this." Dinescu handed Summers an evidence bag containing a watch.

"A nice watch," she said. "Not my taste. Oh, and it's a Rolex. What's Rushton doing with this? It must be worth a bit."

"Between thirty and thirty-five grand, Sarge," said Kirby.

"What! He's stolen it from someone?"

"Rushton also tried to sell it," said Booker. "He went into a few jewellers in Chichester the day Lily died. We've got the CCTV of him trying to sell the watch. They wouldn't touch it. He also went into a jeweller's in Brighton to do the same thing. The shop owner alerted Rolex in case it was stolen."

Burgess's phone rang. "She's here, boss. I'll take her into a statement room." Burgess took the watch and jogged out of the office.

"I saw something when I went to see the Wallace sisters," said Dinescu. "A photograph of Roger Wallace on the wall. His father took it the day before Roger died, and that's where I've seen that Rolex watch before. I believe that watch was Wallace's."

"Wouldn't Heather Collier have recognised it?" said Kirby.

Dinescu shook his head. "She never saw him that last week of Wallace's life."

Summers frowned, confused. "But how did Rushton get it?"

Dinescu went back to the whiteboard. "Let's step back for a moment. I'm going to summarise what we have." He wrote on the board and continued to make notes as he spoke. "We know it's likely that Lily Watson, Henry Rushton, and Raymond Collier met on Monday morning on the footbridge around 07:40. We know Lily's car was on Mill Lane at this time. This was about Lily Watson blackmailing Collier for twenty-five thousand pounds. She thought she had something against Collier, but she didn't think it was enough to convict him. So she forged a confession letter by Collier that he murdered PC Wallace. This was a very naive plan, and it would have failed if it wasn't for the fact that Collier actually *did* murder Roger Wallace."

"Collier did? But the letter was a forgery. I don't get it."

"Do you remember when Heather Collier came in and gave us her statement? She was telling us about Ray's books being left to him by his father."

Summers frowned. "Yes. She put the books in the suitcase."

"Heather Collier told us that was Lily's plan. Lily contrived it all to make Heather believe the letter was real and a key piece of evidence to convict her husband. It was amateur dramatics, all of it. Heather also told us that Ray's father had left him something of much greater value. Ray had put it in the bottom of his wardrobe and didn't even use it."

Summers touched her lips with her forefinger. "Yes, but we don't know what that was... or do we?" She grabbed her desk phone. Within a few seconds, she was speaking to her. "Hello, Heather, this is DS Summers from Chichester Major Crimes. When you came in and gave your statement, you told us about something of value Raymond's father had left him that was in his wardrobe. Can you—?" Summers blinked a few times as she listened and looked over at Dinescu. "Thanks so much, Heather. Did Lily know about it?... You showed it to her... Are you available to put that into a statement for us?... Thanks a lot... I'll be in touch shortly." She ended the call.

Dinescu smiled. "Am I right?"

"The watch! The bloody watch!" said Summers.

"Yes," said Dinescu.

"Sorry, boss, I'm a bit lost," said Booker.

"Raymond Collier showed his guilt by handing over that watch as a blackmail payment. It was what Lily had asked for."

"But it was Roger Wallace's." Booker's confused look turned to a shock. "The bastard took it from Wallace when he killed him." He waved his index finger. "But the fact that he'd stored in the dark all those years means Roger's DNA might still be on it."

"In the links," said Summers. "It's what the crime scene manager told me about Lily's watch. There would be loads of Wallace's DNA caught between the links."

Some minutes later, Sarah Burgess returned to the office with a wide grin. "Penny Wallace has identified the watch as Roger's. She said the serial number would still be registered with Rolex under her father's name. She's put this in a statement."

"Get the watch rushed off to forensics," said Dinescu. "Ask them to compare any DNA found on it to Roger Wallace's."

"But sir," said Booker. "Collier could just say he stole the watch from Wallace's dead body after McKinley killed him. It's a last-ditch attempt, but it would throw in reasonable doubt."

"I agree, Gareth, but that's not all we have. I said Lily thought she had something against Collier but didn't think it was enough to convict him. I've just had some more forensic results in." He went into his office and returned with a printed email and a black book. "I now get what you mean by things coming like buses, Gareth." Dinescu laughed to himself, leaving the others bemused. "On Saturday, I went to the crime scene with DS Summers. Those scratches on Lily's arms bothered me. She had posted something into the pillbox and snagged herself on the brambles in the process."

"The package," said Summers. "Have we got the results back, boss? What was inside?"

"Yes," said Dinescu. "A rusty friction-lock baton made by Armament Systems and Procedures—the ASP. The same type issued to police officers in the early 2000s. It was still in its leather holster. Inside the holster were traces of Wallace's blood and skin, matching his DNA." Dinescu smiled and looked each one of them in the eye. "The rubber handle of the baton had deteriorated, but not completely. Collier had marked the handle of his baton with his warrant number."

"Brilliant!" said Summers, laughing out loud.

"And also inside the package was a note Lily wrote to Joseph." The team went quiet as Dinescu cleared his throat.

Joe,

If you're reading this, then you've received my message. I know you're angry, and you think I've betrayed you. But I haven't. The money was to help Henry with his debt, and to help you get back on your feet. I get why you didn't want it, but Henry really needed it.

I don't trust that bastard Raymond Collier, so I hid this in the pillbox in case anything happened to me. Be careful how you handle it! Leave it in the plastic bag. I think it's what he hit Roger with. I'm not sure if it's enough to prove your innocence, but maybe the police could find something on it. You may need more, and I can help you with that.

I found it in the pillbox a year after the trial. It had fallen down a crack in the concrete. Collier must have dropped it when he went to get your pole with the hook. Take it to the police!

I kept it for all those years because I was angry with you for turning your back on Henry and me. I know why you did, and I don't blame you now. I should have come forward sooner, I know. I'm sorry.

You will always be special to me, Joe.

Love, L.

A breeze cut through the office. They heard a door in CID closing.

"Shit!" said Summers. "I've got goosebumps. We've got him."

Dinescu nodded, holding the black book in his hand in front of Summers. "The diary you found with Lily's things after the burglary." He handed it to her. "It wasn't Lily's diary. It was Collier's—a year diary, appointments for 2004."

"That was it? Have I missed something?"

"You may have misread 2004 as 2024. There's a page missing in January. Other than that, the diary is empty."

"A page missing?" said Summers. She opened the diary and found the remnants left behind from a torn-out page. "He's ripped out Friday, 16th January."

"Look at the next page," said Dinescu.

Summers saw it was only blank at first. Then something caught her eye—a mark in the centre. She held the diary to the light, angling the page to look at the mark. "He's written something and torn it out. It's left an indentation." Summers screwed up her eyes. "It says, *Find the baton*. Lily probably didn't even see this."

"Collier made a note to himself," said Dinescu. "It made no sense to me when I first saw it. Not until I read this note from Lily. He knew his baton was missing."

Silence drifted for a few moments while everyone let that sink in.

"So, we get him back in," Summers said with a smile.

"We do," said Dinescu, handing Summers the email from Forensics. "You and Gareth can do the honours."

Chapter Thirty-Four

With a nod from Summers, Kirby restarted the interview.

"Please tell me what this is about," said the solicitor, placing her silver fountain pen down hard on her notepad.

Raymond Collier sat forward, scowling at Summers as if he were trying to read her thoughts. "They're going to tell us they don't have any more evidence to put to us. The letter was a forgery, so they have nothing."

Summers wasn't intimidated by him. She returned a smile. "I'd like to continue with what you told us about Lily trying to blackmail you."

"Why?" said Collier. "You know I didn't give her any money. You've checked my bank accounts. I told you, I snatched the letter from her and walked off."

"But I put it to you, Mr Collier," said Summers, "that you did pay her something for that letter."

His forehead creased. "Bollocks! You've seen my bank accounts! I paid her *nothing*."

"Tell me what the name Humphrey Collier means to you."

Raymond Collier froze. He didn't answer, turning his shoulder against Summers.

"Humphrey Collier, Ray. He was from Cotisham. I believe he's a relative of yours. Am I right?"

"What does this have to do with my client?" the solicitor asked.

"Shall I suspend the interview again, Mr Collier? I can easily ask your wife who Humphrey Collier was. She's been more than helpful with our enquiries so far."

"My father. Humphrey was my father."

Summers nodded. "He passed away in 2005, I believe."

"Yes, but what does my father have to do with anything?"

"We've spoken at length with Heather. She told us your father left you some items in his will, including some old books you kept on your shelves. Not much of a legacy. I believe my colleague, DC Burgess, has seen one of them—a Jack London book. Heather said she hid the letter inside your old 2004 appointments diary. Then she took it with your father's books to Lily's charity shop. It was a plan to get the letter to her without you finding out. She mentioned that you had forbidden her to talk to Lily. I think we can all guess why."

"What are you getting at?" said the solicitor.

"It's an example of controlling and coercive behaviour."

"Rubbish!" said Collier.

"Heather is terrified of you, Mr Collier. In addition to the books, she also told us about a very expensive item your father bequeathed to you. That's what you told her it was. A Rolex Submariner watch. She said you kept it at the bottom of your wardrobe. She said it never saw the light of day, and you never wore it. Is that true, Mr Collier?"

Collier screwed his eyes. "So what? Yes. I didn't like to get it out. I thought it was ugly."

"Do you still have that watch?" Summers asked.

"I don't know. I haven't seen it for a long time."

"You don't know? It's worth somewhere in the region of thirty to thirty-five thousand pounds, and you don't know if you still have it?"

"I have no idea what it's worth. It's probably a forgery, knowing my father."

"It isn't a forgery. Heather remembers seeing it a few weeks ago in your wardrobe."

"Then I still have it."

The solicitor shuffled. "I don't understand where this line of questioning is going, DS Summers."

Summers nodded to the solicitor. "It's going somewhere very soon, I promise. Bear with me. Mr Collier, do you know Henry Rushton?"

"Who the hell is Henry Rushton?" Collier looked exasperated at his solicitor. "Why don't you do something?"

"Let the officer ask her question, Mr Collier," said the solicitor. "I'm intrigued to know what this is about as much as you are."

"Did you give him your watch?"

Collier grabbed the edge of the table. "I've never heard of Henry Rushton!"

"He's Joseph McKinley's son."

"No, the watch is mine. Why would I give it to a stranger?"

"We have evidence that puts Henry Rushton on Mill Lane and the marshes with Lily when you were with her."

"But it was McKinley."

"You told us you never saw his face. Henry has the same height and build as his father. It would be easy to be confused."

"I..." Collier licked his lips. "I thought it was McKinley."

"We've also arrested Henry, and when we searched his apartment, we found a Rolex Submariner watch. He was concerned that we'd think he'd stolen it."

"It must be a different watch."

"A different watch. Is that your explanation?"

"Well, yes. It must be, as I haven't given the watch to anyone!"

"If I took you to your house," said Kirby, "would you be able to show me that watch in your wardrobe?"

Collier didn't answer. Beads of sweat had formed on his forehead.

Summers tapped the point of her pen on her notepad. "That Rolex Submariner was worth somewhere between thirty and thirty-five thousand pounds. It belonged to Roger Wallace, the murdered police officer. You knew him. He was murdered on Fishbourne Marshes in 2004."

"I know who Wallace was, for God's sake! I arrested McKinley for his murder."

"We seized his watch from Henry Rushton's flat when we arrested him today."

"Roger didn't own a bloody Rolex watch! Not on his wages."

"We've confirmed the serial number with Rolex and spoken to Roger's family. The watch belonged to Roger's father, who passed it on to him as a gift when Roger became a detective. And now, as you've probably already guessed, we are checking for his DNA." Summers paused for a short while, watching Collier's reaction. "How did Henry Rushton come into possession of Roger Wallace's Rolex watch?"

"How should I know? It can't be my watch."

"Your wife has identified the watch as the one you kept in your wardrobe."

Collier turned away, dismissing Summers with a wave of his hand. "I know nothing about it. McKinley must have stolen it when he killed Roger and passed it on to his son. Simple."

"But you arrested McKinley, Ray. You just told us that. Your statement said you caught McKinley with his hands on Roger

Wallace. According to your statement at the time, there was no mention of any watch."

"No comment." Collier clenched his fists and sat back.

"No comment?" Summers smiled. "Tell me now how your father could have bequeathed this watch to you if it belonged to Roger Wallace."

"No comment."

"Heather told me she had once shown Lily the watch and told her how much it was worth. Maybe you'd undervalued it, Mr Collier."

"I… no comment."

"Lily knew about the watch. When she blackmailed you, did she ask for the watch in exchange for the letter?"

"No comment."

"I suggest you gave Lily the watch, and she handed over the letter. You were probably glad to be rid of it. The thing is, you already knew the letter was a forgery because you didn't write it. But Lily had got it right, even though she thought she was making it up. You really did murder Roger Wallace, as she described. Why else would you give her that expensive watch in exchange for the letter?"

Collier stared at the floor. "No comment."

Summers glanced at the solicitor. "Mr Collier, listen carefully to me."

"Why should I? This is all fantasy."

"I'm further arresting you on suspicion of the murder of PC Roger Wallace in January 2004, on suspicion of perverting the course of justice, and misconduct in public office. You are still under caution. Do you have any reply?"

Collier groaned, kicking his legs forward. Summers saw his eyes moving from side to side, trying to conjure an answer from somewhere. His face suddenly changed. A light had come on inside. "Okay. After I arrested McKinley, I took the watch from

Roger. I knew it was valuable, so I stole it from him. I stole the watch, but I didn't kill Roger."

Summers glanced at Kirby and flashed a smile. "We thought you might say that."

"My client has confessed to stealing PC Wallace's watch," said the solicitor, "not to murdering him."

"I understand that," said Summers with a confident smile. She took a sip of water and nodded at Kirby. He removed a sheet of paper from his folder.

"Is this your baton, Raymond?" asked Kirby. He brought out a photograph of the rusty baton and holster sent to them from the forensics lab. "This is produced as exhibit BD/04." He pointed to the photo. "I believe that's your old warrant number written on the side."

Raymond was wide-eyed when he saw it. "How? How did you find it?"

"We didn't," said Summers. "Lily did—a year after you killed Roger Wallace. She didn't think it would be enough to convict you. She wasn't to know we'd find traces of Roger's blood and hair trapped in the holster. You'd dropped it in the old pillbox. How did Roger's blood get on your baton?" Collier froze, barely breathing. Summers could tell from his face that he knew he was done for. He knew it was over. "Answer the question, Mr Collier."

"No comment."

"Come on, Mr Collier! You know how it works—you know you must answer this now."

"I don't know what to say," said Collier, staring at the table.

Collier's solicitor nodded at Summers.

Summers sat back and sighed. "Okay. Let's bring this to a conclusion. If you want to give me an answer, then feel free to interrupt. The watch will go through extensive DNA testing. Since you stored it away so well, we expect to find Roger's DNA caught between the links as well as yours. There should also be fibres, dust, and other particles from the bottom of your wardrobe. From your background in policing and forensics, would you agree with that, Mr Collier?"

Collier nodded. "Yes."

"We already have Roger's blood and DNA on the baton and the holster. As soon as we get the forensic results back for the watch, we are going to the CPS with what we have to charge you with Roger Wallace's murder. The Criminal Cases Review Commission will be hearing from us soon to apply to have Joseph McKinley's conviction quashed."

"That's understood," said Collier's solicitor.

Summers stretched her arms above her head and then reached for her drink. She took a sip. "Now, we must consider if you murdered Lily, too. Perhaps with Henry Rushton's help and with the watch as payment."

"I didn't kill Lily," said Collier. "I gave her the watch, she put it on, and I walked away. The matter was closed. I knew if she tried to sell it, it would flag up as belonging to Roger's father."

"Can we all agree it was Roger's watch, then?"

Collier nodded, his eyes glazed, and his face darkened. "Yes."

"Thank you. Now you know what evidence we have, I will ask you again. Did you murder Roger Wallace and frame Joseph McKinley for Roger's murder?"

"Yes." Collier looked down at the table and spoke slowly. "Heather was all I had. Roger was taking her away from me. He was everything I wasn't. Not only was he good-looking, but he would listen to her. I borrowed an unmarked job car and spied on my bloody wife. Can you imagine what that does to a man? I saw him go into my house, and Heather shut the bedroom curtains. Half an hour later, I watched him leave. I had to do something. I didn't want to lose her. He'd been bragging about that bloody watch and how his dad was so proud of him. All my father gave me was a set of manky books."

"Heather told us about her affair with Roger. Did the idea of working with Roger that week drive you over the edge? Was that the last straw?"

"I had to do something. I called him to join me for a job on the marshes. I was watching McKinley picking up packages. A drugs operation. I knew McKinley was a loser, and no one would miss him. I waited on the footbridge for Roger. I distracted him and then hit him with my baton. I took the watch. That was the only part I was glad about. I dragged his body into the marsh and sank him deep."

"How did you frame Joseph McKinley?"

Collier sobbed angry tears. "After I'd killed Wallace, I went to the pillbox, as that's where McKinley kept that hook thing he used to retrieve the drug packages from the water. I wiped the bloody side of the baton along the pole, but I must have left the baton in there. I had to be quick."

"What did you do with the pole?"

"I threw it into the reeds. I knew McKinley would be turning up soon, and when he came back over the bridge, I called him for help to get Roger's body out of the creek. He did just that. The most stupid thing he's ever done. I nicked him, put Roger's neck chain into McKinley's pocket, and called for assistance."

"You locked up an innocent man in a secure hospital for twenty years," said Kirby.

"I know. But who would miss him?"

Kirby shook his head. "You have no regrets about what you did?"

Collier shrugged. "He was a drug user. Scum."

"When Lily guessed you'd killed Roger Wallace, how did you live with that? Was that too much for you? Too much of a threat?"

"I didn't kill Lily. I left her on the bridge. I knew the letter was a forgery. She was only guessing. She had Roger's watch, and I didn't want it back."

The solicitor put down her fountain pen and sighed. "Unless you have more evidence, Mr Collier has answered your questions. You've had his honest confession regarding Roger Wallace, and I think we'd all like a break now."

Summers nodded and ended the interview. She knew it was all over for Raymond Collier.

Chapter Thirty-Five

Henry Rushton sat with his head on the table, resting on top of his hands. The wound on his forehead was weeping. He had sat like this since entering the room and throughout the entire interview. His solicitor shrugged at Booker.

"Henry," said Booker, "I will continue asking you questions. I'm going to assume, unless your solicitor says otherwise, that your lack of response is no comment. I've gone over how we followed your phone to your mother's car and then your return to Fishbourne on the train. It won't surprise you that we have you on CCTV at Arundel Railway Station, waiting for the Fishbourne train. How would you explain that?"

Rushton lifted his head and sighed. "I owed twenty grand to someone who was going to kill me if I didn't pay it back." He rubbed his eyes and sat back, staring at the ceiling.

"That's serious money, Henry," said Booker.

"Do you think?" he scoffed. "I was dealing rocks from my flat. I had to buy stock somehow, so I got a loan. Then someone broke into my flat. Everything was gone, and if I didn't repay the loan, I was dead. Simple—that's how it works. My birth mother turned up out of the blue one day. She wanted to be all nicey-

nicey and get me back with my real father again. But they dumped me when I was a kid. So, I told her I was in debt from uni. I'd dropped out, but she never knew that." Rushton smirked. "She gave me some money, and I paid back those people to stop them from killing me. But I needed more. Lily said she would give me the money. She said she had a plan."

"Did she tell you her plan?"

"Yeah. Devious really. She'd blackmailed this ex-copper. She said he'd framed Joseph, my birth father. I didn't give a shit about any of that. I just needed the money."

"Tell me what happened when you met your mother on Fishbourne Marshes."

"It was bloody early!" Rushton rubbed his eyes again. "I was there in case the ex-copper got a bit jumpy."

"He was already there when I arrived. The sky was getting lighter, but it was still hard to see. Lily and the police guy— Collier, his name was—talked for a few minutes. He gave her the watch, and she checked it with a torch. Then she gave him something in a brown envelope. He didn't even open it. He said he didn't want to hear from her again and left."

"Did they argue or fight?" asked Kirby.

"Not while I was there," said Rushton. "He could have come back later, I suppose."

"Collier left with the letter, and Lily had the watch."

"What happened then?"

"Lily gave the watch to me so I could sell it. She wanted me to dump her car. She said something incriminating was in there. She gave me her keys, and I drove it somewhere quiet. I made sure I didn't attract any attention. It was nerve-wracking, but I managed to find a secluded spot to leave the car near a train station. I got the train back to pick up my car."

"Lily gave you the watch. Was Lily okay when you last saw her?"

"Yes. She was fine. She said she was waiting for Joseph to come."

"You then drove her car to Crossbush, walked back to Arundel station, and then caught the train to Fishbourne to get your car."

"Yes."

"Why didn't Lily go with you to dump the car?"

"No point. She had to wait for Joseph. Lily was fine when I left her. She asked me to get rid of her car. That's all it was. I didn't ask too many questions. I just did what she asked. I needed the money, and this was my way out. I had nothing to do with her death."

Booker looked at Kirby, who nodded. "Okay, interview suspended at 16:48."

The team had stayed on late, sitting in the office. Burgess had arranged cover for Rosie. She didn't want to miss the results of the interviews. Booker returned with food orders, ranging from fried chicken to burgers. Dirty refs, he called it. It was a working supper.

Summers got off the phone with the CPS, and her expression gave nothing away. "The news is…" She did a short drum roll on her desk. "They've agreed to charge Collier with Wallace's murder."

"Perfect!" Booker raised his hand to high-five Kirby and Burgess, but thought better of it when he saw Dinescu.

"Currently, there's nothing for him murdering Lily," Summers added. "Not enough evidence other than he was there. He wasn't even the last one to leave the crime scene."

"Did Rushton do it alone?" said Kirby. "But we have nothing to negate his cock-and-bull story that Lily wanted him to burn out her car."

"I agree," said Dinescu. "Cocks and bulls everywhere."

Summers laughed. "Not exactly how I would have said it, but yes, boss."

"What did Raymond Collier say about McKinley when he saw him on the footbridge?" asked Kirby.

"He thought McKinley had tried to disguise himself with a hat and scarf," said Summers.

"And carrying a stick behind him," said Kirby. "We now know that was Rushton he saw. What happened to the stick? Was that the pickaxe handle he kept behind his door?"

"Where is this pickaxe handle?" asked Dinescu.

"We seized it," replied Kirby. "Sarah sent it to Forensics. We should get some results back tomorrow."

"Good," said Dinescu, picking up a piece of fried chicken with a napkin. "Then this is what we do. First, we'll enjoy our meal together and relax a little. We've been at this for hours, and some food will do us all good. Then, I will request a custody extension for Rushton. I'm hoping our forensics results will be back soon. Last, after finishing our delicious food, we charge Collier with Wallace's murder and update his wife. I will update McKinley tonight. He deserves to know sooner than anyone. You can all go home. You have all done well. Thank you."

The doors to Dean Court were locked, but Dinescu found a buzzer on the side of the wall.

"Who is it?" said a voice with a crackle.

"It's the police."

"One minute."

A man in a checked shirt and a sleeveless jacket appeared out of the dark and stood behind the glass.

Dinescu showed him his warrant card, and the man opened the

automatic doors with a key. "I'm Detective Chief Inspector Dinescu from Chichester Major Crimes. I'd like to speak with Joseph McKinley."

The man frowned. "Haven't you finished with Joseph yet? He was doing well before all this happened."

"I can understand that. Who am I speaking to?"

"I'm Jeff, one of Joseph's support workers. He's not in a good place at the moment."

"May I speak with him, please? I have some news that may give him some hope."

"Hope? You're not from around here, are you? I'll knock on his door and see if he'll talk to you, but I doubt it." Jeff turned to walk away.

"Tell him we know about Collier."

"Collier? Okay."

Dinescu waited inside. The reception area was dim, lit by a frosted security light, and the air carried a lingering pine anti-septic scent. He sat on a padded chair and looked through his personal mobile phone for messages and emails.

"What about Collier?" McKinley said, standing in the semi-darkness. His voice was gruff and angry. "Are you going to nick me again? Is that it?"

Dinescu stood. "No, Mr McKinley. Far from it. First, you are no longer under investigation for Lily's murder."

"And?"

"Second, I will be contacting the Criminal Cases Review Commission. There has been a miscarriage of justice. This evening, we've charged Raymond Collier with the murder of PC Roger Wallace. He has made a full and frank confession and admitted to framing you. We can prove you are innocent, Mr McKinley."

McKinley gasped, his face contorted. He grabbed the reception desk and looked like he was about to fall. Dropping to his knees, he let loose a loud and heart-wrenching wail. Jeff ran to him and put his arm around his shoulder.

Dinescu watched McKinley, not knowing if he would lash out or compose himself. McKinley's anguish was palpable as he gasped for air. After a few minutes, he brushed off Jeff and made his way up onto his feet again. He wiped his eyes and nose on his sleeve.

"How?" he said.

"The evidence against him was overwhelming. We've charged Collier now, so I can't go into details. Lily had found something, but she didn't realise exactly how important it would be for you. Did you not get her message? She'd kept it to herself at first, but she wanted you to have it in case it could help prove your innocence. She'd left a package for you in the pillbox on the marshes. It was Raymond Collier's police baton."

"Oh, shit!" McKinley sat on one of the sponge chairs to catch his breath. "She sent me a message. She said there was a package in the pillbox for me. I thought it was about the money she was getting from Collier. I didn't want it. I just wanted justice. She said she could give me justice!" He looked up at Dinescu, his face now in shadow. "Collier's baton? Did he hit Roger with it?"

"I'm not at liberty to say, but it will come out in a future trial. It's a shame Lily didn't come forward with it sooner. But, here." Dinescu handed McKinley the note from Lily, and he held it up to the emergency lights so he could read it.

As McKinley read Lily's note, his hands trembled, and tears welled up in his eyes. "She had it all that time?" he choked out, his voice breaking.

Dinescu nodded. "We will be referring your case very soon. I can't tell you everything yet, but we've arrested your son, and enquiries are ongoing concerning Lily's murder."

"Henry? That brat. I don't call him my son."

"Mr McKinley, an apology from me is all I have at the

moment. The best I can do is to see that you are completely exonerated for Roger Wallace's murder."

"It was Collier. Not you. Thank you."

"We will be in touch very soon."

Dinescu left Jeff with McKinley, glancing back to see an innocent man set free before he stepped out into the night. He pulled out a tissue, dried his eyes, and called Lisa.

"I'm coming home," he said. "Let's all watch a film together. Have a family night."

Chapter Thirty-Six

Wednesday

Emily woke to the sound of her radio alarm clock. Rolling over, she covered her face with her pillow and groaned. After a restless night's sleep, she didn't want to face the world today. Her eyes were bleary, and her mind drifted sleepily from work to Kieran, her mother, and then, for some reason unknown, her father.

Something had been going on in her sleep, and she had been dreaming of him, remembering that scene when she last saw him. She was with her mother, who looked beautiful in her blue dress and had golden blonde hair in those days. They were watching her father leave on a ferry heading for Spain. How much of this was a memory and how much was imaginary, Emily didn't know. They stood on the Round Tower in Southsea, overlooking the entrance to Portsmouth Harbour. When her father's ship sailed by, she and her mother waved at the people lined up on the deck. She remembered frantically scanning the faces for her father in his brown bomber jacket. She'd hoped he'd seen her in that bright red dress. She'd imagined he was waving back all her life, but, being honest with herself, she realised she had never seen him there. The memory left her feeling hollow and cold.

She lay there, staring at the ceiling, trying to shake off the unease that had settled in her chest. A thought nagged at her, but she couldn't quite grasp it. She closed her eyes, willing herself to drift back to sleep, but the image of her father's ship lingered, refusing to fade.

As she got out of bed, the nagging thought grew stronger, more insistent. She shuffled to the bathroom, splashing cold water on her face, hoping to wash away the remnants of her dream. But the feeling persisted, a gnawing sensation that something important was just out of reach.

"The red dress?" she muttered. The significance of it tugged at her mind, but she couldn't place it.

A gentle tingling started at the back of her neck and grew, crawling over her as if her blood had turned ice cold.

"The red dress!"

She hurried into the lounge and turned on the light. It was still dark outside, so there was little point pulling back the curtains. She took the open envelope from the bookshelf and read the letter.

"Dad!" she said.

Emily paced the floor, pulling at her hair in frustration. She went back for her mobile to call her mother, but she froze. What if she was mistaken? What would this do to her mother? Would she want to know after all this time? But maybe she knew something Emily didn't about her father—something she had kept secret from her.

The letter trembled in her hand as she read it once again. The words seemed to blur together, her mind racing. She smelled the paper and envelope, hoping for some faint scent of cologne to bring back memories of her father.

Emily didn't know what to do. Was he making contact after all these years? He wanted to meet her. And now she knew where. Did he see her waving goodbye?

$$\sim$$

"How long has Rushton left on his custody clock?" asked Burgess as she put down the tray of coffees.

Summers's mind returned to the room, still thinking about her father. She looked at the time on her mobile. "Three hours and forty minutes. After that, we'll need to give the magistrate a good reason to keep him in."

"No news from Forensics yet, Sarge?" Booker asked.

Summers shook her head. She looked into Dinescu's office and saw he had shut his door—he was on the phone, and his face looked grim.

"Is there anything we could have missed?" said Summers. "I don't want this to fall at the last hurdle. We've come so far."

"We still don't know what happened to Lily's clothes," said Kirby. "We searched Rushton's flat and car, so he may have thrown them on the way home."

"What about in Lily's car?" said Burgess.

"It's a complete burn-out," said Kirby.

Summers's desk phone rang, and she jumped. "DS Summers."

"Good morning. It's Rick Griffin, crime scene manager for Operation Brook."

"Hi, Rick. Do you have something for us?"

"Yes."

Summers held up her hand, signalling the team to be quiet. "Go ahead."

Rick was shuffling papers. "Where shall I start?"

Summers saw Dinescu coming out of his office, so she clicked a button on her phone. "You're on speakerphone, Rick. I want the team to hear this."

"Great. Hello, all. Let's start with the burglary. The lab has found traces of Henry Rushton's DNA on the smashed computer in Lily's bedroom. We found one of his fingerprints on the living room door handle, but none on the computer. They believe Rushton wore gloves when he broke the computer, but he may have touched his face while wearing them, transferring his DNA to the computer on some skin cells."

"Why wasn't he wearing gloves when he touched the door handle?" asked Burgess.

"Good question," said Griffin. "I've seen this before. He could have been to the house previously."

"That's something I hadn't thought about," said Summers. "Anything found on Mellor's jewellery box?"

"No," said Griffin. "So that's all we have on the burglary. Next, Lily Watson's car." Griffin shuffled paperwork again. "As expected, the fire obliterated all traces of DNA and fingerprints. In the glove box, we recovered the remains of a mobile phone. The battery had exploded in the heat. Now, I do have a but…"

"I like a big but," said Summers.

"So do I," said Griffin. "In the boot space of the Mini, we found the burned remains of clothing. Melted nylon from tights. Lumps of melted and charred polyester. Interestingly, we recovered the soles of two black leather platform boots, a size seven, narrow fit. There's a distinctive MK buckle on each boot."

"Michael Kors?"

"That's the one."

"There's a long zip from a coat, and that's it. Oh, and no keys found."

"That's amazing. Thanks, Rick. Do you have the results from the pickaxe handle yet?"

"Not yet. Expecting it back soon."

"Can you tell DCI Dinescu something for me?"

"I'm listening, Rick," said Dinescu.

"Ah, good morning! The fragment of material you found in the bramble bushes had blood belonging to Lily Watson on it. Your guess was right about her being snagged there. We don't believe she was trying to hide from someone. It appears to be from a cuff on a sleeve, possibly poking out from her jacket. That corresponds to the scratches on her arm."

"Thank you, Rick," said Dinescu.

After the call, Summers looked at the notes she had made, and Dinescu walked to the window.

"There's one defence explanation for the fingerprint," said Burgess. "Lily brought him to her house, and she showed him something on the computer."

"But his prints weren't on it," said Booker. "Just his DNA."

"We won't disclose this to his solicitor," said Summers. "Let's see what Rushton says." She looked at Dinescu. "Those boot buckles, sir. They're very distinctive."

Dinescu nodded and smiled. "Who's calling Mellor?"

"Sarah," said Summers. "Call Mellor. What brand of boots did Lily own? Get her to describe them."

Burgess got on her mobile and walked to the window next to Dinescu.

"If this is what I think it is," said Summers, "then there may be enough here to charge Rushton."

"Don't count on it," said Dinescu. "We don't know for certain what Lily was wearing when she was killed."

"I believe we do, sir. Her dress, anyway."

"So when did Lily have a chance to hide the package?" Booker asked.

Dinescu looked at the whiteboard and read out the times from the mobile phone data. "07:34 Lily's phone arrives on the marshes, 07:40 Collier's phone appears, and 07:45 Rushton arrives. She had a theoretical maximum of six minutes to hide it in the pillbox. She could have done it."

Burgess returned, her expression intense. "Yolanda confirmed the boots, Sarge. They're Michael Kors, size seven, with those distinctive buckles. She said Lily wore them often, especially with her favourite dress."

"That's about it, then," said Summers. "We're back at the same question. Was it Collier, Rushton, or both of them working together? Which one do you think, sir?"

Chapter Thirty-Seven

Summers and Burgess waited for Henry Rushton and his solicitor in the interview room. Summers could feel the butterflies that afternoon. A swirling mixture of thoughts and feelings competed for her attention. Her father, this case, and Kieran.

"Are you okay, Sarge?" asked Burgess.

Summers smiled. "I think so, Sarah. The letter I received last week—it wasn't from those men at the nightclub."

"Not Anthony, surely!" Burgess's eyes were wide.

"No. Thank God. It was from my father. He's resurfaced after all these years."

"Your father? I don't understand."

"I'll tell you about it soon. I'm going to Southsea on Saturday to meet him. To the harbour."

"Are you sure? Do you want company? It might be difficult."

"You have Rosie. I can't—"

"I'd like to help, and Rosie will love to see the boats."

"Okay. Thank you, Sarah. I appreciate it. I haven't told my mother yet. I'm not sure how to do that."

The door opened. Rushton entered the room with the same solicitor he had the day before. They settled themselves down, and Rushton's face gave nothing away. He was nonchalant, uncaring.

The solicitor looked at his watch. "You have three hours and ten minutes left on the clock, DS Summers. You will have to charge or release Mr Rushton."

"I know how it works," said Summers. "I've done this a few times before." Summers nodded at Burgess to continue. Burgess restarted the interview, and the detectives introduced themselves for the recording.

"The last time we spoke to you, Henry," said Burgess, "you told us that your mother had asked you to dump her car because she told you it contained incriminating evidence. Is that what you are still telling us?"

"Yes," said Rushton.

"Did she ask you to set fire to her car?"

"Yes."

"To destroy her evidence?" repeated Burgess.

"Yes."

"And then you told us you walked to Arundel railway station, took a train to Fishbourne, and recovered your own vehicle."

Rushton sat forward and smiled. "Exactly as I said."

"How was Lily when you left her on Fishbourne Marshes?"

"Again, she was fine. She said she was waiting for Joseph. She was standing on the footbridge."

"What was she wearing?" asked Burgess.

"I don't remember exactly. A coat, maybe a skirt, and boots."

"What kind of boots?"

Rushton frowned. Summers was glad to see his nonchalance wearing off.

"How would I know?"

"Lily owned a pair of Michael Kors black leather platform boots," said Summers.

"Did that Yolanda woman tell you that?" Rushton scoffed.

"Were those the ones she was wearing?"

"I don't know!"

"Her friend Yolanda remembers she was wearing them when she left the house on Sunday. We've checked some CCTV of Lily standing outside a pub in Chichester on Sunday evening. The boots she was wearing looked very much like them."

"So?"

Burgess smiled and looked at Summers to continue.

"The buckle, Henry," said Summers. "They have a distinctive buckle."

"What are you getting at, DS Summers?" the solicitor asked, not hiding his irritation. "You have three hours and five minutes left."

"A forensics team found the remains of those boots in Lily's burnt-out car. They were her size, and she only owned one pair. We also found the remains of tights or stockings, a coat, and other clothing items. We have requested further analysis of those."

Rushton was pale and clammy. He looked at his solicitor, waiting for him to say something.

"The obvious question coming now, Henry," said Burgess, "is how did Lily's boots get into the back of her car?"

"Maybe she changed, and she had something else on."

"You said she was wearing boots."

"I can't remember what they looked like. In fact, she told me she'd had to change her shoes. She didn't want them to get muddy."

"Lily was wearing only knickers and a bra when her killer left her. Her clothes likely cut from her body."

"That's terrible," said Rushton.

"Did you murder Lily? Did you strike the side of her head, drag her into Fishbourne Creek, and hold her under the water to drown her?"

"No!"

"Did you remove her clothes to hide any forensic evidence you may have left behind?"

Rushton scoffed again. "You people have evil minds, you know that!"

"Am I right in saying you didn't want to share the money you'd make from selling that watch? She was going to share it with your father and you. You wanted it all. Did that annoy you, Henry?"

"No!"

"Can I have some time with my client, please?" said the solicitor. "And he will also need to eat."

Burgess looked at Summers. "Interview suspended."

A detention officer led Rushton and his solicitor into a consulting room, while Summers and Burgess walked back into the custody area. A woman was being booked in with two young PCs standing beside her. Summers found a custody sergeant and slumped her head on the counter of the custody bridge.

"Can you put me in one of your cells?" said Summers. "I'm tired, and I need sleep."

The sergeant laughed. "There are plenty to choose from today."

Kirby found her and Burgess. "Sarge, we've got the forensic results back on the pickaxe handle."

Summers stood upright. "Go on."

"No DNA from Lily. Sorry."

"Bugger!" Kirby's news smarted. "Sarah, let's grab a quick drink and regroup."

"Rushton's asked for his lunch," said the custody sergeant. "We have chicken casserole or vegetable lasagne. Do you want me to delay it?"

"Hmm." Summers grimaced. "Without solid forensic evidence, I can't see how the CPS will agree to charge him. We'll be back in thirty minutes. Tell him to hurry with his food."

Dinescu now had the results back from Digital Forensics on Rushton's phone. When he walked into the Major Crimes office, he saw Summers slumped at her desk, with red marks on her forehead where she had been rubbing it. The other members of the team looked just as despondent. None of them wanted to see Rushton let off. Yet they knew, without the forensic evidence to link him to Lily's death, Rushton's account still had room for doubt.

"Perhaps we've discounted Collier's involvement in Lily's murder too quickly," Summers said. "It's the same MO as Wallace's murder and everything. Collier was trying to implicate McKinley again."

"He's stupid if he was," said Burgess. "It's far too obvious someone was trying to set up McKinley."

Dinescu looked through the window, and a rare moment of sunshine sparked an idea.

"Come on. Everyone get your coats on," he said. "We're going for a walk."

The team looked at each other, confused.

"A walk, sir?" said Booker.

Dinescu was already putting on his jacket. "Yes, Gareth. Follow me. I may even treat you."

Dinescu led his team from the police station and towards the city centre. None of them knew what his idea was, but they were enjoying the fresh air and breaking sunlight despite the cold.

After a short walk, they ended up in a cosy café opposite the cathedral. It had two floors, and the team went upstairs. It wasn't busy, but Dinescu led them to a far corner after ordering drinks and pastries. He didn't want them to be overheard.

"Thanks, boss," said Kirby. "I'm a bit confused, but grateful."

Dinescu looked at his team. "I used to do this when bogged

down by a problem in the Met. A change of scenery helps the brain think differently. It stops us falling into the same thought patterns."

The team received their drinks and pastries with thanks.

"What do you hope to achieve, sir?" Summers asked, looking around her to make sure no one else was nearby.

"Listen carefully." He leant forward and lowered his voice. "Digital Forensics has come back with Rushton's Internet search results. For at least the last three weeks, he's been searching for information on his father and the Roger Wallace case. He's researched exactly how Roger died—a blow to the head and drowning. He searched for how to avoid DNA contamination and how long it takes for someone to drown."

"Shit!" said Summers, with a mouthful of Danish pastry.

"Precisely," Dinescu continued, "and he's looked up the Chichester Harbour tide times."

"Well, that's pretty damning, boss," said Kirby. "I'm hoping for Rushton's bank records to be sent to me by the end of the day. Hopefully, there'll be something in there we can use, too."

Summers pointed at Kirby. "Get straight on to those when they come in, Chester."

Dinescu licked his fingers clean. "The research into the tides is sinister."

"And why would he want to know that," said Summers, "other than to know if the water would be deep enough to drown Lily?"

"We are all too stuck on the weapon that knocked Lily unconscious," said Dinescu. "We may never find it, but there is a lot of other evidence we have. He had the opportunity. We can put him there at the time. We have a motive. Rushton tried to sell the watch to pay off his drug debts. The means of killing Lily was to force her under the water. We have the corroborating evidence of his Internet searches."

"So, we can go to the CPS to charge him, can't we?" asked Booker.

Dinescu tucked his bottom lip under his teeth. He shook his head. "I just feel there's something we're missing, Gareth. I wonder if we're only looking at this from one perspective. It's like someone is making a donkey out of me."

Booker laughed. "No one could call you a donkey, boss. Your ears—"

Burgess nudged him hard, shaking her head.

Dinescu couldn't help but laugh, yet in the back of his mind, the thought was bothering him. Someone was getting away with murder.

Chapter Thirty-Eight

Burgess restarted the interview. The solicitor addressed Summers while Rushton sat back, the smirk returning to his face.

"My client has given you an account of the remains of Lily Watson's clothing found in the boot of her car. He has already told you his mother asked him to look after them. He forgot they were there when he set fire to the vehicle. That is all he will say on the matter, and he now refuses to answer any further questions."

Summers nodded. "Thank you. That's very interesting, but I have a few more questions for you, which I strongly advise you to answer."

"No comment," said Rushton.

"That wasn't a question." Summers sat forward and looked Rushton in the eye. "Digital Forensics has reviewed your mobile phone since we arrested you yesterday morning. They're not entirely done yet, but they've found something interesting. Something in your search history. Do you want to make any comment so far, Henry?"

Rushton looked at his solicitor, who shook his head. "No comment."

"That's your *deleted* search history, Henry."

Henry's eyes flicked up to look at Summers. He shook his head.

Summers continued. "Tell us why you were searching for tide times in Chichester Harbour a few days before Lily's death."

"No comment."

"Why did you research PC Roger Wallace's death, specifically *how* he died?"

Rushton shifted in his chair. "No comment."

"Here we are." Summers produced a sheet of printed paper. "This is a list of your Google searches taken from your mobile phone." Summers held up the sheet of paper to show him. "You can see it's a long list. You had deleted them, but our digital forensic team recovered them. Allow me to read them out. *PC Wallace death Fishbourne 2004*. And, *PC Roger Wallace death McKinley trial 2004, how did PC Wallace die Fishbourne 2004?* Those are just a few of your search queries. Explain them to me."

Rushton glared back at Summers. "No comment."

"Come on, Henry. This is your opportunity to give us your account. Why won't you do that? If this goes to court, the judge may direct the jury to disregard any answers you give at trial if you don't answer now."

"No comment." Rushton looked down.

"The page you opened detailed how Roger Wallace died. How he received a blow to his head that rendered him unconscious. How he was then held under the water in the creek by the footbridge. Why were you interested in this?"

"No comment."

"Listen carefully, Henry." Summers lowered her gaze to meet Rushton's. "Why did you research how to avoid DNA contamination?"

Rushton sighed. "No comment."

"And…" Summers brought out another printed page of a

search entry. "Why did you want to know how long it takes for someone to drown? Can't you see how this looks, Henry?"

"I don't care," said Henry.

"You don't care? You wanted to know how PC Wallace died? It's near enough exactly the same way Lily died, the woman who gave birth to you. Exactly the same. Were you trying to frame Joseph McKinley, your father?"

Rushton clenched and unclenched his hands. He licked his lips as if he were going to answer. "No comment."

"Lily had found the baton that Raymond Collier had used to strike PC Wallace on the side of the head. Did she tell you, Henry? Did she show it to you?"

"No comment!"

"Why were you trying to frame your father?"

"I don't care who he is!" Rushton punched the table. "He's *not* my father."

Sighing, Summers looked at his solicitor in disbelief. "Henry, is there anything you would like to add or clarify with me?"

"No comment."

Summers glanced at Burgess. "We'll soon submit our evidence to the CPS for a charging decision." She checked her watch again. "Your solicitor wrongly believes we only have forty-five minutes to release or charge you. That isn't so. My colleagues are currently speaking with a magistrate. We're awaiting the rest of your phone's data, deleted or not. We will be requesting the full total of ninety-six hours to hold you. We won't need that, hope-fully. You'll be charged with Lily's murder by then. Interview terminated at 16:05."

The team was sitting in the conference room. Dinescu looked around at the tired faces. The magistrate had granted the extension on Rushton's custody clock, and now they were stuck in limbo. They had sent the paperwork to the CPS and were waiting for a response.

"Did they give you an estimate of how long it would take?" asked Booker.

"Four hours," said Burgess. "That would make it gone eleven."

"I have other cases to catch up on," said Booker, rubbing his face and yawning.

"Are you still bothered by something, boss?" Summers asked, tilting her head as she looked at Dinescu. "I can tell. You have that look."

He smiled. "Yes, Emily, I am."

"Donkeys again? Is someone trying to make fools of us?"

"I believe so."

"What could we have missed, sir?"

"I don't know. It's obvious Rushton was trying to implicate his father. The drowning, the location, even the strike on the head."

Kirby's phone pinged. "Late in the day, but better late than never. It's Rushton's bank records. Give me a minute, Sarge. I'll open them on my computer."

Kirby left the room for a few minutes while the others swapped ideas between them.

Summers stared into the air. "You said even the strike on the head, sir."

"Yes. Collier used his baton."

"But Rushton didn't have access to Collier's baton," said Burgess. "It was in the pillbox. He wouldn't have known it was there."

Summers nodded, and Kirby returned to the room with multiple copies of Rushton's bank transactions. They all took a copy and read through them.

"They go back three months," said Kirby.

Burgess frowned. "Why is he three grand better off at the beginning of January?"

"His mother gave him some Christmas money," said Booker.

"That was cash," said Burgess, "and only eight hundred."

"Here!" said Kirby. "A transfer of three thousand pounds on the 6th of January."

"From Yolanda Mellor?" Booker asked. "Why was she sending him money? Was he blackmailing her about those paintings?"

Summers's head was elsewhere for a few moments, calculating. Her lips moved as she spoke to herself.

"Emily?" said Dinescu. "What is it?"

"You're right, boss!" Summers slapped her hands on the table, and the empty coffee cups jumped. "What if Rushton *had* been in the house before the day Lily was killed? And then that burglary on Monday evening! What if he wasn't taking something from the house but was bringing something back? She had no idea."

He sat next to her. "Go on."

Summers lowered her excited voice and turned to face Booker. "Gareth, this is important. Call Mellor and tell her we've got Rushton in for questioning." She went back to Dinescu. "Collier's baton, sir. Lily could have shown Henry, and I wonder if it gave him an idea. I have to go."

"I'm coming with you," said Dinescu. "Sarah, call the CPS and tell them to hold off for now."

Dinescu drove, and Summers fidgeted with her seatbelt. He understood this was a risk she was taking. Whatever it was, he would back her all the way.

For most of the journey, neither of them spoke. The only

sound was the noise of the tyres on the road. He noticed the light of the setting sun through the trees and the subtle change. It was only barely perceivable, but it offered a small hope that the end of winter would soon be here.

After turning off Old Broyle Road and driving through the new estate, he parked the Ford Focus behind Mellor's car in the driveway.

"How do you want to play this?" Dinescu asked.

"I don't know, sir," she said. "She's probably processed the news about Rushton by now. I'm going to wing it."

"Wing it? You mean to improvise?"

"Yes, sir. Wing it. I have a hunch."

"Okay, Emily, I trust you." He smiled to reassure her.

"It's that donkey, sir," she said, laughing. "It's caused all sorts of trouble."

Dinescu nodded.

They got out of the car, and he saw Summers take a deep breath before ringing Mellor's doorbell. While they waited, Dinescu touched the bonnet of Mellor's car.

"It's cold. She hasn't been to work today," he said.

It was only a few moments before she answered with a confused expression.

"Do you mind if we come in, Yolanda?" said Summers. "We have a further update for you."

Mellor hesitated, her eyes flitting between the detectives. "Oh, okay. Please do. You'll have to excuse me. I'm just cooking pasta. I usually like to eat early."

Summers smiled. "Thank you."

They followed Mellor into the house, almost tripping over a small suitcase in the hallway. She led them into the kitchen, where a saucepan of water was about to boil.

Dinescu saw Summers glance into the lounge. "You've done well tidying up everything. Is that a new TV?" she asked.

Mellor frowned a little. "Yes, the old one had a crack in it after being thrown onto the floor." She stirred the boiling liquid. "What did you want to tell me? The officer's already updated me about Lily's son. It's so hard to believe!"

"We're going to charge him for Lily's murder," said Summers. "He wants to tell us everything."

"Really?" Mellor raised her eyebrows. Her neck and face flushed. "Did you say his name was Henry?"

"Henry Rushton. You haven't met him before, of course."

Mellor grabbed a tea towel as the water in the pan bubbled. Dinescu felt his palms sweating—something wasn't right.

Summers strolled into the lounge and stopped in front of the glass cabinet. "This was your grandfather's leaving present, wasn't it?" She was looking at a presentation case inside the cabinet.

"Yes," said Mellor. "He served in Pulborough and Petworth and then in Chichester." She glanced into the kitchen.

"Look at this, sir," said Summers, pointing at the case.

Dinescu came over. He knew she was trying to do something, but he was unsure what. He looked at the display case inside the glass cabinet. A whistle and some epaulettes lay on dusty black velvet, with a dark wooden truncheon beside them. The truncheon had PC Mellor's old warrant number engraved on its side.

"Very nice," said Dinescu.

"See, sir, even back then, officers used to write their warrant numbers on their kit in case they got nicked."

He understood what Summers meant.

"I'm so glad you've caught Lily's murderer!" said Mellor. "I can rest easy now, can't I? Or is there something else?"

"He's not the only one," said Summers, smiling. "Another person is outstanding. The brains behind it, as they say."

"Really? Who?" asked Mellor, wrapping her tea towel around her hands.

"You," said Summers. "I believe you planned the whole thing."

Mellor stepped back, then turned. She rushed into the kitchen. Dinescu saw it coming. He grabbed Summers's shoulders and twisted her around, throwing her into the lounge. She fell onto the coffee table, which collapsed beneath her. Dinescu had dodged most of it. A boiling, syrupy liquid stuck to his jacket, and the heat had begun to sear his arm. He threw off his jacket. Mellor tried to push past him, car keys in hand. Dinescu struck the side of her neck with the heel of his palm. She collapsed in a heap on the floor, unconscious.

Summers groaned, and Dinescu pulled her up. The back of her blouse was ripped and bloody.

"Are you okay?" he asked. "We need to get you an ambulance."

"I'm okay, sir. How about you?"

"I've felt worse."

Mellor was stirring. Dinescu handcuffed her and sat her up against a chair, still stupefied.

"The truncheon," said Dinescu.

Summers lowered her voice to a whisper. "Yes, boss."

Chapter Thirty-Nine

Thursday

Summers was none the worse for having been thrown onto the coffee table the previous evening. Thanks to her boss's intervention, she had only a few minor cuts and bruises. The only major casualty was Dinescu's jacket.

"Glad you're both okay," said Booker as he brought the team a tray of morning coffee. "What a nut job!"

"It was a close call," said Summers. "Boiling sugar solution is like napalm. I'm so grateful to the boss for realising what it was."

"What's the plan?" Burgess asked, sitting next to Booker.

Summers looked at Dinescu, who was leaning against her desk.

"Chester and DS Neil conducted the first round of interviews with Mellor last night. She's broken and telling all. She told Chester she knew we'd be coming for her when Gareth told her we had Rushton. It was risky, Emily."

"I know, boss," said Summers, "but I didn't expect her to try and maim us."

"It worked, though," said Dinescu. "Well done."

"What has she said about Rushton, boss?" asked Booker.

"She'd already hired him to kill Lily weeks before. Their argument brought things to a head. She called Rushton after Lily stormed out, and Rushton came over to Chichester to meet her."

Summers nodded. "So they finalised the plan then. Rushton used Lily's blackmail scheme as the perfect cover."

"Yes," said Dinescu. "Mellor's in pieces. We're getting a mental health nurse to go in there. It was all about being spurned by Lily. She thought she had a connection with her, especially after she painted those erotic portraits of her. She realised that it meant nothing to Lily. When Mellor found out she was having an affair with Justin, that was the moment she decided to kill her."

"The woman needs help," said Burgess.

"She does," said Dinescu, "but we're waiting to charge her with conspiracy to murder and attempted Section 18 GBH on DS Summers and me."

"I'm ready to go back in there with Rushton, sir," said Summers, "and the CPS have been updated with what we have on him."

"What's that?" asked Burgess.

"It's going to take another couple of days for the DNA to come back on the truncheon, but they found a spot of blood on it and a thumbprint of Rushton's. He wiped the grip before returning it to the display case, but must have touched it again."

"Idiot," said Booker.

"Wish us luck," said Summers. She felt a slight twinge of nerves in her gut. She wanted to see this through to the end.

Summers and Burgess grabbed their folders and, after calling ahead, went to the Custody Suite. Outside, they met Rushton's solicitor, who was vaping and scrolling through his phone.

"We need to get in there with Henry now," said Summers.

The solicitor nodded. "Not looking great for him, is it?"

Summers smiled. "We'll see, shall we?"

"Nothing more to disclose?"

"A fingerprint and blood on a truncheon, a payment from Lily Watson's friend to kill Lily, and more to come from his phone data. And the friend is telling all." Summers shook her head. "As you said, it's not looking great for him now."

The solicitor nodded and smiled. "I thought as much. He'll grass up Lily's friend, no doubt. What was it, unrequited love?"

Summers nodded.

"I'll tell him, but he won't listen to me. He will try to fight it, but there'll be a full and frank confession in the end, DS Summers."

"I hope so."

When they opened the door, Rushton was already in the interview room with a detention officer who had given him a beaker of water. His head hung low, and his eyes were focused on somewhere far away. As Burgess drew a breath, Rushton glanced up at his solicitor as he took his seat.

Burgess started the interview process while Summers got her notes together. Summers found Burgess's voice calming. That smooth lilt of her Caribbean accent filled the otherwise drab, cold room with warmth.

"Thank you, Sarah," said Summers. "Henry, I'd like to show you something." Summers pulled out the printouts of Rushton's bank account. "Your bank account transactions. Do you agree?"

Rushton looked at the printed sheets. "Yes."

"I've highlighted one transaction in yellow." She pointed to a line of text. "Three thousand pounds came into your account on Saturday, the 6th of January this year, two days before Lily Watson's murder. Referenced as *services*. Tell me about that payment, Henry."

Rushton shrugged.

"I need an answer."

"No comment."

"You won't tell me about three thousand pounds moving into your account. Were you expecting it?"

Rushton folded his arms and looked away. "No comment."

"Was it payment for something? What services were they, Henry? It must have been important. That's a lot of money."

"No comment."

"Let's take a look at who gave you this money." Summers pointed to another line of text. "*Y. Mellor*, it says. Is that Yolanda Mellor?"

"No comment."

"Still no comment. We double-checked, and it is Yolanda Mellor. What was she paying you for? You didn't know her, or did you?"

Rushton began picking at his nails. "No comment."

Summers nodded to Burgess.

"Tell us about when you met your mother in Chichester," said Burgess softly. Rushton looked at her.

"What do you mean?" Rushton asked. "I've already told you —I met her on Monday morning. She wanted me there with her to meet Collier."

"No, not on the Monday she died," said Burgess. "Before that. When did you start visiting Lily at home?"

"I've never been there," said Rushton. "She came to me."

"I would strongly advise you to answer no comment," said the solicitor to Rushton.

"You've never been to Lily's house?" Burgess pressed. "The one she shared with Yolanda."

Rushton shook his head. "No."

"Okay, I'm glad we've cleared that up." Burgess smiled and looked at her notes. "On the day Lily was murdered, you then went into Chichester city centre and tried to sell the Rolex Submariner watch you had taken from your mother."

"Did I?"

"Yes, Henry, you did. We have you on CCTV visiting various jewellers in the city and statements confirming you tried to sell them the watch. Was that part of the plan, too?"

"My mother wanted me to sell the watch. We were going to split the money."

"Did you steal the watch from her and kill her for it?"

"No!"

"Did you want all the money for yourself? Perhaps to pay off the people you owe money to and have some left over for yourself."

"No. Half of the value of the watch would have been enough."

"What did you do when you failed to sell it?"

Rushton looked at his solicitor. "I went home."

"Did you go back to Chichester?"

"No, Brighton."

"Did you try to visit Yolanda?" Burgess sat back and tilted her head.

Rushton smiled and shook his head. "No."

"Yolanda Mellor was your mother's housemate, wasn't she?"

"You know she was. Why?"

"Her house was burgled on Monday evening. The place had been ransacked."

"I'm sorry to hear that, but why are you telling me?" Rushton squinted, trying to keep a smile.

"Your DNA was found on Lily's computer. How did it get there?"

"No, it wasn't," Rushton replied, spitting out the words.

"Yes, it was. I have the evidence from the forensic laboratories here. It's a match to your DNA—one in ten billion. It's not a familial match—it is *your* DNA. If you've never been to Lily's house, how did it get there?"

"No comment," said Rushton, shifting in his chair.

"Why were you at Lily and Yolanda's house that evening?"

"No comment."

"You were there, Henry," said Burgess. "How else would your DNA be on the computer?"

"I don't... no comment."

Burgess glanced at Summers, who sat forward to take over.

"We can prove you were there," said Summers. "There's no point denying it. Shall we review the evidence we have against you? You were with Lily when she was killed. You had the thirty-five thousand pound Rolex watch Collier had given her. You tried to sell it in Chichester and later in Brighton. You took Lily's car and later burned it out to destroy evidence, including Lily's clothes. Yolanda made you a three thousand pound payment, and you were at Yolanda's house."

Rushton shook his head. "No comment."

"I put it to you, Henry, that you didn't go to Yolanda's house to burgle it."

Rushton's face flushed. "What do you mean?"

"No, you didn't, Henry. You were there to return something, and you covered your tracks by making it look like a burglary. What do you say to that?"

Rushton kicked his chair back as if he were about to stand up. "This is stupid!"

"We have the truncheon you previously took from Yolanda's display cabinet. It's currently being examined for both your DNA and Lily's DNA." Summers saw the panic in his eyes. "You've been to Yolanda's house before. Am I right?"

"No."

"Perhaps with Lily, or perhaps it was during a previous

meeting with Yolanda. I believe you took her grandfather's truncheon without her knowledge and used it to strike Lily on the head. Was it your back-up plan, Henry? Can you tell us about that?"

"I don't know anything about any truncheon!"

"I believe you faked that burglary at Yolanda's house to return the truncheon. She knew nothing about it, did she? It was your insurance. If Yolanda tried to turn the tables on you, you could point the police to the truncheon, incriminating her."

"I said I know nothing about it."

Summers smiled. "Really? We've already found your thumbprint on it. How did it get there, Henry?"

Rushton shouted, "Yolanda hated Lily! She's the one who wanted to hurt her."

"She was in love with her." Summers slowed everything down and lowered her voice. "We've arrested Yolanda for conspiracy to murder and attempted Section 18 GBH on two police officers. She's been interviewed, and she doesn't seem to care anymore. She's telling us everything. She told us all about you and how she hired you to kill Lily. She pretended she didn't know you existed, but she told us she found your birth certificate and your phone number. She told us about your money troubles too. I bet that watch was a bit of a bonus, eh? A bonus you didn't want to share. I reckon you grabbed it off Lily's wrist. Her other watch ended up in the creek. Very careless of you."

Rushton slumped into his chair, his head cast down and his arms wrapped around him. "I was in so much trouble. They were coming for me."

"I put it to you, Henry, that you were paid by Yolanda to kill Lily, your birth mother. Yolanda had had enough of Lily spurning her affection. And when she found out about you and Lily's affair with Justin, she snapped. She contacted you after learning from Lily that you were desperate for money. I believe you met up with

Yolanda at some point, and she convinced you to kill Lily for her. Is that right? Was the three-thousand pounds a down payment for murdering Lily?"

"You don't know half of it," said Rushton. He rocked in his chair, his forehead sweating.

"Henry, did you kill Lily for Yolanda?"

Rushton nodded. "Yes."

～

Dinescu took Summers with him to Portchester to meet Roger Wallace's sisters. In his pocket, he carried a small bag containing something that had remained in storage for twenty years.

It was now dark, and from where Dinescu had parked, they could see Portsmouth Harbour below them. In the distance were the curves of the Spinnaker Tower, lit in red, white, and blue. Thousands of twinkling streetlights traced the paths of the roads. On the horizon was the Isle of Wight, again sparkling with lights.

"This is big," said Summers. "Can you imagine dealing with this after twenty years?"

He shook his head. "I can't. But we've done well getting to the truth. Don't forget that, no matter how they react."

"Yes, boss." She nodded, biting her bottom lip. "I'm hungry. Fancy a monster burger on the hill after this?"

He chuckled. "Where do you put it all? You're so slim."

"The benefits of youth, sir."

"Are you calling me old?"

"Ha! I wouldn't dream of it, sir."

"Come on. Let's do this. They're waiting for us."

Penny and Jeanette welcomed Dinescu and Summers with anxious expressions, unaware of the news he was bringing. He dispensed with the pleasantries of tea and idle chat and went straight into why they were there. The sisters sat together, glancing at the photograph of Roger on the wall.

Dinescu put his hand in his pocket and pulled out the plastic bag. He handed it to Penny. She puzzled over it, but then her eyes filled with tears. She passed it to Jeanette.

"I thought it was lost," said Penny, wiping her eyes. She ripped open the bag and held the gold chain up to the light. "I bought this for him using my savings." She ran her finger over the links until she came to those that were stretched and broken. Her face showed horror at first but then hardened to resolve. "We can get that repaired."

"It was in the evidence stores," said Dinescu. "On behalf of Sussex Police, I can only apologise that we never returned it to you."

Penny nodded. "He only wore it for one day."

Jeanette looked puzzled. "How did you find Daddy's watch? We thought that was lost, too. Was that in your evidence stores?"

He shook his head. "We didn't have it. It was with the person who murdered Roger."

Penny glanced at Jeanette. "McKinley returned it?"

"No. Joseph McKinley didn't murder Roger. I'm sorry to say that there's been a terrible miscarriage of justice."

"I... I don't understand. Jeanette? What is he saying?"

Dinescu continued. "Raymond Collier framed Joseph McKinley for Roger's murder. McKinley is innocent." He felt like he had delivered a punch. "Collier admitted to killing your brother. He's up before the magistrate tomorrow. I have no doubt the court will remand him. There'll be a press release later. Now we've charged him, I'm not at liberty to go into any detail about what happened." By the time he'd finished speaking, the sisters were in each other's arms, sobbing. "I know this was difficult to hear, but I wanted to tell you personally. You will be able to have the watch back soon. I promise you."

As Dinescu and Summers stood to leave, Penny reached out her hand to his, and she squeezed it. He nodded, and no more words were said as the detectives left the house.

Summers put her arm around Dinescu as they walked to the car. "Well done, boss."

Dinescu smiled and fought back the tears. "I'll have a double-cheese monster burger. I've earned it."

Chapter Forty

Friday

Raymond Collier, Yolanda Mellor, and Henry Rushton were up before the magistrates in Portsmouth and Worthing. CID had lent its resources, and the Major Crimes Team was attending court. They had submitted the remand files, which had reached the courts on time.

Only Summers and Dinescu stayed behind. They sat together in Dinescu's office, drinking coffee and eating a cream doughnut.

"I needed this," Summers said. "A successful result, boss."

"Down to you and the team, Emily. I'll make sure your name is mentioned. I have a press conference later. Do you want to do it for me?"

"Me! That's the one thing that would kill me, being up in front of a camera."

"I was joking. Don't worry. I'm surprised you couldn't tell."

"Your face is inscrutable at times," she said.

"Inscrutable," Dinescu repeated. "I like this word."

Summers looked out of Dinescu's window and saw a tall man

in a full-dress uniform enter. "Shit! It's McBride. The Chief Constable's here."

"I know," said Dinescu. "He told me he was coming. He has Professional Standards with him."

Summers went pale. "Is everything okay, sir?"

"It's all okay, Emily. Please don't worry."

Tom McBride knocked on Dinescu's door and entered. Dinescu and Summers stood.

"Sir," said Summers. She realised she had fresh cream from her doughnut on her chin.

"Did you get one for me?" said McBride.

"No, sir," she said, wiping her chin. "Sorry, sir."

McBride laughed. "I wouldn't worry. There are a few of us coming. Emily Summers, isn't it?"

"Yes, sir."

"I've heard a lot about you. Good things, that is."

Summers blushed. "That's good to know, sir."

"Are you ready, Ben?" asked McBride.

Dinescu winked at Summers as he left, hiding his apprehension, then followed the Chief Constable.

Dinescu entered the conference room and saw DCS Faraday and DI Irving already sitting opposite each other at the table. Two others were present whom Dinescu hadn't met before. They introduced themselves as a chief inspector and sergeant working for Professional Standards. Dinescu missed their names. One was a bald man wearing reading glasses, and the other was a stern-looking woman with grey hair. Dinescu sat at the end of the table and pulled down his shirt cuffs. McBride began.

"Thank you all for coming. Let's get straight to it. Sadly, I'm not here to bring good news today. This is the part of my job I hate."

The corners of Faraday's mouth lifted. He locked eyes with Irving for a moment.

"Would you like me to begin, sir?" said the chief inspector in the glasses.

"Yes, please, Graham," said McBride. "We may as well get it over and done with." McBride waved a hand. "DCI Francis is going to make a statement. I'd like you to listen to him."

Faraday and Irving both turned towards Dinescu, but he remained calm, ready for what would come.

"This isn't a meeting where we are hearing evidence," said DCI Francis, "but only to inform you of pending action. It will give you time to obtain legal advice." He cleared his throat and shuffled some papers in front of him, handing copies to the chief constable. "We are here to serve papers for gross misconduct. We have gathered evidence after being made aware of a situation where a senior officer has acted in a manner that has brought disrepute to our service." He looked up. "Detective Chief Superintendent Faraday, I am serving you with a formal notice of investigation for gross misconduct."

Faraday's head snapped around in shock. "What did you say?"

"Namely, abusing your rank and influence to advance the career of a more junior officer in exchange for sexual favours, breaching standards of professional behaviour. Additionally, you have fraudulently completed paperwork to secure a new post for that officer, including falsifying the signatures of senior management. You are hereby suspended from duty. Consequently, I am arresting you on suspicion of misconduct in public office. This case will be referred to the Independent Office for Police Conduct for further investigation."

Dinescu studied Irving's face as Faraday was being cautioned. It was as if she'd realised everything was over for her. She knew she would be next. She turned to Dinescu and nodded, mouthing "*I'm sorry*" to him. Faraday was on his feet, pointing his finger at Dinescu and shouting obscenities at him. But Dinescu wasn't bothered. He'd learned as a child how to switch off from vicious tirades, remembering his old teacher in Harrow.

"For God's sake, sit down!" Irving shouted at Faraday, slamming her palms on the table. "You're making an even bigger fool of yourself and me. Have some dignity. It's over. Can't you see that?"

Faraday went silent, staring at Irving. "I just wanted… After everything I did for you, Daisy."

DCI Francis raised his voice to interrupt Faraday. "DI Irving, I'm also serving you with a formal notice of investigation for gross misconduct, specifically conspiring with DCI Faraday—"

Dinescu stood to address the Chief Constable.

"One moment, Graham," said McBride, holding up his hand.

"Would you mind if I left the proceedings at this point?" said Dinescu. "I don't believe I am required to be here. Thank you, sir, for listening to me. I am grateful. This has given me no pleasure."

McBride nodded. "That's fine, Ben. On behalf of all of us, please accept our apologies for this. We are more than satisfied with your team and how you operate here in Chichester." He shifted in his seat, his face reddening. He had more to add, glancing at Irving and Faraday as he spoke. "Some people don't realise the type of man you are, Ben. I know your history and your incredible bravery. Thank you for showing dignity here today."

Dinescu nodded. "Thank you, sir." He left the room without looking at Faraday again.

Epilogue

Storm Isha was about to take hold of the country. Emily and Sarah had decided to travel to Southsea without Rosie, leaving her to play with Jordan and Marie. Emily was driving. She would have been too nervous as a passenger, thinking about meeting her father again.

"Can you remember what he looked like?" Sarah asked, watching the rain tracks weave a path down her window.

"Roughly," Emily said. "I mean, yes. But it's a bit vague. It was a long time ago. I was a girl. But why now, Sarah?"

"That's a good question, Sarge—sorry, Emily. There has to be a reason."

"Perhaps he's dying," said Emily, breaking the silence.

"Don't say that."

"There must be some life event that's made him consider contacting me after all these years."

"Why not your mother?" Sarah asked. "Surely, she'd be the first person he would have gone to."

Emily took the M275 and headed through Portsmouth and into Southsea. The rain stopped, and after a few minutes, they passed the cathedral and were in Old Portsmouth. They found a parking space near the old Hotwalls, a tall, defensive wall that overlooked the Solent Water. Behind the wall, through the old gates, was a narrow, stony beach with granite sea defences along the edges. The walls themselves housed small artisan shops built into the old arches.

They sat in Emily's car in silence. Everything in her wanted to turn and drive back out again. This can of worms was going to hurt when she opened it.

"You don't have to do this," said Sarah. "He doesn't deserve you for what he put you through."

"I know. But if I don't meet him, I'll never know why. He left us behind without saying goodbye. What was more important to him than us?"

"You're courageous, Emily. Take your time. Don't promise yourself anything."

Emily smiled. "Come on, then! And if it doesn't work out, we can go shopping."

Sarah laughed. "Perhaps we can go shopping anyway?"

They left the car and climbed the stone steps to the top of the Hotwalls. A footpath led them through an enclosed area and out onto the Round Tower. From there, they could see Gosport across the harbour entrance. The water looked grey and choppy beneath a dark, stormy sky. To their left was a stone staircase that went down onto the street.

"This is where I last saw him," said Emily. "He was on a ferry heading to Spain. I was with my mother, wearing the brightest red dress, so he could see me waving. I never saw him."

Sarah placed her arm around Emily. "Are you ready to meet your dad?"

"No. But I'm here." Emily squeezed Sarah's hand. "Thank

you." Her hair had come loose, blowing in the wind. She felt sick to her stomach while waiting. She lifted her watch. "Well, it's noon. Where is he?"

"I'm going to go back onto the Hotwalls," said Sarah. "This meeting is between you and him, and I may be scaring him off."

Emily smiled and nodded as Sarah headed away. Emily was alone. The wind was getting stronger. Perhaps the weather would have put him off, or maybe he got cold feet. She tried to imagine what he would look like now. He wasn't tall, but well-built, and had fierce blue eyes. Dinescu's eyes were like her father's. Maybe that's why she always felt safe around him.

She heard footsteps coming up from the stone stairwell. They were scuffing as they climbed—slow and deliberate.

Emily's mind cleared. It was like someone had thrown a switch. Why now? After all this time? She wasn't ready to play catch-up with a stranger she barely knew.

"No," said Emily. "Not today."

She turned and went beneath the covered walkway to find Sarah leaning over the wall, the wind blowing her hair like a colourful, wild mane.

"I need to go," said Emily. She felt a surge of relief come over her. She turned to Sarah, and they hugged. "He missed my whole life, Sarah. I'm not ready for him today. Our boss is more of a father to me than he ever was."

"That's good," said Sarah with a broad smile to reassure her. "Now you know how you really feel. Shopping it is, then."

The two of them walked back the way they came. Emily glanced over her shoulder and caught a figure with grey hair in a suit in the distance. He was way off, but she saw he was carrying flowers. She realised afterwards that it might not have been him—just a coincidence. Now, she'd never know.

Sarah took her arm. "How about Gunwharf Quays for shopping? I need to buy a sexy dress."

Emily frowned and then grinned as she realised. "Sarah?"

"I have a date. He's someone I met the other day. Nothing serious—just a tryout."

Emily's eyes grew wide with excitement. "Does your tryout have a name?"

Sarah nodded. "Of course he has a name! Louis."

"Does he play the trumpet?" Emily asked.

Sarah rolled her eyes. "Can I call you weird when we're not at work? But how about you and Kieran? Is that going to happen?"

Emily sighed with a smile. "Maybe. Kieran is a great friend, but I don't know about romance yet. We'll see. You know how it is—one day at a time."

Sarah nodded. "Nice and easy does it."

Joseph McKinley stood on the footbridge over the creek, watching the red rose drift away towards the outlet of the Fishbourne Channel. It had gathered all his thoughts and memories of Lily and taken them on its journey into the wide water. Would it reach the sea? Maybe.

"Goodbye, Lily," he said. "I forgive you." The wind was strong enough to whistle through the reeds, and he thought he heard Lily's ghost calling his name as she went on her way.

He turned at the sound of heels on the bridge. A woman stood facing him. She was tall, elegant, and attractive, wrapped in a long coat against the wind. She approached him as if he were a dangerous beast. She was uncertain of him but lifted her head, finding courage from somewhere.

"You must be Joseph," she said.

He frowned, and his face creased. "What of it?"

"I hated you for many years for taking away the one person who loved me. Now I know I was mistaken. And I'm sorry. It was someone else in my life who did that. He took away your life, too."

Joseph raised a bushy eyebrow. "You must be Heather." He looked her up and down. "Better looking than Lily described you."

Heather Collier smiled in relief. "I am truly sorry, Joseph."

He cleared his throat. "You don't need to apologise. It wasn't you. Your husband had it in for me."

"Thank you."

He nodded. "He was a handsome fella, that Roger."

"He was. I loved him."

"All the women did. Even my Lily."

"Pardon?" Heather took a step back.

"My Lily loved him, too. He got her pregnant. Roger was Henry's father." He looked down at the dark waters below.

"What the hell are you saying? Roger was in love with me!"

"Roger Wallace stole what Lily and me had! Any woman was fair game to him, and so were you."

Her voice cracked. "I don't believe you. How could you be so—"

"It was twenty years ago! Get over it. You were screwed by Roger as much as I was. He lost interest in Lily when she told him she was pregnant. So he moved on—just like that. He moved on to you."

"Me?"

"It must have been a shock to Lily when you told her about you and Roger."

She opened her mouth, but nothing came out. The realisation had hit her.

He turned away, the weight of his words hanging in the air between them. He gazed at the creek; the rose was now a distant speck. "Lily was everything to me," he continued, his voice softer. "I never wanted to believe she could betray me. But Roger... he had a way with women. Probably couldn't help it. He saw someone lonely and vulnerable, and in he went. That's how he worked." He turned back to Heather. "You weren't the only one living a lie."

She took a breath to compose herself. "Looks like Lily made a fool out of me, too. I came here to make peace, Joseph, not to dig up more pain. I'm truly sorry for what Ray did to you. You didn't deserve that. But maybe we both need to let go now."

Joseph nodded slowly. "Perhaps you're right. Goodbye, Heather." He walked past her, leaving her standing on the footbridge. A curlew circled above them, its cry blending with the whispering wind. The red rose continued its journey, carried gently towards the sea.

To the Reader

I'm truly grateful for your support, and it would mean a lot to me if you could share your thoughts by leaving a review on Amazon. Your feedback is invaluable, as it helps other readers find books they might enjoy. Also, if you enjoyed this story, tell a friend.

Thank you for being part of my writing journey.

Acknowledgments

First and foremost, thank you to **Val Evans** (valerie-evans.com), my wife and editor, for her love, encouragement, and support. Also, thank you to all **my wonderful family** for being there and being my greatest fans. Thanks to my beta readers: **Bob Lock, Beth Leeworthy-Evans, and Caitlin Gale.**

Thanks for specialist support goes to:

- My friend, **PC Darren Triggs,** for your patience and research on some of my more tricky police procedural problems.
- My friend and police drone pilot, **PC James Steer,** for listening to me drone on about drones.
- My dear friend **Dr Matthew Crisp**, thank you for your insights on GP procedures.
- Author **Fiona Forsyth** for your wisdom about spooky Roman beliefs. See her website (fionaforsythauthor. co.uk) for details on her splendid Roman mysteries.

Any factual errors that remain after publishing are entirely my own

Rick Griffin was the winner of a competition for me to create a character using his name. So, well done, Rick.

About the Author

Matthew lives in Chichester, West Sussex, UK. He is married to Valerie and has three children and two grandchildren. He served as a police officer (Regular and Special) in Hampshire and Sussex for 19 years and is now retired.

Matthew is a musician (meditative folk). He composes and records his own work and performs on albums for others.

Email: matt@matthewjevans.co.uk
Website: www.matthewjevans.co.uk

Visit my website to subscribe to my newsletter, where you can read my latest updates, find out about new releases, and get exclusive inside information on my creative processes.

Also by Matthew J. Evans

The Chichester Crime Mysteries Series

The Dead Beneath Us

Our darkest places are never far away.

When a brutal murder strikes a prestigious private school, DCI Dinescu finds himself entangled in a complex investigation, including the mysterious disappearance of a schoolgirl in the 1980s. How are these two cases connected? Confronting his deepest fears, Dinescu must uncover the dark secrets of the past to bring justice and closure to the present.

The Max Fortis Thrillers

Heel of Achilles

Private detective **Max Fortis** is a former Met Police protection officer and MI5 agent. When a mysterious woman comes to Fortis for help, he becomes embroiled in a ruthless vendetta against him. Partnering with reporter **Ella Munro**, he takes on an investigation the police won't touch and uncovers a sordid underworld of murder, sex trafficking, and modern-day slavery.

Fortis must confront the demons from his secret past and form an unexpected alliance to bring down a ghost—a forgotten enemy bent on revenge—before it destroys him.

In this dark and fast-paced crime thriller, will the secrets and lies of the past exact their chilling revenge on Fortis, or will he overcome and serve justice on his enemy?

Printed in Great Britain
by Amazon

45749141R00189